96
MILES

96
MILES

J. L. ESPLIN

A TOM DOHERTY ASSOCIATES BOOK
NEW YORK

This is a work of fiction. All of the characters, organizations,
and events portrayed in this novel are either products of the author's
imagination or are used fictitiously.

96 MILES

Copyright © 2020 by Jenny Esplin

A Starscape Book
Published by Tom Doherty Associates
120 Broadway
New York, NY 10271

www.tor-forge.com

Library of Congress Cataloging-in-Publication Data

Names: Esplin, J. L., author.
Title: 96 miles / J. L. Esplin.
Other titles: Ninety-six miles
Description: First edition. | New York : Starscape, a Tom Doherty
Associates Book, 2020.
Identifiers: LCCN 2019044525 (print) | LCCN 2019044526 (ebook) |
ISBN 9781250192301 (hardcover) | ISBN 9781250192295 (ebook)
Subjects: CYAC: Survival—Fiction. | Brothers—Fiction. | Diabetes—Fiction. |
Electric power failures—Fiction. |
Nevada—Fiction.
Classification: LCC PZ7.1.E846 Aam 2020 (print) | LCC PZ7.1.E846
(ebook) | DDC [Fic]—dc23
LC record available at https://lccn.loc.gov/2019044525
LC ebook record available at https://lccn.loc.gov/2019044526

Our books may be purchased in bulk for promotional, educational,
or business use. Please contact your local bookseller or the Macmillan
Corporate and Premium Sales Department at 1-800-221-7945, extension
5442, or by email at MacmillanSpecialMarkets@macmillan.com.

First Edition: February 2020

Printed in the United States of America

0 9 8 7 6

For my parents, Gus and Mary Morgan.

And in memory of Scott Esplin—brother-in-law, friend, and fellow writer.

96
MILES

1

DAD ALWAYS SAID if things get desperate, it's okay to drink the water in the toilet bowl. I never thought it would come to that. I thought I'd sooner die than let one drop of toilet water touch my lips. Yet here I am, kneeling before a porcelain throne, holding a tin mug for scooping in one hand and my half-gallon canteen in the other.

Don't worry, I'm going to boil it first.

Behind me, my brother, Stewart, is making gagging noises. "I'm gonna throw up," he says, which is something Stew says all the time, but does he ever actually throw up? No. He doesn't do most of the things he says he's going to do lately, like run away, or kill himself, or kill me.

"C'mon, John," he says, the whine in his voice setting my teeth on edge, "do we really need this?"

I stop mid-scoop and stare up at him, holding back the pink padded toilet seat with my elbow. "No, we don't need it, Stew. I just thought, 'Oh, look—water from a toilet. That sounds refreshing, let's drink it.'"

His sullen, dark eyes narrow at me, and I thrust the

canteen into his hands. He kneels down to help me, but adds in a mumble, "We have two canteens of water already."

And that's a perfect example of how my brother thinks. Two canteens of water, and we have a three-day walk down an empty stretch of desert highway before we reach Brighton Ranch, our last chance for help. I'm no math genius, but before this ugly pink toilet came along, I figure we were short in the water department.

It isn't Stew's math skills I'm questioning, though. If we'd found a pantry full of Aquafina in this abandoned shack of a home, Stew would have been the first one to start filling his pack. He knows how desperately we need water. What I'm questioning is his willingness to do anything hard—or in this case, anything revolting—in order to save himself.

Yet we were raised by the same dad, who preached self-reliance on pretty much a daily basis.

I wouldn't have predicted this about Stewart. He's younger than me by two years, but he's always had a lot more determination when it comes to stuff like this. My dad calls it "a strong mental fortitude."

I couldn't say what my strengths are. I guess I'm good at yard maintenance and, according to my school counselor, using sarcasm to avoid conflict—and now that I think about it, I'm not exactly sure she meant that as a compliment. But my point is, in the face of a real natural disaster, or a terrorist attack, or a zombie apocalypse, or whatever the heck happened twenty-one days ago that caused all the power to go out, I would have predicted that *Stewart* would be the one talking *me* into doing hard things. Not the other way around.

Anyway, it's not like I *want* to drink toilet water, boiled or not, but what choice do we have? What's the alternative? It's not like we're at a restaurant and the waiter is asking

Would you like the bottled water, or the toilet water from the creepy abandoned bathroom?

My mug scrapes the bottom of the porcelain bowl as I scoop the last of the water, and before I can stop myself, I give the bare toilet a quick inspection. It looks clean for the most part. Other than the faint, rust-colored ring where the water level once was. The water itself doesn't look bad either. Still, it's the stuff we can't see that we have to worry about.

Stew is doing a bad job of holding the canteen over the bowl—that's no surprise. He's got this disgusted look on his face and he's checking out the dirty corners of the small bathroom. I already told him not to look too closely. The place kind of creeps me out, with its cracked vinyl floor and sun-bleached lace curtains. Like something frozen in time. Like something out of an old horror movie.

Not to mention it's hotter than Hades, and the air is as still as death in here.

"Move closer," I say impatiently, motioning for Stew to bring the canteen over the bowl. He does it with a shaky hand, so I end up spilling toilet water on his fingers. His fault.

"Ah! Gross!" he says, jerking the canteen back. He switches hands and then wipes his wet one down the side of my pant leg before I can stop him.

"Real mature," I say.

"*Real mature*," he mimics.

We've been together too long.

Before I realize what he means to do next, Stew is on his feet, upending the canteen, dumping all that water I just collected back into the toilet.

"Stop!" I yell, jumping up and making a grab for the now-empty canteen. "*What are you doing?*"

"We don't need this," he insists, hiding the canteen behind his back like he's ten years old or something—he's eleven, which may not seem *that* much older than ten, but I swear, under normal circumstances, he's the oldest eleven-year-old I know. "We could end up finding one of those hot springs along the way," he says. "You never know."

"Or we could find a chocolate factory with a chocolate river inside!" I say. Stew looks like he wants to hit me. "What? Am I not allowed to come up with any what-if scenarios?"

He does this heavy-sigh thing that he's been doing a lot lately. "I think we should stop at the reservoir for water," he says. "It's only a short detour."

The "short detour" he's talking about is sixteen miles out of the way. I don't know if he's thinking about this in terms of walking, but I've already made up my mind that we aren't stopping at the reservoir. With the supplies we have (and I'm including the toilet water), we'd be lucky to last three days out there in the desert. So we've got three days to get to Brighton Ranch. We can't afford to add sixteen more miles to our already insanely long walk.

"We'll decide about the detour when we get to the turn-off, all right?" I say.

He nods reluctantly, but I can tell he sees right through me.

"For now, we have to take as much water with us as we can." I hold out my hand for him to give me the canteen. He sighs again . . . without handing it over.

I should be the one sighing, not him.

"Do you want us to survive or not?" I say, throwing my hands up in frustration. But one look at Stew's face, and I regret I asked.

"What is the *point* of surviving?" he shouts at the low ceiling.

His question freaks me out. It really freaks me out. Because I'm not sure there *is* a point to all of this anymore. But I'm not going to tell him that. Instead I say, "I told you I would get you across this desert, all right? All you have to do is trust me."

"You mean *all* I have to do is lie to myself. *All* I have to do is pretend like I'm not already a goner."

My chest tightens with familiar dread. "Don't say stuff like that. That was part of our deal, remember? I'm going to get you across this desert, and you're not going to say stuff like that."

He stares right at me, and he's thinking about pushing me a little further—I can tell by the tic of his jaw. But then he just says, "Fine, I trust you."

I don't believe him. He doesn't trust me at all. I mean if he did, he wouldn't be acting like this, right? He wouldn't be calling himself a goner. But I decide to drop it, pretend I believe him.

It's like that annoying dry spot at the back of my throat that won't go away. If I pretend it isn't there, then it doesn't bother me so much. But if I let myself think about it, even for a second, then I become obsessed with working my tongue against the roof of my mouth, trying to gather up enough saliva to quench it. But you can't cure a thirst this powerful with spit, and all I end up with is a tongue that aches, a sore mouth, and the spit never seems to hit that dry spot anyway.

So yeah, sometimes you're better off ignoring things you can't do anything about anyway.

"Listen," I finally say, "I'm going to give you my clean water." I go to the pack I left leaning against the chipped bathtub and unhook my one full canteen. I walk it over to him, but he won't take it. He just stares at me with hard eyes and a clenched jaw. I squat down next to his pack and find his empty canteen opposite his full one, and switch it out for my full one. "Your pack's evened out now." Without looking at him, I add, "I don't mind the toilet water."

Positioning myself in front of the bowl again, I unscrew the plastic cap on Stew's canteen, grab my mug, and start filling.

"Stop it, John," Stew says in a quiet voice.

"Stop what?" I say, focusing on the narrow opening of the canteen, ignoring the obvious drop in Stewart's mood. Anger I can deal with, but not this.

"Stop acting like I'm some helpless baby and it's your job to save me."

I open my mouth, ready to disagree with him, but nothing comes out. I've never thought of Stewart as helpless before. But lately, that's exactly how he's been acting. So I guess I've been acting like it's my job to save him. Isn't it, though?

Before I can come up with a response that will snap him out of this mood, I hear a noise outside. Stew hears it too. I can tell by the look on his face, the way his whole body tenses up.

If this were just your average, everyday massive power outage that we were dealing with, the sound of footsteps on gravel outside wouldn't exactly send up alarm bells. But two days ago, everything was taken from us. I mean, *everything* that Stew and I needed to survive this blackout. Including a decade's worth of dry and canned goods that my dad had been hoarding away, and all six of his fifty-five-gallon water tanks.

If my dad had been around, he would've taken a bullet for those water tanks.

Maybe Stew is remembering our water tanks, because he's suddenly eager to protect what we found first—the toilet water. He crouches down next to me and picks up the empty canteen he tossed aside moments ago and motions for me to hurry and finish with the one I'm working on. Like it's all of a sudden Evian.

I got everything I could out of the bowl, so I set down my mug and quickly close the canteen, handing it off to Stew. Then I shut the toilet seat and quietly lift the lid off the back tank. As I'm doing that, I check out the window, craning my neck both ways, but the early morning sun is glaring off the dirty glass and I can't see who's out there. I hear them, though. It's a shack of a home, an abandoned double-wide trailer in a patch of trees about a mile from our property line. The walls are like papier-mâché, the whole house like a giant piñata waiting to be crushed.

I can hear muffled voices speaking to each other now, and footsteps treading through the gravel around to the side where the entry is. I hear the rusty spring of the screen door opening, then the high-pitched squeak of metal hinges.

Stew's beside me with the mug and the empty canteen, and he motions for me to get out of the way so he can take over. I nod and move silently to my pack, wiping away the sudden trickle of sweat at my brow. I unzip a side pocket and pull out my long hunting knife. Adrenaline has kicked in, and I feel blood rushing just below the surface of my skin. Still, my hand is visibly shaking.

I grip the knife and position myself in front of the open bathroom door, ready to strike, ready to take down who-ever comes around that corner . . . I think. But then I hear something that causes me to make a split-second decision.

Standing up straight, I reach behind my back and hide my knife, slipping it blade-down into the waist of my jeans so I appear unarmed. And just as I do, a kid wanders into view.

He looks younger than Stew, scrawny, dirty, with messy blond hair, and he's looking around the connecting bedroom, inspecting a few of the dusty knickknacks and figurines sitting on the nightstand and dresser. He thinks he's alone. Well, except for whoever's banging around in the kitchen, opening and shutting cabinets and drawers. He doesn't notice me or Stew, and we're not even more than five feet away.

A girl's voice calls out, "Will?"

The kid turns, and that's when he sees us. He sort of jerks to a stop, his small chest inflates like he's about to scream, but then he completely freezes up. I hold out my hands to show him I'm harmless, but the girl is suddenly there, wrapping an arm around him from behind and pulling him back protectively. She's got what looks like a steak knife in her hand, pointing it at me. She stares at me with wide blue eyes.

She's kind of pretty.

Her dirty blond hair is pulled back in a messy ponytail at the base of her neck, she's covered in road dust, and she looks slightly crazy, with red-rimmed eyes like she hasn't slept in days. But even with everything that's going on, I can't stop the stupid thought from going through my head that she's pretty.

And then this weird moment passes between us. It couldn't have lasted longer than three or four seconds, but I lock eyes with her. And when we hit that half second where it would have been awkward *not* to look away, we just keep looking.

I swear I'm not usually this overdramatic.

As soon as our eyes unlock, her vision seems to expand to take in the whole scene before her, and her expression turns to one of horror.

"What are you doing?" she asks, like she just caught us drowning puppies.

I look over my shoulder at Stew and see him hovering over the toilet tank, water still dripping from the canteen. He's got this guilty look on his face that isn't helping, and I turn to the girl again, wanting to tell her that we're going to boil it first—

"That is disgusting!" she says, adjusting the grip on her steak knife and pulling the kid closer against her chest. "You are disgusting!"

Okay, on second thought? She's not that pretty.

"Get out of our house!" she yells. "Now!"

Stew makes a scoffing sound behind me, because clearly, nobody has stepped foot in this place in a long time.

"This is your house?" I say as if I don't know the truth. "Not to be rude, but maybe you should hire a maid." I nod at the wall just left of her, where a really big cobweb hangs in the space between a cracked mirror and the low ceiling. It almost looks like a prop from the same horror movie that was filmed in the bathroom, it's that scary.

She doesn't look, and she's still pointing that knife at me. Not that I'm worried she's actually going to stab me—it's just harder to break the ice when someone's pointing a steak knife at you.

I force a smile and say, "We're your neighbors to the west, then. It's nice to finally meet." And she looks at me like she's trying to figure me out. I hear Stew wrapping things up behind me. I add, "I hope you don't mind that we're borrowing the water from your toilet—"

"We're *taking* it because we know you don't live here, and we found the water first," Stew says, not politely.

"We *do* live here," the little kid fires back with more

nerve than I expect from him, "and that's where we pee, you sicko!"

The girl grabs him by the upper arm, because he's pulled free of her grip, and leans down to whisper something to him without taking her eyes off us.

Stew pushes past me. He's got his pack on, and he doesn't bat an eye at the steak knife, would have walked right into it if she hadn't backed up. "Don't worry, we're leaving now. So you can have your *house* back," he says. He heads out of the small bedroom, the floor shuddering with every step.

I turn to get my pack off the bathroom floor. Stew has already hooked on my canteens, and even though one is slightly fuller than the other, it feels like he's shifted some stuff inside my pack to even the weight. I take the knife from my waist and put it back in the side pocket, then lift the pack onto my shoulders. I fiddle with the straps and adjust the sides, but really I'm just stalling.

The girl and the kid are sitting on the edge of the sagging double bed now, watching me. The mattress is so old and worn out that they are sunk pretty low. She still has that knife in her hand, but she's resting it on the bed beside her, as if she's run out of the strength needed to hold it up.

We know pretty much everyone who lives within a hundred-mile radius of us, and since the girl looks about my age, I'd definitely know if she lived in the area. I wonder where they came from and how they ended up way out here. I can tell they've been on the move for a while. They're both dyed in desert dirt from the shins down.

I notice for the first time that the girl has a gray backpack slung over her shoulder, and it's kind of deflated. They're probably relieved to have found this shelter. Probably eager for Stew and me to get out of here so they can crash on that old bed. I know I have to say something to her. At the very least, warn her that there is nothing here for them.

I walk over to stand in front of her, gripping the shoulder straps of my pack, jittery and wound up. "You're not planning to stay here, are you?"

Her chin tilts up, and she just sort of squints at me like it's none of my business.

"Because you can't. It's a shelter, but that's it. It won't do you any good if you don't have food and water." *Unless you're looking for a tomb.* She doesn't volunteer the information, so I ask, "Do you have food and water?"

I already know the answer. They are half dehydrated, half starved. And I'm suddenly very aware of what little food I have left in my pack, the two canteens hanging from the sides. . . .

The girl is still squinting at me like she's trying to keep something deep inside her from coming out, and the boy's face is starting to crumble, like he's on the verge of bawling his eyes out.

Stew calls from the other room in an almost bored voice, "Let's go!"

Every instinct in my body is telling me to walk away now. Just leave. Don't ask any more questions. I can't help them, so what's the point? But something compels me to turn my head and call back to Stew, "Just trying to be neighborly." I look back at the girl and press my mouth into a smile, and though she's still squinting up at me with that same expression on her face, her eyes start to well up a little.

I check out that cobweb on the ceiling for a minute.

Finally, she says in a quiet voice, "We're just resting for a while. Then we'll move on. We have somewhere to go."

I want to feel relieved. Really, I do. I wait for the relief to wash over me, but nothing happens. So I say, "Where? I mean, maybe I can point you in the right direction."

She hesitates, and then says, "Jim Lockwood's house? My grandparents know him and said he would take us in. For a while."

I force myself to nod, but otherwise hold back my reaction to her answer. "Who are your grandparents?" I hear myself ask. Though it doesn't even matter.

She starts to answer, then tears up for real this time, so I walk out of the bedroom and leave them alone.

I swear it's ten degrees hotter in the room where Stew is waiting for me. Sunlight filters right through those pathetic window curtains, catching bits of dust suspended in the air. Stew's sitting on the armrest of a faded old couch, his feet flat on the ground, his forehead dotted with perspiration. He's taken off his pack, and he's giving me this look because he overheard everything the girl just told me.

Holding up my hand, I separate my dry lips with my tongue and say, "I'll hear you out, but then you have to listen to me."

He says in a not-so-quiet voice, "You gonna leave them here to die?"

Warmth flushes through my chest, and I glance over my shoulder before moving to stand closer to him. "Thanks, Stew," I say, lowering my voice. "That's really fair."

"I'm just wondering," he says with a shrug, as if he's not trying to push my buttons.

I go through a mental checklist of our food—it's a short list, so it doesn't take long—and we *definitely* don't have enough to keep four people alive for three days. I mean, maybe if we were staying in one place, we'd be okay. But walking through a desert in the middle of summer? We'll burn through a crazy amount of energy. There's small game out there, wild jackrabbit. But we don't have time to trap them.

Anyway, I don't know why I'm even thinking about food when the real problem is water. Or lack of it.

I drag my palm across my mouth, wiping fresh beads of sweat from my upper lip. "I'm not leaving them anywhere, all right? I already warned them not to stay here."

"Yeah, I heard." Stew looks up at me with dark eyes that match mine. "They're going to Jim Lockwood's."

I don't break his stare. It's just our eyes that match. Any similarity between my brother and me pretty much ends there. "I probably don't need to remind you," I say carefully, "but we just scavenged water from a freaking toilet."

He doesn't say anything, because, let's face it, he really doesn't care.

I feel old anger rising to the surface. I'm the one responsible for getting us across this desert, not him. Stew knows it. And it's not just because I'm the oldest. The minute I put up the fight to leave home, insisted that it's totally possible to walk three days across a desert with barely any food and barely any water, we both understood that the responsibility to actually get us to Brighton Ranch alive was mine. And things are already going badly for me.

I'm telling you, it's like Stew's *hoping* I'll fail, *hoping* we don't make it, just so he can prove that he was right all along.

I finally say, "I want to help them. You know I do. But we are in no position to help anyone. I have to get *us*"—I motion between us—"to Brighton Ranch. Not them. I can't . . . do . . . both." I emphasize each word so he'll get how serious I am.

Stew bites at the side of his dry lips like he's thinking, then sort of shrugs. "Dad would do both."

Yeah, my brother knows exactly how to push me.

"Well, Dad's not here," I say, forcing the words out calmly so he won't have the satisfaction of knowing he's getting to me.

"You gonna at least tell them?" he says.

"Tell them what?" I snap, frustrated that he's twisting the conversation in another direction.

"You gonna tell them that Jim Lockwood is our dad?"

I hear the floor creak behind me, and shut my eyes for a second before opening them again and meeting my brother's.

His eyebrows are pinched together like he's really curious about this. "I mean, before they walk all the way to our place. Are you gonna tell them that our dad isn't here and everything is gone? The food is gone, the water is gone, and if they thought they were this close to filling that empty pit in their stomachs, they've just hit a major setback."

I was going to tell them. I swear I was.

"Your *dad* is Jim Lockwood?" says a voice from the bedroom doorway.

I turn and the girl is standing there, holding the boy's hand so tight I can see her white knuckles from here.

Her eyes are narrowed at me, like she's accusing me of something—lying, I guess. Even though I was *going* to tell them.

"Yeah, about that—" I start to say.

"Yep, he's our dad," Stew says, pushing away from the couch. He lifts his pack up off the floor, heaves it onto one shoulder.

"Wait," she says, "where are you going?"

Stew raises his eyebrows at me, like he expects me to answer that question.

Before we left home, I promised myself that I would get

my brother across this desert. Promised myself that I'd do whatever it takes.

But I didn't expect something like this. I didn't expect a choice between getting my brother to Brighton Ranch alive or helping two complete strangers.

And the worst part is that Stew is right. He's exactly right. Dad would do both.

2

TWENTY-ONE DAYS AGO. The morning before the blackout, the morning my dad left town, I woke to the sound of him pounding out his usual rhythm on my bedroom door.

It sounded like a marching band was about to bust in.

I winced, groaning at the noise. Flat on my stomach, arm hanging over the side of my mattress, pillow gone to who-knows-where. The door swung open and my dad leaned in, bringing with him the familiar scent of bar soap mixed with his aftershave.

"I'm leaving in fifteen minutes!" he said, tapping the wall to stress this point. "Stewart's already up—" He stopped, his eyebrows knitting together in confusion as he took in the strange blue tint lighting my room. "What is that doing up there?"

I craned to look back at the flag I'd tacked up over my blinds the night before, cobalt blue with an emblem in the upper left corner. At least, it'd be in the upper left corner if the flag weren't hanging sideways. Instead, it was in the bottom left corner—a silver star, two sprigs of green sagebrush.

A scroll with the words BATTLE BORN written in small block letters.

"Take that down, John. Our state flag is not a curtain."

"I found it in a box in the garage—"

"I don't care. Take it down." He didn't sound mad exactly, just kind of frustrated or disappointed.

I sighed and collapsed back down onto my mattress, pressing my palms into my eye sockets. "I didn't know it was a big deal," I said, but my dad isn't the type to stick around and listen to excuses.

"Get a move on, John," he called back, already halfway down the hallway.

I climbed out of bed and shut my bedroom door before dragging the metal chair from my desk to the window.

"Apparently," I mumbled, wriggling out the pushpins, "I'm supposed to know *every random thing* about flags. . . ."

I folded up the flag as carefully as I knew how and set it on my desk next to a plate of dried-up old pizza. Then I changed into a pair of jeans I picked up off the floor and grabbed the least wrinkly T-shirt I could find in my drawer.

In the kitchen, Dad was eating a bowl of Grape-Nuts cereal over the sink, an open canister of sugar on the counter beside him with a spoon handle sticking out.

I avoided looking at him directly—maybe I didn't think it was a big deal to turn our state flag into a curtain for my bedroom window, but my dad did. And there was nothing worse than the feeling that I'd disappointed him.

"Where's Stew?" I asked on my way to the cupboard.

Just then, a rumbling sound started up out back, a lawn mower engine turning over.

"He wanted to get it over with," my dad said with a shrug in his voice.

I rolled my eyes, took down a cereal bowl. That drought-resistant stuff my dad called grass wasn't exactly growing out of control.

"It's not even seven A.M.," I pointed out.

"Best time of day to get something over with, don't you think?"

What I thought was, *Stewart is a suck-up*. But I didn't tell my dad that.

I got a spoon from the drawer and went around to sit at the breakfast bar, facing the sink. I was about to grab for the box of Grape-Nuts—the stuff tasted like cardboard, but if you dumped a bunch of sugar on top, it wasn't so bad—but froze when I spotted what was sitting next to it. A number 10 can of powdered milk.

I dropped my arm. "Great. We're out of milk again," I said matter-of-factly.

My dad's eyes shifted toward me, then to the can of powdered milk. "That is milk."

"It's disgusting."

"You're not mixing it right. Put a little more sugar in it."

"Why can't you just get real milk?"

He raised an eyebrow at me. "That *is* real milk. But look," he continued before I could keep carrying on about it, "I'll grab a jug of milk for you in Alamo on my way home."

"So . . . three days from now?" I said, folding my arms on the breakfast bar, pushing them forward so I could rock back and balance the barstool on two legs—something that I knew drives my dad nuts.

He dropped his bowl in the sink, ran the faucet. "I'm sure the Yardleys have milk in their fridge. You could be drinking it by breakfast time tomorrow."

"Can't wait." I slid my unused bowl and spoon across the

countertop, and my dad put them back in the cabinet and drawer without missing a beat. "What about our bikes?"

"I promise I'll get the parts we need and we'll fix them when I get back."

"So we have to walk to the Yardleys'."

"It won't kill you, John."

Over the lawn mower rumble out back, I could hear Stew bellowing out lyrics to an old Rush song—listening to Dad's playlist on that ancient iPod. *Total suck-up.*

"Remember," my dad said, starting his usual instructions, "the Yardleys are looking out for you, but they aren't your babysitters, all right?"

"Not our babysitters. Got it."

"No lazing around their place in the morning, clean up after yourselves, and come home to take care of your chores here."

I pushed my stool back farther, resting my chin on my arms. I watched my dad move around the kitchen, clearing off countertops, wiping loose sugar into the sink, his suntanned forearms dark against the rolled sleeves of his crisp white button-down. Clipped to his front pocket, his Ely Granite Company work badge.

I tried to imagine him "lazing around" anywhere.

"You need to take care of that room of yours too," he added, returning the powdered milk to the top shelf of the pantry. "I don't want it to look like that when I get back. I haven't seen your bedroom floor in so long I can't even remember what it looks like."

"Brown carpet," I reminded him.

"Yeah, well, I want to *see* the brown carpet."

He came around the breakfast bar and I sat up, letting the stool drop down on all four legs. I twisted to face him but didn't raise my eyes. The hum of the lawn mower was growing fainter outside, Stew already working his way to the outer edge of our yard.

"You know," he said, his callused hands low on his hips, "your mom *hated* powdered milk. Five years, and I couldn't get her to come around to it."

"I can't guess why," I said dryly, though I always liked when he talked about my mom, the way his voice went kind of soft. I was so little when she died, my only memories of her were *his* memories of her.

"Watch over your brother, all right?" he said, getting back to it.

I stared at the knot of his thin tie. "Don't I always."

He sighed. "John, I know I've been gone a lot lately—"

"Fourth work trip in less than two months."

"—but this job will be over soon and then I won't be traveling so much. I'll be working on-site in Ely by the end of August."

"The end of *summer,* you mean."

"We've got that trip planned with the Brightons before school starts up again. It's not like we have nothing to look forward to."

Stew and I were excited about the trip—Stew especially. Camping with Jess, hiking the Narrows in Zion National Park. But there was no way I was going to admit that to him now.

"John," my dad said again. And this time he waited so long that I finally lifted my eyes to meet his. Dark eyes. Like mine, like my brother's. "You just can't use it as a curtain," he said, talking about that flag again.

"Dad, I know—"

"But if you want to hang it properly, emblem upright, 'Battle Born' where you can actually read it . . ."

I dropped my eyes. He closed the short distance between us and I felt the weight of his hand on my shoulder.

"I think it'd look pretty good on your bedroom wall," he said, gripping the back of my neck, pulling my head to his chest.

It was just a flag. I didn't care. Wasn't even sure I wanted it in my room anymore. But for just a few seconds, I let him hold my head there, listening to his strong heartbeat against my ear.

Door to door, it was only about a mile's walk to the Yardleys' place. We'd left our house around sunset, after an exciting day of chores, arguing over the Xbox, and playing H-O-R-S-E on the driveway until we couldn't stand the heat.

I still hadn't gotten around to cleaning my room.

Mr. Yardley answered the door with his one-year-old baby, Freddy, on his hip, and cradled in his other arm, a big bowl of microwaved popcorn for the movie marathon we'd planned. "Finally!" he said. "I thought you guys would never get here."

Stewart flashed me an *I told you so* look. "John made us wait," he said, pushing past me with that overstuffed pillow of his.

"They aren't our babysitters, Stew," I called after him, as if I weren't only following Dad's instructions.

Mr. Yardley raised an eyebrow at that, the corner of his mouth tugging up in a grin. "Definitely not babysitters."

"We walked here," I said, closing the door on my way in. "That's what took so long."

"Bikes still out of commission? I could have picked you up."

"It's fine. My dad was technically right, it didn't kill me."

Mr. Yardley laughed, giving Freddy a little bounce to stop him from fussing. "I'm guessing Jim gave you his 'personal responsibility' lecture before he left?"

"Pretty much," I said. The morning conversation with my dad replayed in my mind, and I couldn't help but add, "He expects too much from me sometimes."

"Could be," Mr. Yardley said. "Or maybe he's just got a knack for knowing what you're capable of before you even know it yourself."

I stopped short of rolling my eyes, and half a grin slid onto Mr. Yardley's face. "Okay, don't give me that look. Your only responsibility tonight is to eat a lot of popcorn."

"That, I can do," I said, following him to the back of the house, making faces at Freddy, who pulled his two fingers out of his mouth long enough to babble a *J* sound.

"*John,*" I pronounced for him. He rewarded me with a slobbery grin, clapping his chubby hands before plugging his fingers back into his mouth.

Their house was set up like a mirror image of ours—one story, but with the bedrooms in the front, and the kitchen open to a great big family room in the back. They had this old sectional that took up half their family room, so soft and comfortable you could barely sit on it without sinking down and drifting off to sleep.

"Davis, why are you eating that right before my dinner is ready?" Mrs. Yardley said from the kitchen. She dropped the towel she'd been drying her hands with, marched over, and wrestled the bowl of popcorn out of Mr. Yardley's grip.

"I have room for both," he said teasingly, grabbing half a handful before she could get it completely out of reach.

She sort of smiled and rolled her eyes at the same time. Then she looked at me and said, "I've been *craving* home-made ice cream for weeks."

My eyebrows went up. "Oh yeah?" I was trying not to stare at her belly. She looked about ready to pop open with that second baby.

"Davis *finally* got me one of those old-fashioned ice cream makers. Only," she added under her breath, "it just looks old-fashioned. It has a motor that does all the work. Come see."

So while Mr. Yardley set up the Blu-ray player for our marathon and Stew stacked wooden blocks on the family room rug for Freddy to knock over, I went into the kitchen to see this ice cream maker. It looked like a giant wooden bucket. But inside was a stainless steel cylinder, tall and skinny with a motor on top that churned the ice cream inside. The space between the cylinder and the bucket was packed with melting ice.

"You have to sprinkle rock salt on the ice to make it melt," she explained. "That's what lowers the freezing temperature. Can you smell it? Vanilla and fresh strawberry."

"It smells amazing," I said, nodding, but all I could really smell was that plate of chicken, fresh off the grill, sitting on the kitchen island, and the baked potatoes in the oven. They were making my mouth water.

This was the best part about staying over at the Yardleys'. Dad had been so busy with work lately, he hadn't had much time for summer barbecues.

The oven timer beeped, and Mrs. Yardley was chopping chives now, so I grabbed the oven mitts off the counter and pulled out the potatoes. They were the biggest, fluffiest-looking things I'd ever seen, golden brown jackets glistening with butter and sprinkled with coarse salt.

I couldn't really blame Stew for being mad that I made us wait.

Later that night, after Mrs. Yardley put Freddy to bed,

we stretched out on the sectional for our movie marathon, all the lights out, wrapped in blankets, eating popcorn even though we were already stuffed. My eyelids were just starting to grow heavy. When suddenly, the TV blinked out. Along with everything else.

It's weird but you never notice how much noise electricity generates until everything shuts off at the exact same time. And I'm not talking about the big stuff, like a movie blaring on the television, or the second round of popcorn popping in the microwave. I'm talking about the stuff in the background; the stuff you didn't even realize *was* making so much noise. The whirl of an overhead fan, the whoosh of the air conditioner, the soft buzz of a refrigerator. Whirl, whoosh, buzz, all coming to a stop at once. Creating the most complete silence you've ever heard.

Everyone sort of groaned and Mr. Yardley jumped up from the couch. "Don't panic, I just got new flashlights."

These were good flashlights. The kind that felt heavy in your hand and had a strong beam, not like those self-powered flashlights my dad had. While Mrs. Yardley checked on Freddy and Mr. Yardley went to check the circuit breaker, Stew held the flashlight under his chin and made zombie noises. I rolled my eyes and bit the inside of my cheek to keep from smiling.

"Okay, it's not a tripped switch," Mr. Yardley called from the entryway. "Looks like the power is out everywhere."

Out on the front porch, it was a typical warm summer night. Micro-swarms of tiny winged bugs whispered by; a breeze rustled the branches of the tall mesquites lining the Yardleys' property. But it also seemed different somehow.

"This is pretty cool," Stew said, leaning on the porch railing and looking up at the sky.

"Turn off your flashlight," Mr. Yardley said. "This is what zero light pollution looks like."

The houses in and around Lund didn't put out a ton of light, not like the lights of a big city, but I'd never seen it so dark. There was no moon out, just an explosion of stars in the sky, all of them varying in brightness and size and even color.

"Boys, help me move this out onto the grass," Mr. Yardley said, taking one side of their stand-alone porch swing. We got it down the porch steps, set it in the middle of the lawn, and took off the canopy so we could see the whole sky. Mrs. Yardley came out with bowls of that homemade ice cream on a tray, her flashlight tucked under her arm.

"I got it," I said, jumping up to help her with the tray.

"Look what we have a front-row seat to, Lizzie," Mr. Yardley said, motioning up to the sky. "This is *better* than Blu-ray."

Stew threw his arms out, as if presenting the sky to Mrs. Yardley. "A long time ago, in a galaxy far, far away . . ."

Mrs. Yardley laughed, taking in the sight with her head tilted up, one hand braced against her lower back, the other cradling her stomach. "It's pretty incredible," she agreed.

We ate melting ice cream under all those stars, squished together on that porch swing, talking and telling stories and laughing until we sometimes couldn't breathe.

We forgot all about our movie marathon. Forgot all about the power being out.

It was a peaceful summer night. It was the last time I remember feeling completely at ease.

3

"DO YOU THINK Dad will still be home before dinnertime?" Stew asked. He sat down on a case of bottled water that we'd brought out to the end of our driveway with us, scratched a dry spot on his leg until it turned chalk white. "I mean, since it's the zombie apocalypse?"

"Of course he'll be home," I said, ignoring the part about the zombie apocalypse.

Three days into the blackout, and we still had no idea what had caused it or when the power would be back on, but I was pretty sure zombies had nothing to do with it.

An emergency community meeting was being held in town today. Mr. Yardley said he'd pick us up, and we were waiting for him under the shade of the desert willow by the road, shirt collars stiff and itchy with dried sweat. I'd had a jittery feeling in my chest all morning, anxious to get to this meeting to find out what was going on, find out how soon we could expect things to go back to normal—which couldn't happen soon enough.

I was sure when my dad got home, he'd want to know what was said at the meeting too.

I jammed the toe of my shoe into the packed dirt, kicking loose a big rock. Then squinted up the empty road, watching for a truck.

"Planes can't fly into airports with no power," Stew said, speaking of Dad again.

I held in an irritated sigh. Stew had been acting weird today. Sort of quiet, barely touching the breakfast Mrs. Yardley had made us before we left their house early that morning.

"There's more than one way to travel," I explained as patiently as I could. "He probably already rented a car and is most of the way home."

"But why do you think we haven't heard from him?" Stew asked, which was the most annoying question ever, given the circumstances.

"I don't know, Stew, the power's out. Maybe the Pony Express will deliver a letter."

He gave me a quick stare, but seriously. We'd tried everything we could think of to get ahold of Dad, to get ahold of *anybody* outside of Lund after that first day. On a good day, internet and cell service was spotty out here. But we'd never had a problem calling out on landlines. Until now.

One thing we did know, this blackout was big. That first morning without power, Mr. Yardley drove all the way up to Ely to find out what was going on, find out how soon we could expect the electricity up and running in Lund.

The look on his face when he told us it wasn't just Lund without power.

"There he is," Stew said, looking past me. A red truck was coming down the road in the distance, sunlight glaring off the windshield.

"All right, don't ask him if he wants it," I said, "just—"

"Yeah, I know."

Mr. Yardley pulled up with the windows rolled down, arm resting on the doorframe. He lifted his hand as if to wave, but stopped short when he saw Stew with the case of water.

I pretended not to notice the way his eyes dropped uncomfortably, went around to the passenger side while Stew loaded the water in back.

"Mrs. Yardley's not coming?" I said, moving to the center of the bench to make room for Stew. Even with the windows down, it was about a thousand degrees in his truck.

"She wasn't up for it." He leaned forward to watch Stew in the rearview mirror, adjusted his sweat-ringed baseball cap, and draped his arms over the steering wheel.

He glanced over at me. "Thanks, John," he said with a nod.

"It's payment for dinner the last few nights," I said, though we both knew it had nothing to do with payment and everything to do with the fact that they were already running low on water.

It didn't always seem like it, but Mr. Yardley wasn't really from around here. I mean, he had been our neighbor for a few years now, but he grew up in a city just south of Las Vegas called Henderson. Mrs. Yardley was from Ely, which isn't exactly like living in Lund either. Somehow they ended up out here, buying that property next to ours that had been for sale for ages.

"Stewart, thanks for the water," he said when my brother jumped in.

"It's no problem," Stew mumbled, adjusting the air vents in front of him, though no air was coming out.

"Sorry it's so hot in here." Mr. Yardley glanced out the back window, as if there was any chance a car might be coming, and turned the wheel as far as it would go, the tires grinding in the dirt. "I'm not running the AC. Thought I should probably try to conserve gas, in case this drags on for another day."

I groaned. "I don't think I can take another day of this."

"Miss your Xbox that much, huh?" he teased.

"Maybe a little," I said, which was an understatement, and Mr. Yardley knew it. He chuckled. "Okay, a lot," I admitted. "But Stew and I have been playing this game with a tennis ball around the house that isn't so bad."

"Oh yeah?"

"Yeah, you throw a tennis ball against any wall in the house as hard as you can, making it bounce off the opposite wall. Bonus points for distance and multiple hits in a row. Minus points for knocking down pictures or getting whacked with the ball. I've been kicking Stew's butt."

"Is that true, Stewart?"

"He cheats a lot," Stew said, staring out the open window.

I rolled my eyes.

Mr. Yardley turned onto State Route 318 and sped up, warm air streaming in through the side windows and swirling out the back, like a deafening whirlwind. Stew put his head against the doorframe and shut his eyes. I relaxed against the warm seat, feeling the wind gust up through the damp hair on my neck.

The meeting was in the school library. Mrs. Rudman, the school librarian, was waiting at the entrance, cheeks flushed, fanning herself with a clipboard.

"Glad you boys could make it," she said, glancing at her watch.

"Well, the power's out at our place, and we had nothing better to do. . . ."

"Funny, John." She gave me a tight smile. Her sharp blue eyes glanced to Mr. Yardley, then moved past him to the empty hallway behind us, and softened. "Your dad still isn't back?" she said, flipping through the papers on her clipboard.

"Not yet," Mr. Yardley said, clasping my brother's shoulder. Stew was staring at the floor, counting the blue flecks in the tile or something.

"He'll be back tonight," I quickly added.

Mrs. Rudman pursed her lips in concentration, Mr. Yardley watching with interest as she found our names and marked them off with a pink highlighter.

There wasn't much pink on those papers.

"I guess we're not the only ones running late?" Mr. Yardley said. He removed his baseball cap, swiped his forearm across his hairline.

"That, or they aren't coming," Mrs. Rudman said grimly.

Stew leaned close to my ear. "Zombies already got to them—"

I nudged him back with my elbow.

"What was that, Stewart?" Mrs. Rudman said, setting down the clipboard behind her.

"Nothing."

Mr. Yardley had tucked his cap under his arm. One of those orange Igloo water coolers that we used in gym class was sitting on a desk outside the library door, and he was reaching for the stack of foam cups.

"Oh—" Mrs. Rudman stopped him with an apologetic smile. "Davis, that's empty. But here." She took a paper from the small pile next to the watercooler and handed it to him. "Every household is filling out one of these. Front and back."

"Thanks," he mumbled, staring at the paper with a small crease between his eyes.

"Don't forget to take a pen," she added before looking

back to Stew and me. She kind of hesitated, then took a second paper from the stack and handed it to me. "I guess you're the head of household while your dad is away, John. Front and back."

It was a list of handwritten questions, taking inventory of the things we had in our house. Questions that my dad would be answering, not me, if he were here right now. And the first one . . . I tried to figure out why it bothered me, why it started this strange little flutter in my chest.

"What is it?" Stew asked, crowding in to get a look.

"Just a bunch of questions," I said, nudging him away again, forcing the unease from my mind.

"Boys, you ready?" Mr. Yardley said.

We took a shortcut through the maze of bookcases. Loud voices were talking over each other, Mr. Ramsey already struggling to get everyone's attention.

"If you could all *just* quiet down for a moment—" he was saying, standing on the "story time" stage at the back of the library. Behind him, a wall-to-wall mural of Great Basin National Park, a blue banner painted across the top with the title of our state song, HOME MEANS NEVADA.

Around a cluster of "silent reading" tables, a heated argument had broken out, a chair skidding across the floor as Mr. Johnson leapt to his feet. "Don't tell me what I *do* and do *not* know! I'll take care of my family the way I see fit." He jabbed his finger at his chest.

"Everyone, please," Mrs. Clarke said over the yelling. My favorite school counselor—also, the *only* school counselor. She had taken down one of those stiff posters that were tacked up all over the library—the one with a panicked-looking cat hanging from a tree branch, with the words HANG IN THERE! written above—and was standing by an open window, fanning outside air into the room.

Mr. Ramsey put his hand in the air. Like he had a question or something. "If you all wouldn't mind—"

"Oh boy," Mr. Yardley said under his breath, taking in the scene.

"Why is no one listening to him?" Stew asked.

"Not everyone can command a room like your dad," Mr. Yardley said, and through the nervous fluttering in my chest, I felt a small swell of pride.

"Dad would have this room under control in a heartbeat," I agreed.

"Let's sit with Mr. Neilson," Mr. Yardley said, pointing to a round table set farther back from the others.

Mr. Neilson—our closest neighbor after the Yardleys—was sitting alone, shoulders hunched, collar damp with sweat. Mr. Yardley patted him on the back to let him know we were joining him, and he turned, kind of startled, but then smiled warmly at each of us, unfamiliar gray stubble on his cheeks and chin.

"Your dad still not back?" he said, looking past me as I pulled out the chair to sit beside him.

"He'll be back tonight," I said, though I was starting to get tired of repeating this stuff.

Mr. Neilson patted my hand, gave me a concerned smile that did nothing to help the fluttering in my chest, then glanced toward the stage. "Apparently, Ramsey used to work for Nevada Power and knows a thing or two about power grids."

"Yeah?" Mr. Yardley said distractedly. He squared the questionnaire on the table in front of him, picked up the pen.

"He was just starting to explain it—"

An ear-piercing screech came from some little kids chasing each other around the library. Because I guess the room wasn't loud enough.

"For Pete's sake," Mr. Neilson grumbled.

Most of the older kids—kids our age—were hanging out in the courtyard. Goofing around. *Not* filling out emergency-preparedness questionnaires. I could see them from the east-side windows.

"Did the Ericsons come back from Tahoe?" Stew asked, his eyes scanning the courtyard.

"They were supposed to be back yesterday," I said, remembering our plans to go over to Ryan's this weekend for an old-school video game tournament.

"I don't see them," Stew said.

"Well, maybe they aren't here yet."

"The Ericsons are *never* late. They show up early for everything—"

"Stew, not now, all right?" I said, cutting him off. I leaned on my elbow, hand braced across my forehead, blocking out the noise around me. I read the first question again and . . . I decided to skip it for now. I went straight to the second one.

#2. How much water do you have for your family?

This was an easy question for me. The rule of thumb is one gallon of water per person per day, but I didn't need to do the math. I already knew that with our water tanks, and the cases of water bottles that we always rotated through our food storage, we had a six-month supply for the three of us.

I wrote in my answer.

#3. Do you have a supply of nonperishable food?
How much?

Another easy answer that I didn't have to think about. Six-month supply.

#4. Do you have a generator (solar or gas)?

As if we wouldn't have a generator.

The first morning of the blackout, right when we got home, Stewart and I moved my dad's gas-powered generator out of the shed, ran a long extension cord through a window in the kitchen. Plugged in the fridge so nothing would go bad in there, plugged in a big box fan—

"If I could get your attention—" Mr. Ramsey said, raising his voice.

Mr. Neilson sighed beside me. "He should probably put his hand down. Looks like he's waiting for someone to call on him."

I focused on the next question, blinking down at the paper.

#5. Do you have the medication you need, a first aid kit?

I pressed my fingertips into my temple, slick with sweat. Filled in my answer.

"Hey, Davis," someone called from across the noisy room, "isn't your Lizzie due to have that baby any day now?"

I lifted my eyes to look at Mr. Yardley. He was staring steadily at his questionnaire, which was still blank. In fact, I didn't think he had moved since he picked up his pen.

I read through the remaining questions quickly.

#6. Does your home provide adequate shelter from the heat?
#7. Do you have a radio?
#8. Do you have batteries?

#9. Matches? A reliable light source?

#10. Sanitation supplies?

I filled in my answers.

We were prepared for this. My dad had made sure of it. We had everything on the list, and then some. So I didn't know why the fluttering in my chest had turned to a pounding.

Then I heard something through the disorderly room. My dad's name.

"Don't get started on Lockwood again. He didn't predict any of this!"

It came from the front of the meeting, near those silent reading tables, but I didn't look up this time. I just made my hand into a fist, fingernails biting into my palm.

"At least he practiced what he preached," someone answered, "which is more than a lot of us can say."

"The man isn't a saint. He's a pack rat—"

Stewart stiffened beside me, and my head shot up, chest inflating with air, but Mr. Neilson stopped me, covering my fist with his weathered hand. "You know what I always admire about your dad?" he said to us in a low voice, the weight of his hand heavier than I expected. "Up against a hothead like Mike Johnson who doesn't know up from down, Jim never takes the bait. Just stays cool as a cucumber."

A heart-leaping whistle broke through the chaos, sharp and high-pitched, and Mr. Neilson's hand left mine.

Mrs. Rudman was standing red-faced on a chair in front of the bookcases. "The power may be out," she said in a stern voice, trembling with anger, "but this is *still* a library. *Quiet!*"

Seizing the moment, Mrs. Clarke dropped the cat poster

and hurried to the front of the meeting. "Excuse me, every-one. I know tensions are high right now—"

"I came here to get answers," Mr. Johnson shouted, "not a lecture from my neighbors—"

"I agree," Mrs. Clarke said smoothly. "If you would take a seat, then I think we can *all* agree to give Mr. Ramsey the floor, and get our questions answered. And, parents, let's have the children play in the courtyard. They don't need to be in here for this anyway."

"Is she talking about us?" Stewart asked, as parents began breaking up the game of tag and ushering kids out of the library. He leaned forward on his folded arms, heel tucked beneath him.

"Nah, she's not referring to you boys," Mr. Neilson said, "just the kids running around screaming."

"What a relief," I said dryly, as if I wouldn't rather be goofing around in the courtyard than listening to a bunch of adults have a shouting match. But then I caught a hint of Mr. Neilson's expression and immediately regretted my sarcastic response.

Definitely not cool as a cucumber.

"John," Mr. Yardley said, the directness in his voice catching me off guard, his attention off the questionnaire and on me for the first time since sitting down. "You should stay and listen to Mr. Ramsey."

He'd said it like he was apologizing for something. *Sorry, John, but you have to stay here and be "head of household."*

I agreed with a shrug, like it didn't bother me.

Stew straightened. "If John's staying, I'm staying."

"Parents," Mrs. Clarke called from the front of the room, "do not get upset—of course, I am not referring to your little ones. Nursing babies, toddlers can stay."

"Well, there's your answer, Stew," I said, his eyes narrowing at me, "you can stay."

"All right," Mr. Ramsey started as the room quieted, giving Mrs. Clarke a nod of thanks. "As I was saying before, the Western Interconnection is a power grid that spans more than the eleven westernmost states, parts of Mexico, and up through Canada—"

"So, you're saying the whole grid is down?"

"What I'm saying is, we've already confirmed blackouts in Arizona, California, Utah, Idaho . . ."

There were a few gasps as the list went on, and though news of this had already spread, hearing it again was just as shocking as when Mr. Yardley first told us. Still, I tried to focus on the fact that, when the blackout started, my dad was outside this area, all the way in North Carolina.

I figured that was a good thing. Wasn't it?

"Does that mean the whole grid is down?"

"Well—"

"What could cause an entire power grid to go down?"

"Zombies," Stew said in my ear. I gave him a sharp look, not in the mood. "*What?*" he mouthed, his hands up in a shrug, like he wasn't even kidding.

"Answering that question would require a lot of speculation," Mr. Ramsey said, "the kind of speculation that isn't helpful. Let's work with what we do know—"

"Who *cares* how it happened," Mr. Johnson snapped. "I just want to know why the power isn't back yet."

"Yes, what is the holdup, exactly?"

"Let's keep it orderly," Mrs. Clarke said. "One question at a time! Mr. Ramsey, when can we expect the power to be back on?"

"Well, I suppose it could come back anytime. But"—he

interrupted the collective sigh of relief—"if you aren't prepared for the worst, then I would start considering your options."

"What do you mean?" Mrs. Clarke said. "What options?"

"Well, if you don't have at least a three-month supply of food and water—"

"Three *months*?" Mrs. Clarke said over the shouts. "Are you saying we won't have power for *three months*?"

The room erupted then, but all I could do was watch Mr. Ramsey. He rubbed his jaw, his eyes concerned, like he was just coming to the realization that a lot of us didn't understand something about this blackout.

"Listen," Mr. Ramsey said, putting both hands in the air this time. "*Listen*," he repeated. "Even if the power comes back on tomorrow, food production, shipping, *everything* has already come to a halt across the entire western United States. There's already a fuel shortage in Ely, we can assume that's true of most cities. And with no fuel, nothing is moving up or down our highways. Think of it like a chain reaction. And way out here in Middle-of-Nowhere, Nevada, we're on the end of that chain."

He paused, like he expected more interruptions, but at that moment, all I could hear was the pounding in my own ears.

He cleared his throat. "Now, you were given a questionnaire when you walked in. If you'll flip it over and take a look at the back . . ."

I looked down and turned the paper over for the first time, surprised to see it was mostly blank. Except for the words written at the top: PLAN OF ACTION.

"This is where you can work out a plan for your family. Think about the answers to those questions on the front. If you don't have at least a three-month supply of food and water, then consider the first one. For a lot of you, that question might be the most important. It represents mobility. As you've probably noticed by the low turnout here, a lot of folks have already taken advantage of it." He paused for a moment. "'How much fuel do you have?' Enough to temporarily evacuate your family out of Lund?"

I sat by the window on the drive home, staring at the blur of sagebrush and dust.

"Why don't you boys come over for dinner again tonight?" Mr. Yardley said. His hands were gripping the steering wheel, his eyes fixed on the empty stretch of highway in front of us.

"Our dad will be home before dinner," I reminded him.

Stewart was silent.

Mr. Yardley looked like he wanted to say something else, but he didn't.

When we got home, Stew went straight to his room, which was fine by me, because I went straight to mine. I picked up everything off the floor, made my bed, cleared off my desk.

The state flag was still there from the morning my dad left town, and I made a split-second decision about it. I unfolded it, got some thumbtacks, and hung it on my wall properly. Like Dad said I should.

I stood back and stared at the emblem.

Against the opposite wall, the wall I shared with my brother, a tennis ball thumped. A steady *thump, thump, thump.* My heart beating twice as fast.

Dad would be home that night. I let myself believe it was possible. I let myself believe that a massive power outage on one side of the country wouldn't affect travel on the other side of the country. One side grinding to a halt, but not the other.

I let myself believe it, until I couldn't anymore.

It was late, probably past midnight, when a knock sounded on my door.

Lying on top of my comforter, I took a breath and stopped all the overwhelming thoughts in my head, forced my mind to be still. I rubbed my palms over my eyes, wiped my nose on my sleeve. "I'm awake," I called in a steady voice.

My brother cracked open the door, and I made room for him on my bed. I gave him my pillow and tucked my arm beneath my head.

"We're going to be on our own out here for a while," I said.

"I know," he whispered back.

My hand was on the flashlight resting against my leg. I thumbed it on with a click, lifted it, and shined it at the flag, at the words in the upper left-hand corner. BATTLE BORN.

My dad was right. That flag did look pretty good on my bedroom wall.

The Yardleys were at our house the next day.

"We brought dinner," Mr. Yardley said, carrying in a pot of cooked pasta. "The only problem is, we have no pasta sauce."

"I kept meaning to get more sauce," Mrs. Yardley said, holding tight to Freddy's little wrist as he tried to wriggle away. He squealed as she pulled him back, grabbing him under the arms and lifting him to her hip.

"Don't worry. We got a whole shelf of pasta sauce in the garage," Stew said.

Mrs. Yardley smiled in response. And then for some reason, she put the back of her hand to her mouth, shut her eyes, and burst into sobs. Freddy took one look at his mom and stopped wriggling. He stuck out his lower lip, his clear blue eyes brimming with tears.

"Geez, it's just sauce," Stew said as Freddy let out a wail. "Take as much as you want."

Mr. Yardley put his arm around his wife and kissed the side of her head, rested a hand on her pregnant belly. Then he looked at me. "Let's go talk, John."

Out back, the sun was setting and the sky was streaked with shades of red and orange, like the distant mountains were on fire.

The view didn't exactly help ease the feeling of dread growing inside me.

"We have plenty of food and water," I started to say, "enough to share—"

"It's not just that, John. Lizzie could go into labor any day now. She'll need help."

I nodded like I understood these things.

"I'm just trying to decide if I should be talking you into coming with us," he said, "or talking you into staying here on your own."

I knew it was coming. I knew they'd have to leave. But my heart still dropped when he said it. I told him, "You don't need to do either. We're staying here."

"All right," he said after a pause. And while we watched the sunset fade, we went over everything. He wanted to make sure we were really prepared for this. Stew and I had plenty of food and water, and we had that generator. How much fuel did we need to keep the generator running? How much fuel did we have stored on our property? How much fuel did Mr. Yardley need to get up to Ely, to Mrs. Yardley's sister? How much fuel did he need to get back here, back to us, after the baby was born and it was okay to travel?

I tried not to let my mind go too deep into all this. Tried not to think about how my dad should have been talking about this stuff with Mr. Yardley, and not me. Tried not to think about how long we'd be on our own. And at the end of it, he gave me a way out. "Are you sure you can do this? If you're not sure, we can figure out something else."

I'd never felt more unsure in my life. But I just scrunched up my forehead like I was giving it more thought—then I nodded. "I'm sure."

His lips pressed into a smile. "You know, John, you're a lot more like your dad than you think."

"If you say so, Mr. Yardley," I said, like I agreed with him.

He took his eyes off that sky, regarded me directly. "John. You can call me Davis, all right?"

Some things Davis and I never went over: What to do if I was startled awake in the middle of the night by a stranger. What to do if in one night, the food was gone, the water was gone. *Everything* was gone.

4

BETWEEN US AND Brighton Ranch is this stretch of highway that my dad calls "the *actual* loneliest road in America." Highway 50 in Nevada holds the official title, but my dad says the second it was named the Loneliest Road in America, state officials put up signs and used it as a marketing campaign to attract tourists. This was way back in the 1980s, so maybe there was nothing better to do back then but visit an uninhabited length of asphalt. Anyway, my dad calls Highway 50 a tourist trap, and he calls State Route 318 the *actual* loneliest road in America. Except for a rather unpopular reservoir with a campsite near one end, there is nothing but this highway, dirt, and some poky-looking plants. No gas stations, no bathrooms, no fast food.

The highway is mostly flat and mostly straight, the kind that tapers off to a pinpoint on the horizon that you never reach. It cuts through a wide desert basin covered in woody, silvery-green sagebrush. Sometimes you'll see what looks like a tree, but it's actually just *big* sagebrush. They've got these crumbly-looking trunks that have been twisted and bent by the wind, like freakishly large bonsai trees in need of a good pruning. Rising from both sides of the basin are distant, barren mountains.

"How far is it to this ranch?" the girl calls through the wind. She's holding the boy's hand and they're trailing several feet behind me and Stew.

Dad would do both.

I swear, if I weren't so determined to keep us both alive, I'd pound my brother for putting those words in my mind.

Not that the girl had waited for an invitation to come along or anything.

"Hey," the girl calls again. "How far is it to this ranch?"

I glare sideways at my brother. "Did you have to tell her about Brighton Ranch?"

Stew shrugs. "You think she would have stopped asking?"

He has a point.

I yell back over my shoulder, "It's about three days!"

If I tell her exactly how many miles, she might think we can take more than three days to get there. And we can't.

"Three *days*?"

I motion for them to catch up to us because I can't hear her too well back there with the wind roaring in my ears. And as soon as she's next to me, on my left side with the boy beside her, I feel this weird sense of doom.

The boy looks like he might be eight or nine years old. He's got one of those kid haircuts that hangs over your forehead and into your eyes—real babyish. The wind is blowing it straight back and his forehead is several shades paler than the rest of his suntanned face. He'll be burned within an hour. His lips are red and chapped, because he keeps on licking them. One of the stupidest things you can do when your lips are chapped in a dry wind, not that I blame him.

Every once in a while, I notice the girl tug on his hand, like she's trying to keep him alert and awake.

He'll be the first one to slow us down.

"What are your names?" I finally ask. I don't think any of us are exactly in a friendly mood, but I guess names are a good place to start.

"Cleverly," she says. "And this is my brother, Will."

I must look confused because she says her name again, louder and slower this time. "Clev-er-ly."

Stew, who's walking to my right, leans around me to ask, "Like the verb?"

"You mean *ad*verb. And no. Like, named after my grandparents, whose last name is Cleverly."

Stew and I share a look because we know who she is now. I mean, we don't know *her*, but we know the Cleverlys. They live just north of Lund, maybe ten or fifteen miles from here. I wonder where her grandparents are, what happened that brought her and her brother here, but I decide not to bring it up for now.

"Cleverly," I repeat. It sounds strange to call her that, like I'm calling out to a teammate to pass me the ball or something. "Clev?" I try, but can tell immediately it's not gonna work.

"Don't call me that," she says, and her little brother snorts.

"Clever?" I try again.

"I know it's a mouthful, but you must speak all three syllables."

"She doesn't like nicknames," her brother says.

"Will, I like nicknames fine, just not for *my* name."

"What if someone needs to shout out your name real quick, to warn you of danger or something?" Stew asks. "Then what do they call you?"

"What are *your* names?" she asks abruptly. "Or should I keep referring to you as Toilet Water Boys, like I've been doing in my head?"

You'd think that if you'd gotten desperate enough to scavenge water out of a toilet bowl, people wouldn't hold it against you. You'd think.

"You can call him Toilet Water," I say, aiming my thumb at my brother, who rolls his eyes. "T.W. for short. And you can call me John."

"How boring," she says.

"Thanks. I picked it out myself."

Will grins, but she just says, "How far are we walking today, John?"

She's trying to do math. But I can out-math her. "A third of the total distance."

"You're kind of annoying, aren't you, John?"

Stewart laughs out loud, the traitor. I can't remember the last time I heard him laugh, so I let it go. "I'm Stewart Lockwood," my brother says, leaning around me to raise his hand like she's taking attendance or something. "Or just Stew."

"Hi, Stew. Maybe you could tell me how far it is to Brighton Ranch?"

"Sure, it's about ninety-six miles from our place," he says without hesitation, which really bugs me. He could have at least hesitated.

Cleverly stops in her tracks with Will beside her, but I don't break pace, just keep pushing through the wind. "Ninety-six *miles*? That's like . . . that's like three and a half marathons!" she says as they hurry to match my pace.

Math, again. "I'm pretty sure it's only a marathon if you run it, with one of those numbers pinned to your shirt." I wave my hand over my chest.

"Is it even possible to walk that far in three days?" she asks, ignoring my logic.

"Oh, most definitely," I say.

Stew leans around me again and says, "Probably not."

What a punk! Leave it to Stew to remind everyone that we're in the middle of a life-or-death situation.

"Wait," Cleverly says. "Wait a minute." She grabs the sleeve of my shirt, pulling me to a stop. "Is this our best option?"

I'm starting to think that our best option is leaving them behind. "Oh no, we have better options," I tell her. "I just thought we'd go with Option B: scavenge drinking water from a toilet and walk for three days down this highway."

She just kind of stares at me for a second while the wind does funny things with the loose pieces of hair around her face. Then she looks at Stew. "Is he always like this?"

"He's gotten worse lately," Stew says.

I roll my eyes at that. *I've* gotten worse?

"Listen," I say, yanking my shirt out of her grip, "nobody is forcing you to come with us. If you have a better option, then great, go for it."

I start walking again, Stew by my side, though he keeps looking over his shoulder. I don't. I'm trying to set a three-mile-an-hour pace, which is kind of brisk. I'm not sure how long they plan to walk behind us, debating their options, but right now it feels like there is this invisible rope around my waist and that I'm pulling them with it. It's already wearing me down mentally. That, and the fact that I've heard Will say at least twice that he's thirsty.

I can't help thinking about our water supply. Just before the end of today's leg, about thirty-one miles from where we started, is the turnoff that leads to the reservoir. I don't want to take it, no matter what Stew says about it.

It's a waste of energy and time. We'll just have to stick with the plan, ration what water we have, and walk straight past it. Which means, if we split our water evenly, we have enough for eight cups of water each. That has to last us three days. Eight cups, three days.

Okay, stop thinking about water.

Cleverly and Will catch back up with us, that invisible rope going slack, and I lengthen my stride, trying to keep our pace up in the wind. Will leans close to his sister and I hear him ask, "When can we get a drink?"

Cleverly shushes him.

"Stew," I say, "you still have that ChapStick?" He digs it out of his pocket and I pass it on to Will. "Here, use that."

"Thanks." He takes it shyly, but then drops his sister's hand and eagerly applies it to his lips and half his face.

"Just hold on to it," I say when he tries to give it back to me.

"So, Jim Lockwood—I mean, your dad," Cleverly says, her forehead creased in thought. "Where did you say he was?"

"Good question," I say lightly, as if thinking about where my dad is doesn't bother me at all.

"You mean, you don't know where he is?" she says.

"My guess is somewhere between here and North Carolina," I say.

"We haven't heard from him since before he left town for a work trip," Stew says.

"Oh."

A mile marker is coming up on the side of the highway, a white reflective sign that indicates we've gone another mile, so I pull a black permanent marker from my shirt pocket and take the cap off with my teeth. I add a second line to the tally I started on the inside of my forearm.

"Where are you from?" I ask, tucking my pen back into my pocket, mostly to get off the subject of my dad.

Cleverly's looking at the marks I've made on my arm and frowning because she has probably figured out that we've gone only two miles, and she has probably done the math and realized that we have thirty more to go before the end of the day.

It's Will who answers. "Las Vegas. But Cleverly and I were staying with our grandparents when everything went dark."

"We should call it the Great Power Outage," Stew says. "Or the *GPO!*" He crosses his arms and makes some sort of unintelligible symbol with his fingers. Very rural Nevadan. Then he gets ahead of us, turns and throws his arms out, and yells, "Or simply, *The End*!"

I glare at him, but otherwise ignore him. "So, your parents are in Las Vegas right now?" I ask.

Will looks up at his sister, and she reaches down to squeeze his hand. "They were in Hawaii on vacation," she says.

"Oh," Stew says. "Bad timing."

The wind is really starting to pick up, even more than before. Microscopic bits of dust and dirt blast through the air, stinging our exposed skin. We move off the shoulder to walk down the middle of the highway, where the dust is less irritating. I roll down my sleeves to my wrist and turn up the collar on my shirt, then slide my hands into my pants pockets and tuck in my chin. Stew does the same. Will has this thin, oversized gray hoodie tied around his waist, and we slow down for a minute so he can put it on. Cleverly is wearing only a Tshirt and jeans.

"You got a jacket or something in there?" I lean close to ask her through the wind, motioning to her backpack.

"No," she says, shaking her head.

On one hand, I can't blame her. It's summer; it's the desert. The wind is too warm to give a chill. But long sleeves are actually ideal right now. Something lightweight and breathable, light in color so it won't absorb the heat of the sun. And if it makes you sweat a little . . . well, that's a good thing. That's your body cooling you down.

The white noise grows so loud that we don't talk at all after that, except every so often when Cleverly yells, "This is crazy!" I try to keep us moving at the same pace, but I feel the energy draining out of me. I can't even tell how fast or slow we're walking anymore, but we have to be slowing down. It's hard to walk, hard to hear and see, hard to breathe. It seems like it's been forever since we saw that last mile marker.

"This sucks!" Stew yells.

"Yep," I say back. My ears are starting to ache.

"We gotta stop," he calls over the wind.

"Why? The wind isn't going away."

"I have to pee."

I turn my head to look at him, shielding my ear with my arm. "Didn't you go before we left?"

"I have to go again."

I stare at him for a while, trying to figure out if he's messing with me, because it's been less than an hour since we left.

"Are we stopping?" Cleverly says from my other side.

"Yes," I finally say.

Stew takes that as his cue to run back the way we came, powered by airstream, and we all turn our backs to the wind and huddle into our shoulders while we wait in the middle of the highway for him.

I watch Stew veer left and pick his way through the knee-high sagebrush, which looks like a field of soft wheat bending and swaying in the breeze, except it takes more than a strong breeze to bend sagebrush.

I cup my hands around my mouth and yell, "Don't pee into the wind!"

Stew yells something back but we can't hear it.

It's kind of a relief to have the wind beat against our backs instead of our faces. But my hair has grown out longer than I usually keep it, long enough to get in my eyes and annoy the heck out of me in a windstorm. I tuck in my chin and stare down at my feet. Cleverly moves to stand in front of me, her bare arms crossed protectively over her stomach, letting me block most of the wind with my body.

I hesitate, then let my pack drop off one shoulder. "I have a hoodie you can wear."

"I'm fine," she says, loose hair whipping violently around her face. Will moves to stand behind his sister, his hood pulled up, burying his face in her backpack.

"It's really lightweight," I say.

"I don't need it."

"I'm not offering it just to be nice," I tell her bluntly, which is partly true. "It's not just the wind. Long sleeves will help you stay cooler. You're gonna get fried in this sun. You get sunburned, your temperature will go up, which will make you more dehydrated—"

Eight cups of water each. That's it.

She twists her mouth to the side. "Okay, I'll take it."

I dig my arm deep into my pack, pushing stuff aside.

"It's kind of weird that we're standing in the middle of a highway," she says.

I was thinking the same thing earlier. This may not have been the busiest highway in Nevada, but it's not like you could have taken a walk down the middle of the 318. It's actually a shortcut between Ely and Las Vegas. Anyone willing to take the route with no gas stations, no rest stops, and no cell service could shave forty-five minutes off their trip. There were plenty of takers.

"Warn me if you see a car coming from behind," I say, spotting my light blue hoodie and pulling it out for her.

"I will. Then I guess we'll run out there in the desert and hide behind some sagebrush."

She'd said it jokingly, but neither of us laughs.

We don't talk about the reasons why, but I guess we're both aware of the fact that seeing a car could be more cause for concern than for celebration. The last time I saw a running vehicle . . . well, let's just say it didn't end well.

Anyway, the chance of us seeing anyone come down this highway is pretty much zero.

Cleverly takes off her backpack and gives it to Will to hold, takes the hoodie from me and pulls it over her head. She tries to put the hood up, keeping her hair tucked back, but it keeps blowing down, her hands fumbling with the drawstrings. I finally grab the drawstrings and tie it for her.

"Thanks," she says.

"You're welcome," I mumble, shoving my hands in my pockets. I squint off to the side at nothing, because it's weird seeing her wearing my favorite hoodie.

"So," she says in a long, drawn-out way, like she's trying to fill an awkward silence. "I'm craving a cheeseburger like you wouldn't believe."

"I believe you," I say.

"That's because you don't know how much I hate cheeseburgers. But right now, I could literally skin and eat a cow."

"You could *literally* skin a cow? That's pretty disgusting, actually."

"Is it more or less disgusting than drinking toilet water?"

I pretend to think about it. "More," I say. "In fact, I think I just lost my appetite. I've been trying to get rid of it for days now, so I guess I owe you one."

She presses her lips together, like she's trying to hold in a smile, and I realize I'm doing the same thing. I look down at my feet and sort of kick at the asphalt.

Then she says, "I assume Brighton Ranch has cows that we can skin and eat?"

A small laugh escapes from my chest, but not for the reason she thinks. "Mr. Brighton doesn't have any cows."

"What kind of ranch doesn't have cows?"

"Don't worry, other than live cows, they have plenty of food. He's a self-reliance freak, like my dad. Probably even more so. He's built up this mind-blowing food storage—"

"This sounds familiar," she says, looking at me with a thoughtful frown, and I realize she was already promised the same thing once before. Her grandparents probably described Jim Lockwood's place in much the same way, a place stocked with food and water, yet here she is, standing in the middle of a deserted highway, *not* eating a freshly butchered cheeseburger.

Then Will starts laughing. I glance up to see Stew about ten yards away, with his back to us, and I start laughing, too, because a stream of urine is sailing straight out in front of him, like a fluid yellow ribbon caught in the wind.

"Unbelievable," I say.

"That is sick," Cleverly says, but Will keeps laughing.

Stew finally comes loping back through the brush, his tan button-up shirt plastered to his chest, pumping his fists in the air. "Did you see that?" he calls.

"Unfortunately," Cleverly says.

"That was pretty awesome!" Will says.

"Okay, we gotta get going." I'm feeling antsy, like we're wasting time. But before Stew gets to us, he reaches to his side and unhooks one of his canteens from his pack.

"What are you doing?" I call.

He starts walking backwards away from us, and unscrews the cap. "Signing the Declaration of Independence," he says, putting two fingers to his forehead in salute.

I drop my pack and move quickly past Cleverly and Will, but before I can stop him, Stew brings the canteen to his mouth and tips it back, recklessly chugging water, his throat working to keep up with how fast he's guzzling. I watch—almost stunned—as lifesaving water streams along the sides of his cheeks and down his neck.

"Stewart, wait!" I yell. I stop walking and hold up my hands to him in surrender, because that's all I can do. He's about ten feet away from me. I would rather chase him down, grab him by the throat, and punch him in the face, but I'm worried he'll do something even stupider, like dump the whole canteen.

Finally, he comes up for air with a gasp and swipes the back of his hand across his mouth. I don't know how much water he drank, or how much is left in his canteen, but I'm sure he's used up the day's water ration, and then some.

I'm kind of shocked. Stew can be a stubborn jerk when he wants to be, but he's not an idiot. He's annoyingly brilliant for an eleven-year-old, in fact. He wanted my attention, and now he's got it.

"I guess it's time for a water break," I call to Stew as calmly as I can.

He shades his eyes from the sun and wind. "Yep. Might as well eat too."

I bite down on my back teeth, and then agree with a nod.

Cupping my hands around my mouth, I turn and call out to Cleverly and Will, who are still standing where I left them. "We're gonna stop for a minute!"

They look relieved. I don't think they realize that Stew has just staged a mini water rebellion, and won.

5

THE CAP IS off Stew's canteen and it's making me nervous.

"Stew," I call to him evenly, as if I'm not still really angry about the water, "you wanna see if we can make some sort of shelter from this wind?"

He hesitates, like he's trying to decide if I mean to trick him. Finally, he shrugs one shoulder and replaces the cap.

I'm still nervous about him holding the canteen, but I look away from him—as if I trust him, as if he doesn't need me to keep an eye on him with that water—and I go back to my pack and get to one knee on the warm asphalt to find our shelter supplies inside.

My dad made these disaster packs for each of us years ago—originally with about three or four days' worth of food, water, and emergency supplies inside—and stored them in the cool crawl space beneath our hall closet.

If he hadn't, our chances of making it out of here would be zero percent.

After moving some stuff aside in my pack, I find the blue

tarp I'm looking for folded at the bottom. I also take out four metal stakes and my hatchet.

"Over here!" Stew yells, and I see he's found a somewhat clear area of dirt within the sagebrush, which will also help block some of this wind. Cleverly and Will are already with Stew, huddled together and waiting for me.

I grab my pack and run down there, dropping it next to Stew's pack in the swirling dust. Then Stew and I get to work setting up a tarp shelter, which would normally take us about two minutes, if we weren't working in a freaking tornado. We nearly lose the tarp twice before we finally get a handle on it. With it folded in half the long way, we lay it out on the dirt, and Cleverly and Will stand on it to keep it down. Stew holds a stake in place through the first grommet on one corner while I use the hammer side of my hatchet to pound it in. But the ground is too hard, and I'm not exactly full of energy these days—I'm operating on the handful of granola that I had before the sun came up. The stake barely makes a dent in the packed dirt before it slips to the side.

"Hold it really tight," I tell Stew impatiently, but after a few more hits and slips, he gives up. He drops the stake and sits back on the tarp like he's exhausted or something.

I'm beyond frustrated with him. Really, he had the easy job. I grab the stake and hold it in place myself. I get in a couple of decent hits, but it's not going in, and I realize that I can't gather enough force behind my swing if I have to worry about holding the stake too.

Then Cleverly is in front of me, kneeling down and taking the stake from my hand. She holds it in place with both her hands and looks me in the eyes. "Don't break my fingers, John," she says with deadly seriousness.

This causes me to smile nervously, so I quickly assure her, "I won't. Okay, you ready?"

She looks like she has a firm grip on it, firmer than Stew was holding it. She nods. With my focus on the stake, I pull my shoulder back and swing the hammer down hard, using any upper body strength I can muster. She flinches a little, but then adjusts her grip and nods for me to go again. I pound the stake, again and again, until it finally, *finally,* starts to go in. Cleverly lets go and moves back while I finish it off.

I'm sweating by the time I'm done, out of breath, and feel a couple of blisters forming on my hand, but I don't really care. I'm just glad it went in. I take a second to roll up my sleeves, and then we move on to the next one.

Will squats down to watch us, holding the extra stakes. Stew just sits on the tarp with his head buried in his knees. But once we get all four stakes in place, pinning down the bottom layer of the tarp, he has the decency to get off without waiting for me to ask.

Lifting up the top layer from two corners, Cleverly and I make a sort of V-shaped cave, with a floor, and a roof that the wind will hopefully glide right over—yeah, right. Normally, I'd prop it open at the corners with a couple of telescoping tent poles, but they wouldn't hold up in this wind. Even with us holding it up, the tarp is flapping violently.

"Now what, genius?" Stew says. He's got this smirk on his face.

Cleverly is looking at me, probably wondering the same thing. There is nothing to tie the tarp to, no tree or big sagebrush. All we have is our packs. They're almost three feet tall and reinforced with an aluminum frame, weigh about twenty-five pounds without the canteens, so they normally stand upright without a problem.

"Get our packs," I say to Stew, and he shakes his head like that's a dumb idea. But he still walks over to his and drags it across the dirt to Cleverly's side. The dragging really bugs me, and I almost yell at him to pick it up, but then Will runs to get mine and does the same thing, so I just roll my eyes and forget it.

"Thanks, Will," I say, unzipping a utility pocket and putting away my hatchet.

"No problem." He grins up at me, and then runs his tongue along those red, chapped lips of his.

"Don't lick your lips. You have that ChapStick, remember?"

"I lost it."

"*What?*" I say, thinking he must be kidding. But he's not—I can tell by the way his eyes drop. "I just gave it to you!"

"I think it fell out of my pocket when I put this on," he says, pulling at the front of his oversized hoodie.

"It's fine," I say, gritting my teeth a little, because he looks close to tears. "Don't worry about it right now."

In the front mesh compartment of my pack are a couple of thin ropes, and I take out a short one and uncoil it. I feed it through the corner grommet of the tarp, and use a few half hitch knots to tie it to the top of the aluminum frame of my pack. Will watches me closely the whole time, crouched down with his hands on his knees. I carefully let go of it, to see if it will hold, and it immediately blows over.

"This isn't gonna work!" Stew yells from the other corner.

"Just tie your side!" I prop my pack up again and sort of angle it upright against the wind until I get it to stay. Then I go help Cleverly and Stew with their side. Stew didn't even try to make it work. He's tied a couple of sloppy overhand double knots, and the rope is too slack. Probably because he thinks my idea sucks.

It's going to take me some time to get the knots undone; so I hold up the corner for them and say, "Go ahead and get in." Stew, Cleverly, and Will all duck under the sloping tarp.

When I finally get it undone, a big gust of wind hits me in the face, snatching my breath away and making me stumble a little. Holding both the tarp and Stew's pack in place, I wait for it to pass and then tie the rope and angle his pack the same way I angled mine, until it looks like it's gonna stay.

The whole shelter is crap—I know that. The roof is low and rippling like crazy; the packs make it completely unstable. But it's blocking the worst of the wind, and it only needs to last us thirty minutes, tops. That's plenty of time for a food-and-water break. Thirty minutes, then we can get on our way again.

Stew and I each have a gallon-sized ziplock bag of food in our packs, but they contain different things. Stew has a lot of high-protein crap that he actually likes but I can't stand. Plus almost everything he has left contains some sort of nut, and I have a mild nut allergy—the kind that makes my throat itch, not the EpiPen-to-the-thigh kind. I have typical hiker's food in my pack—granola, dried fruit, crackers, a couple cans of Vienna sausages. We both have jerky. These weren't intended to be three-course meals. In fact, I never actually believed we'd be eating this stuff at all. If I had, I might have talked my dad into something that actually tastes good.

Unzipping Stew's pack without disturbing the tarp, I take out his food, as well as his tin mug, and then I go to my pack and get my food too. I grab one more thing—sunscreen for Cleverly and Will—then I hunker down, duck my head under the tarp.

My breath catches, and I freeze in place.

Sunlight hits the roof of the shelter, casting everyone in a blue pool-like glow. Like the flag over my bedroom window. The morning my dad left. The smell of his aftershave, the lawn mower fading in the distance, his heartbeat echoing in my ear.

John, I know I've been gone a lot lately—

It starts to happen again. That thing where my chest tightens, like a balloon is inflating in my rib cage, squeezing the air out of my lungs—

"John," Cleverly says, and I blink at her, clearing my vision. She puts her knees up and scoots closer to Will, patting the space next to her, like I'm just waiting for an invitation to sit.

Think of something else. Not Dad leaving again. Not me being responsible for everything that's happened since, being responsible for my brother . . .

"Nice shelter, John," Stew says.

I look at my brother, sitting cross-legged with his forearms on his knees, his head tilted to the side. That cowlick at his hairline pushing his hair the opposite way, his mouth pressed in a sarcastic grin.

I take a breath, force air into my lungs. "Thanks," I say to him, and crawl inside, sitting next to Cleverly, right on the edge with my ankles crossed, knees bent upward like bat wings.

"Kind of hot and cramped in here," he continues. "It will probably collapse. But otherwise, nice shelter."

"Exactly what I was going for." My heart rate is already returning to normal. I take another breath.

"It's not bad, right, Will?" Cleverly says, nudging her brother. And I realize she's trying to defend me. She's also eyeing the low, flapping ceiling like she thinks it's going to collapse any second.

"Yeah, I think it's amazing," Will agrees, nodding encouragingly.

Those words are barely past his lips when the pack on my side starts to topple over, pulling the roof down with it. Reacting fast, I roll forward onto my knees and grab it, propping it back up from the inside.

Stew laughs. "Amazing that it stayed up as long as it did," he says.

I don't really care that the shelter sucks; I just want to get this break over with. I toss Stew his pouch of food and he catches it. I give Cleverly the sunscreen. "Your whole face, your ears, the back of your neck."

She cringes but takes it.

"Won't it make us sticky?" Will says, squeezing his eyes shut and scrunching up his nose as she wipes down his face.

"There are worse things, Will," Cleverly says.

I pull open my ziplock bag and take out three individually wrapped packages of dried fruit, taking one for myself and passing one to both Cleverly and Will. My dad stored this stuff away so long ago that it's best not to check the expiration dates, but I can tell by the packaging alone that this flat rectangle of fruit leather is *old*. Still, Cleverly and Will open it with so much enthusiasm, you'd think they were biting into a fresh-picked Washington apple, with the juices trailing down their chins.

I hesitate, then go ahead and take out two pieces of jerky from my pouch, and zip it closed. I hand it to Cleverly and her brother. "It's not a cheeseburger, but . . ."

"Thank you," she says, and I can tell she means it. Will immediately tears into the jerky with his back teeth.

I peel away the wrapper on my fruit leather and bite into it. It's so tough that I have to work my teeth back and forth to tear off a bite. In this dried form, the sweet tang of apple is really strong, almost sickeningly so. It sits heavy on my tongue, absorbing all the moisture in my mouth like a sponge. I chew on it for a while, and it goes down like a lump of pasty oatmeal.

On Stew's lap is the canteen he was drinking out of earlier. "How about you share your water with them?" I say, holding out his mug to him, but he doesn't take it. He has the wrapper pulled down on a protein bar and is about to take another bite, but he hesitates.

"Why can't you share *your* water, John?" he says in this confused, thoughtful tone.

He knows why—he's just trying to be difficult. My water is still contaminated. I could have boiled it before we left the shack house, but I was so anxious to get going . . .

Maybe it wasn't the best idea.

Stew is waiting for my answer, and I realize ignoring him isn't going to make him shut up about it, so I go ahead and say it. "I haven't boiled it yet."

"Oh yeah," he says real slowly, like I just jogged his memory, "that's right. You gave me all the clean water, and took all the toilet water for yourself, like a real hero. And now it's way too windy for a fire. Who knows when you'll have a chance to make it drinkable—"

"All right," I say, mostly because I don't want to argue with him. "I screwed up. I should have boiled it right away. Can we drop it now?"

"So, you *do* make dumb decisions?"

I glare at him. "On rare occasions, yeah."

Stew looks so satisfied by my answer that I suddenly realize that was all he was trying to get me to admit. I, John

71

Lockwood, sometimes make dumb decisions. So what? What's his point?

He stuffs the rest of his protein bar in his mouth, crumbles up the wrapper and jams it in his pocket, and then leans forward and grabs the mug from me.

"Start with half a cup each, all right?" I say.

"Did you hear that?" he says to Cleverly and Will, his mouth still half full. "You each get a whole half cup of water!"

Will has a concerned frown on his face, and Cleverly turns to give me an *Are you kidding me?* look, her eyebrows arched over her widened eyes. Because half a cup of water is nothing. It's backwash. And she isn't complaining about it, even though we both know it's not enough water to keep anyone walking. That look is because she's beginning to realize just how desperate our water situation is.

I could point out to her that her first clue might have been when she caught us scavenging water from a toilet, but I decide not to bring it up. For obvious reasons.

Stew gives both Will and Cleverly their water ration, and then takes the mug back, pours a third cup, and holds it out to me before I can stop him. "Pour it back. I don't need water right now." Once it's out, I realize it's kind of a stupid thing to say. My mouth is so dry that my lips stick together when I talk. Almost without realizing it, my tongue glides along my bottom lip, and then begins the spit-gathering-and-swallowing ritual.

Cleverly is eyeing me thoughtfully, chewing on a piece of fruit leather like it's bubble gum. "You don't need water? Is that another one of your dumb decisions?"

Stew laughs again. "I'd say so. But if he's not gonna drink it . . ." He shrugs, and then tosses back the half cup in a single swallow.

An obvious attempt to get under my skin. I grit my teeth and swallow more spit.

But Cleverly leans past her brother and hits Stew on the knee. "Hey, he needs that. Pour him another cup."

"I'm fine," I say, barely containing my annoyance.

"We *all* need water."

"Not John," Stew says. "He can survive without water. Right, John? Because you're so much stronger than the rest of us, right? Only the strongest idiot survives!"

I've had enough at this point, but before I can tell Stew to shut it, Cleverly comes to my defense again. "Could you have set up this tarp shelter?" she asks, narrowing her eyes at my brother.

"I could do better than this—"

"I'm not asking if you know *how* to set up a tarp shelter. I'm asking if you could have set up *this* shelter, right here, right now. Because a few minutes ago, you seemed pretty much useless."

"I'm only useless when I want to be," Stew says, which might be true, but he's definitely losing ground here.

Will is gnawing on his jerky, watching them go back and forth like it's a tennis match.

Cleverly shakes her head. "You couldn't even hold the stakes in place, let alone hammer them into the hard ground. John got them in. So stop acting like his strength isn't important to our survival."

I immediately feel blood rushing to my cheeks, and I'm not typically a blusher. I mean, I shouldn't be blushing over this at all. That's the worst part. Because I know she's just trying to take Stew down a notch—and it worked, because it shut him up. But my body is reacting as if she had just given a speech on the wonders of my right biceps.

"Why are you grinning like that?" she asks me in this

exasperated tone. Then she sighs and says, "Look, it's kind of freaking me out that you won't drink half a cup of water. I get that there is not much of it, but—"

"Enough," Stew interrupts.

"What?"

"Enough," he repeats. "I'm just correcting you. You said there isn't *much* water, and the truth is we don't have *enough* water. To make it to Brighton Ranch, I mean. We have less than two gallons to get us there. Or *not* get us there, I should say."

No, Stew, you shouldn't say anything. Really, you should keep your mouth shut!

I see the look on Cleverly's face and I want to insist that everything will be fine, that we can make it through the desert on what water we have left. But I know she won't believe me. She *shouldn't* believe me.

It would be a complete lie.

Even if Stew hadn't messed up the ration, even if he hadn't guilted me into letting two strangers tag along with us, we just don't have enough water to make it. That's what Stew's little water rebellion is all about, isn't it? Getting me to admit that we don't have enough water?

It's Will who finally breaks the silence. Staring off at nothing, he says in this wooden voice, "Last night I dreamt I jumped into a swimming pool and started gulping down the water. I drained the whole pool, every last drop, but I was still thirsty for some reason. I don't know why I was still thirsty. I drank a whole pool."

I look out in front of me at a row of sagebrush that are beating wildly against each other, their long pointed stems waving violently toward the sky, like some sort of crazy battle. I let the scene mesmerize me as I think. I guess there comes a time when you just stop fighting and accept the inevitable.

"Okay, Stew."

"Okay?"

I nod. "Okay," I say again. "We'll stop for water at the reservoir."

Stewart hesitates with his hand on the cap of his second canteen. "You're sure about this, John?"

I give him a look. Because apparently, *now* he cares what I think.

"I mean," he says, "since we're stopping at the reservoir, drinking the rest of our clean water now just makes sense, right?"

"Makes sense to me," Will says with a nod.

Cleverly nudges him with her elbow. "What do you think, John?"

I meet my brother's eyes, and I think . . . he's testing me. I think the only thing that matters right now is that Stew believes me. I *need* him to believe me. I don't want a single doubt in his mind that I'm serious about stopping at the reservoir to refill our canteens.

And I am serious about it. It's just not going to happen in exactly the way he thinks.

I hold out the mug. "Fill it to the top."

He grins and unscrews the cap.

I drink the water in a few swallows and pass the mug to Will.

"Thanks," he says, taking it eagerly.

"So, after we drink this," Cleverly says, "there's no water left except—"

"The toilet water," I finish for her, and she makes a face. "Don't worry, I'll decontaminate it as soon as I get a chance."

"Then first thing tomorrow," she says, "we'll head to this reservoir of water, that was actually between us and Brighton Ranch the whole entire time?"

I know what she's getting at. But I don't give her an explanation, just answer, "Right."

She stares back at me, her eyes narrowed like she's thinking about something.

"Ugh," Will says, swiping his hand across his mouth and passing the mug to Cleverly. "It tastes like old bathtub water."

"Don't complain," Cleverly says. "And how do you know what old bathtub water tastes like anyway?"

He shrugs. "I'm just saying, I wish the water was colder."

Stew takes the mug and says, "Here, Will, do this." He pours himself another cup. "Let it sit on your tongue for a minute before you swallow." He demonstrates, holding the water in his mouth, cheeks puffed out like a chipmunk. Then he swallows. "Ah!" he says, smacking his lips. "So refreshing!"

We all try Stew's method, and I admit it helps a little bit. But the constant thirst at the back of my throat? It's still there. I'm guessing I could drink the swimming pool from Will's dream and it would still be there.

As soon as the water's gone, I stretch out my legs and say, "All right, it's time to get going—" But Stew lies down on the tarp, curls onto his side, and I freeze mid-stretch. "Stewart. Get up."

"I'm just closing my eyes for a minute," he mumbles, his head resting in the crook of his arm. "Don't freak out."

Don't freak out?! We've gone less than three miles, and you need a freaking nap!

This is exactly why I didn't want to stop at the reservoir. He's proving my point, though I'm sure he doesn't care. Keeping my brother walking for ninety-six miles is hard enough, without adding sixteen more miles to our already insanely long walk.

"I'm breaking the shelter down in five minutes," I snap, grabbing my food pouch. I reach past Cleverly for Stew's.

"I got it," she says, passing it to me, along with his mug.

I crawl out from under the tarp before I explode in frustration.

The wind hits me hard, catching me off guard even though it shouldn't have. I guess my shelter wasn't completely worthless after all. Cleverly follows me out, stands beside me with her arms crossed and her head ducked against the wind as I crouch next to each pack.

I get the feeling she's getting ready to bombard me with questions about the reservoir, and why, until ten minutes ago, I was planning to walk right past it. So when I'm done with the packs, I turn and move away from the shelter, stepping through the knee-high brush.

I don't have to go far to hide our voices—the wind is still pretty noisy.

"Go ahead," I say, because she's hesitating, and in about four minutes, I'm dragging Stew out of that shelter by his ankles.

She looks at me with this little crease between her eyes. Then says, "Your brother is kind of crazy."

I snort out a laugh, surprised that *I'm* not the one she's calling crazy.

"He's not, actually," I say, though I don't know why I'm defending him.

She pulls her sleeves over her fists, shoulders hunched against the wind. "He is definitely crazy," she says, shaking her head. "But he was right about the water. There's not enough of it."

I unclench my jaw enough to say, "Yep."

"So what I'm wondering is, why weren't you planning to stop at the reservoir in the first place?"

I put my hands low on my hips like my dad does when explaining things, trying to look confident, like I know what I'm talking about. "It's out of the way," I say.

"Yeah, going out of the way for water sucks. But so does dying from dehydration." She says it like she's weighing the two sucky options evenly, which only shows how stupid the second choice is.

"Right," I say shortly. "Which is why I changed my mind."

She doesn't react to my attitude, just looks over her shoulder at the shelter. I follow her gaze. Will is lying down opposite Stew now.

"Perfect," I mumble, breathing out a sigh.

"How out of the way did you say it was?" she asks.

Maybe she actually gets it. Maybe she understands why I'd ignore all common sense and lead us ninety-six miles across a desert with less than two gallons of water, rather than walk the extra miles to the reservoir and back.

"It's a sixteen-mile detour," I tell her.

Her eyes jump back to her brother, curled up under the tarp. "One hundred and twelve miles," she says, almost to herself.

"If you're adding up miles, you might as well subtract the two and a half we've already walked."

She chews one side of her lower lip, then says, "It might take us longer than three days to walk that far."

"It won't," I say quickly.

"*Seriously?* You want us to walk over a hundred miles in three days? That isn't realistic—"

"Will doesn't have to do it," I blurt out, just so she'll drop it.

She frowns. "What do you mean?"

"The detour. Will doesn't have to do it. Neither does my brother. And neither do you. It only takes one person to walk to the reservoir to refill our canteens."

That's the solution I came up with while staring out at that battling sagebrush. Because there's no way Stewart can walk an extra sixteen miles. He couldn't even go two miles without taking another break. And if I'm being honest, the way I'm feeling now, I don't know if I can walk the extra sixteen miles either. But I'm not going to think about that right now.

Cleverly's looking at me like she's trying to decide if this is another one of my dumb decisions, so I turn and head back to the tarp.

I'm actually looking forward to dragging Stew out by his ankles more than I should. But a few steps from the shelter, Cleverly shouts, "John!" her voice sounding panicked. I look back, and she's got one hand shading her eyes, blocking the wind, and the other is pointing north. Back toward the direction from which we came.

I stop, my breath catching, squinting my eyes to make sure I'm seeing what I think I'm seeing. Rolling south down the 318, in a swirling cloud of dust, is a silver pickup truck.

6

IF THINGS WERE different, I wouldn't think twice about waving down that truck and asking for help. But having a gun pressed to your forehead kind of changes how you see the world.

That morning, the day our world changed, Stew and I had linked together some longer extension cords, plugged one end into the generator, and moved the box fan into the family room. It was rattling like a freight train, tilted back, leaning against a chair so the air would blow up toward the ceiling and not disturb the cards we had laid out on the family room rug.

"You're cheating!" Stew yelled, throwing down his hand for the second time.

"Will you knock it off—I'm not cheating! You're being a bad sport!" I rolled forward, gathering up my chips, careful not to let him see the card I had hidden under my knee.

The rattling fan, the fighting. That's probably why we never heard the truck pulling up our drive, probably why we heard nothing at all until the knock at the front door, and the doorbell ringing.

We both kind of jumped. But it was followed by big smiles of relief.

"They're back!" Stew shouted. And we leapt up, slipping on cards and shoving each other in our race to get to the door.

It'd been over two weeks since the Yardleys had left. Two weeks of uncertainty, two weeks and still no power. A fifty-pound boulder that had been weighing on my shoulders, gone with a single knock at the door.

Stewart got to the doorknob first, yanked open the door, both of us out of breath.

But it wasn't Davis Yardley on the porch. It was a man we'd never seen before. Relief turned to something else.

It's funny how your body warns you when something isn't right, even before your brain understands why. And the first thing your brain does is try to explain away your body's reaction. *Calm down,* your brain says. *You are overreacting. He doesn't look scary. He's smiling at you, nodding hello.*

"Name's Clayton Presley," he said, holding out his hand for one of us to shake. I hesitated, then reached past Stewart and took it. His handshake was firm, his fingers warm and dry.

"Did Mr. Yardley send you?" Stew asked, his forehead creased in confusion.

Presley frowned a bit, like he was trying to place the name. Then he hooked his thumb through one of his belt loops and shook his head. "I'm just out checking on folks in the area. Down from Ely. Actually surprised to find people still out here." He looked over his shoulder at nothing, then back at us. "Your dad around?"

My body was back at it again, heat blooming from my chest. And this time my brain didn't argue. Our place was a mile back from the highway, and the last house before you hit a long stretch of nothing. You wouldn't come out here unless you knew where you were going.

And there was something else. Something about the way he asked about our dad. People who don't know who we are, people who haven't known me and Stew since we were babies—well, I'd expect him to ask about our parents. Either one of them. He knows it's just our dad.

"We're expecting him home any second," I lied, moving to stand fully in front of my brother. I felt vulnerable, standing there in nothing but a pair of basketball shorts. I wasn't even wearing shoes. But I tried not to let it show.

I looked back at Stew, nudged my head toward the back of the house. "Why don't you run and get him a drink."

Stewart's eyebrows drew together in a frown. "Bottled water, or—"

I widened my eyes at him, and he shut up and took off down the hall. Not toward the kitchen off to the side, but back to my dad's bedroom first.

I looked back at the man on our porch. He seemed around Mr. Yardley's age, younger than our dad. Average height with light-colored hair and scruff on his jaw. The corners of his mouth were dried and chapped. Behind him, parked a ways down our driveway, was a silver pickup truck.

His gaze followed mine. "Not much to look at, but I paid cash for it."

I wasn't exactly wondering how he paid for his dumb truck. I was wondering why he'd use up gas driving way out to the edge of nowhere to check on some strangers.

He smiled and said, "You boys got everything you need out here?"

I shrugged. "We're doing all right."

"Is that a generator you got running?" he said, leaning to look past my shoulder.

That rattling fan. "We got a small one," I admitted, because there was nothing I could do about it at that point. I brought the door a little closer.

Stewart came back right about then. He ducked under my arm, leaned between the door and me, and handed a water bottle to Presley.

"Here ya go," he said, breathless.

Presley's eyebrows shot up because it was cold, wet with condensation. And too late, I realized I should have answered Stew's question, told him to grab a glass from the kitchen and pour the man some of the warm, flat water from one of our water tanks.

But it wasn't important. What was important was that pressed against Stew's back, sticking out of his waistband, was the grip of my dad's semiautomatic pistol.

"Wow," Presley said with a chuckle. "Can't remember the last time I had a cold drink."

I watched him take a nice long swig, then said, "We were kind of in the middle of something. Is there something else you want?"

He swiped the back of his hand across his mouth and eyed me for what felt like a full minute. "Nope. Like I said, just checking on folks in the area." He looked down at the water bottle in his hand, pressed his mouth into a smile that didn't quite reach his eyes. "But it looks like you boys are doing just fine." He held up the water bottle, taking a few steps backwards. "Thanks for the cold refreshment."

I didn't take my eyes off him as he walked down off the porch and out onto the gravel driveway.

"See ya later!" Stew called with a wave.

I elbowed him in the side, shut the door and bolted it.

"*Really?*" I said, turning on him. "'See ya later'?"

"It's just an expression," he said, though his eyebrows were pinched with worry. He followed me to the front window.

We watched Presley start his truck, back it down our long driveway.

"Is the safety on?" I asked.

"Yeah," Stew answered, his voice wavering a little.

"I'll be right back. Yell if you catch one glimpse of his truck."

I ran back to my room and got dressed. I didn't care how hot it was. Next time we had a visitor "checking on folks in the area," I'd be wearing pants, good running shoes, and a shirt that would conceal my dad's gun.

And before I went back to the family room, back to Stew, I stopped, got down on one knee, just for a minute. Tried to catch my breath. Tried to stop my hands from shaking.

I didn't think I'd sleep that night. I didn't plan on it. Stew and I stayed in the family room, turned off that stupid fan, moved the couch right up against the window. We kept my dad's loaded pistol next to us the whole time, within grabbing distance on the end table. But hours of night went by, and Presley didn't return. My brain started to argue with my body again. *See,* my brain said, *I knew you were overreacting. He's not coming back.*

Still, I didn't think I'd sleep that night. I didn't even realize I *had* fallen asleep, until I woke up with my dad's pistol pressed hard against my skull.

Clayton Presley's voice in my ear. "I'm sorry, kid, but we need what you got."

Shock, heat from my chest, my heart pounding. On our

knees in the dark. Stewart right beside me, his face as white as a sheet as more headlights came up our drive. Four or five sets of them.

I heard men getting out of their trucks, heard their foot-falls on the gravel as they went around to the garage, their muffled voices, laughing, my dad's name coming from their mouths.

Those fifty-five-gallon water tanks? They were so heavy that I always assumed they were pretty much unmovable. I was wrong about that. Turns out you only need about seven or eight jerks to move them.

"Please," I said like a whisper.

"I'm sorry, kid," Presley said again, standing over me, my dad's gun never leaving my head. "We'll be out of here soon. We don't wanna hurt you."

Nothing he said made sense to me, and I repeated my plea, almost mindlessly, until finally he said, "If you don't shut up, I'm gonna have to blow your brains out."

I stopped talking, just focused on every breath coming in and out of my lungs. I strained to hear the voices that were now in the kitchen, strained to recognize any of them. Then came the silence of the generator shutting off. That rumbling hum from outside the kitchen window, going dead.

"Hey," Presley called out, "stick with the plan!"

There was yelling back and forth, a disagreement, but I wasn't listening to them anymore. My brother's head was down, his face buried in his knees, and I could feel his shoulders shaking next to me.

"Stewart," I whispered, my head near his, sweat trickling down the side of my face, tasting the salt in my mouth. "It's okay. It'll be okay."

I don't know why I said that, knowing it wasn't true. But once the words left my mouth, a stillness came over me. And it wasn't that I didn't have any more terrifying thoughts, thoughts of jumping up, attacking this jerk who was holding a gun to my head, holding *my dad's* gun to my head.

But I also felt something deeper. A deep need to survive what was happening, for my brother to survive what was happening.

And we did. We stayed there on our knees. We survived the night.

7

"IT'S NOT THE same truck," I say aloud without thinking.

"What?" Cleverly asks.

I glance at her. Then back to the silver pickup truck heading in our direction. I'm sure it's not Presley's. This one's smaller, older, a bigger piece of crap.

"Nothing," I say, unclenching my fists, flexing my fingers.

She shades her eyes. "Are they . . . driving down the center of the highway?"

I squint up the road, a feeling of dread in my gut. "Wow. Like they're the last truck on earth."

"My parents wouldn't do that. Even if they were driving the last truck on earth, they'd stay on the right side of the road."

"Same with my dad," I say. And I guess that's why I know we can't trust whoever's driving that truck. Once a person starts ignoring normal laws that they used to follow, it becomes easier and easier to break other laws, and next thing you know, you're doing something crazy, something you'd never thought you'd do. Like robbing kids at gunpoint.

I watch, holding my breath, until the truck passes, and barely catch a glimpse of the two people in the cab, their heads turning to look back at us—it happens too fast to really see them.

"Holy cow, that's a lot of stuff," I say.

The bed of the truck is loaded up with a ton of crap—boxes, a mattress, a couple of chairs—all tied in a sloppy mess of ropes. Like they are moving a small apartment across the state.

"They aren't stopping," Cleverly says.

I can't tell if she's disappointed or relieved.

"I guess we won't be bumming a ride," I say. The words are barely past my lips when, through the cloud of dusty haze, the tail end of the truck lights up in a red glow.

Brake lights.

My stomach drops. Okay. They are stopping.

"What do you think they want?" Cleverly says, her voice wavering a little.

"Not sure," I say, even though my guess is they want whatever we have. It isn't much, but we do have some food and water to protect, as well as our packs. We've got some decent gear in there, gear that we very much need to hang on to. They, on the other hand, have a truck loaded with supplies—maybe scavenged, possibly stolen. Not to mention gas in their tank.

A split-second idea comes to me, and I run for the tarp, high-stepping it through the sagebrush.

"John! What are you doing?" Cleverly calls from behind me.

"I need a prop!" I call back.

I duck under the tarp. "Stewart, wake up!" I nudge him with the toe of my shoe.

He groans and sits up on his elbow, looking irritated and tired. I spot the empty canteen tucked against his side.

"There's a truck," I start to explain, and then forget it and just say, "Give me your canteen."

"Why? What truck?"

"Just give it to me," I say impatiently. Will sits up, and he looks as groggy as Stew, but he doesn't hesitate. "Here," he says, passing it to me.

I come up against Cleverly and she stumbles back a step. "I don't think they stopped to help us," she says. "All that stuff loaded on the back—"

"Yeah, and I'm gonna convince them we have nothing left to take."

I grip the empty canteen; weave my way through the brush, my eyes never leaving the tail end of that truck. The brake lights have dimmed, the truck idling in the middle of the highway. I don't want to see the reverse lights come on. I want to approach them before they come to us.

Too late, I remember my hunting knife, tucked away in one of the side pockets of my pack, and I briefly consider turning back for it. But then my feet hit the asphalt and I take off in the direction of the truck, sprinting against the high wind.

"Hey!" I scream at the top of my lungs, waving Stew's empty canteen in the air. "Hey! We need help!"

The brake lights flash and then dim again. I'm not sure why, but it makes me think they are already having second thoughts about stopping. I push myself to run harder, wind roaring in my ears, not caring that this will probably wear out my energy-starved body.

"Hey!" I yell into the wind again. "Please, help!" My voice cracks mid-yell. The wind makes my eyes water, and the tears stream along my temples, mixing with the sheen of sweat across my brow.

As I get closer, the dusty haze clears, and I catch a glimpse of something in the bed of the truck on top of a pile of boxes that both surprises me and lights a fire in my chest. A bright red metal gas can.

It's one of ours, a five-gallon can that we use to fill the lawn mower. I know this because my dad spray-paints a black letter *L* on all our cans, for Lockwood.

These people, whoever they are, have just come from our place. And they took a gas can.

It's empty. All the full ones were stolen three nights ago.

What else did they take? Did they go through my bedroom, my closet, all my stuff? Did they go through Stew's and my dad's stuff?

This gets my blood pumping, and I don't need it pumping right now. I need to calm down. I need to appear like I'm unaware of any danger that I might be in. I need to seem completely desperate.

When I reach the back of the truck, I pound once on the rear wheel cover with my fist—I don't know why, I guess just letting out some pent-up anger. I can only hope it comes off as a desperate move, even though it angers the man inside. I hear his muffled shout of, "Hey, what do you think you're doing?" right before I collapse against the open passenger window.

"Sorry," I say, out of breath, leaning in, clinging to the hot metal frame. "Thanks for stopping."

"Get the hell out of my truck!" the guy says—the driver. And scooted all the way next to him is a woman. A very pregnant woman.

In the space of one second, I'm taken back. Back to Mrs. Yardley on that porch swing, holding her stomach because she's laughing so hard, then an image of the last time I saw her, pulling away from me, smiling through the tears in her eyes—

"I said get the hell out of my truck."

I blink, let go of the window frame, and hold my hands up, the empty canteen clutched in one. Still trying to catch my breath. "We're out of water—"

"We don't have anything for you, kid," the man interrupts.

Then why did you stop? I want to challenge.

He's a freaking bodybuilder—head shaved, a sleeve of colorful tattoos up one arm. His upper torso is twisted toward me, his thick, tattooed forearm leaning against the steering wheel, his cold blue eyes narrowed at me in annoyance.

The pregnant woman, on the other hand . . . She won't even look at me. I figure that's a bad sign.

"Please. Sir," I start again in a stronger voice. "We need water. If you could just fill this canteen." I hold it out to him through the open window, and the woman cringes away from me.

"Get that out of her face!" he yells, leaning around her belly to shove my hand back. "Ever heard of personal space?"

I clench down on my back teeth to keep from mentioning our gas can in the bed of his truck. Then I open my mouth to plead again, but something catches my attention. A red parking permit with an Ely Granite Company logo, swaying from the rearview mirror. Not my dad's parking permit, but one just like it.

My dad's name coming from their mouths. Strangers to us, but not to my dad. They knew he was away on a job for the Ely Granite Company. They knew it was just Stew and I on our own—

"What are you doing out here, kid?" the man says, and my eyes jump to his, thrown off by the question.

He stares at me with this expression that I can't read, and my pulse kicks up, a fast staccato beating in my ears. I blurt out the only thing I can think to say. "W-we need help."

"Yeah, you said that already."

Sweat gathers at my hairline, rolling slowly down my jaw, and I wipe at it nervously.

"You're headed south, aren't you?" he asks, but it's not really a question. "Why would you go south for help? Makes more sense to head north to Ely."

I swallow the dryness at the back of my throat, confused by his apparent irritation with our direction of travel. Why does he care? And why is it any of his business?

I rack my brain for some explanation that makes sense, without mentioning Brighton Ranch. Because there is no way I'm leading this jerk and his wife to the Brightons' place.

The problem is, he's kind of right. If we didn't have Brighton Ranch to go to, it would definitely make sense to head north to Ely. Even though we'd have to pass through a mountainous stretch of terrain, Ely is still closer than any town to the south.

Going south, just past Brighton Ranch, is Hiko, but it's actually more of a ghost town—no services there, just a small farming and ranching community. After that, there's Alamo. Alamo actually has a couple of gas stations, a small grocery store.

"Well," I finally come up with, "we have family in Alamo."

"You ought to turn around, kid," he says, dismissing my lie.

I don't blame him. I don't lie well under pressure.

"Wherever it is you think you're going," he adds, "it's a bad idea."

I feel my eyes start to narrow, and quickly nod to hide my suspicion. My body is firing off warning signals, but I don't need them to know that something is very wrong here.

"Thanks for the advice," I say, and his stare hardens. I should just agree that he's right, fake like we're turning around, and let this guy drive away and forget he ever stopped. But even though I know I can't trust him, I feel compelled to ask one more question. For my brother. Even if it's risky, even if I'm only inviting trouble.

I lean in through the open window again. "But if we decide to head south, do you think you could give us a ride?"

The woman turns to him sharply. Her hand, resting on his leg, tightens, her knuckles turning white. "I told you not to stop," she says through gritting teeth. But the guy doesn't take his eyes off me. For a second, I think he might reach past the woman, grip my shirt in his fist, pull me into the cab, and pound my face in.

"What do you have?" he snaps, his pregnant wife groaning, sinking lower in her seat. "A tarp? What else?"

I recognize the subtle threat, but play it off like he's actually proposing a trade—we give him something, he gives us a ride. *Yeah, right.*

I wipe away the sweat trailing down the back of my neck. "I have a hunting knife," I say. I don't want him to think we're completely defenseless—even if it is back in my pack. "It's a good one. It's yours for a thirty-mile drive down the highway."

"What else?" he says, unfazed by my mention of a knife. I'm not sure what he's looking for, and I don't want to

93

accidentally tell him we have something that he wants. My eyes go to the bed of his truck, as if I can pick out what he's missing from their hoard of stuff in a single glance.

"Well," I say, lowering my voice, "if the knife doesn't interest you, I also have a gun."

He doesn't even flinch at my lie. Before I know what he's doing, he leans back, reaching behind his sun-faded bench, and swings around a .30–30 Winchester rifle.

The woman yelps, shrinks back against the seat.

My hands immediately shoot up and I take a step back, all pretenses of a fair trade gone. Then his eyes go to the canteen in my hand, and I'm filled with dread.

"How about that?" he says, nudging the butt of his rifle at the canteen.

"Please, I need this. My brother—"

"Kid, your brother, someone else's mom, someone else's dog . . . I can't save every person on the planet."

He seems genuinely annoyed by my neediness. As if I asked for any of this to happen. As if I have control over even half the things that have led me to this moment.

I grit my teeth, my arms still up where he can see them. "I'm not asking you to save every person on the planet. And a dog isn't technically a person." This earns me a glare, and I quickly say, "We'll turn around, find help in Ely, just let me keep the canteen—"

His chin goes up. "Drop it on the seat," he says, motioning with his rifle.

I give a brief thought to my options, which are pretty much nonexistent, and then toss the canteen into the cab of the truck. It rolls and comes to rest against the woman's bare leg, and she pushes it onto the floor like it's nothing.

"Now turn around and head to Ely," he says, setting the rifle across the woman's lap.

She cringes.

I rush back to the open window. "We won't make it either direction without water. We need that canteen."

The guy smirks, his brow going up. "You're ten, eleven miles from Lund. I'm sure you can borrow a canteen from one of your friendly neighbors, once you turn around." Without waiting for me to step away, he puts the truck in gear and adds, "You better hope I don't see you again."

He accelerates before I can say the same thing back to him. I say it anyway. "You better hope I don't see you either!" I yell, watching that bright red gas can until I can't see it anymore. Then I holler out a few more choice words at the top of my lungs, because I know I've just screwed up colossally.

I didn't need a freaking prop to convince that guy we had nothing worth taking. He hadn't stopped because he saw a couple of kids on the side of the road worth robbing.

He'd stopped because he saw a couple of kids headed south. Headed in the direction of Brighton Ranch.

STEW, CLEVERLY, AND Will are all standing together on the shoulder of the road, shading their eyes and watching me walk back to them. Stew calls out something, his hands cupped around his mouth, but I don't catch it. I figure it's something sarcastic, something about me coming back empty-handed, because Cleverly shoves his shoulder, and then they all go back to the tarp and start taking it down. Or at least they try to.

I take my time walking back, mostly because my adrenaline has worn off and my feet suddenly feel like they weigh twenty pounds each, but partly because I'm thinking, deciding what I'm going to tell them and what I'm going to keep to myself.

Some jerk threatening me with a rifle isn't going to stop me from doing what I have to do. We're not turning around. If anything, his threat makes me more determined than ever to get to Brighton Ranch.

That guy has no idea what it took to get Stewart as far as I have. He has no idea it took me two days to convince my stubborn brother to even leave our house after we were robbed. *Two days.*

During the robbery, I kept thinking that all I had to do was survive the night. Just kneel there on my family room rug with a gun pressed to my head, and survive the night.

We still had those emergency packs in the hallway crawl space. We still had a *chance* to go for help. And that was the only thing that stopped me from doing something stupid that night. Like jumping up and trying to wrestle my dad's gun out of Presley's grip.

I'm not usually one to hold a grudge, but I hope that guy chokes on a grotesquely large chunk of canned chicken and dies.

When it was over, I went straight to the hall closet. I had to get the packs ready, lay everything out, see what we had. Purge stuff we didn't need, move food and things we could use from my dad's pack into ours.

Then I gathered my nerve and went to face my brother. The sky was just starting to lighten with the promise of morning, and Stewart was still in the front room on the couch, blank eyes staring out the window.

"We have enough food and water to get us to Brighton Ranch," I told him, which was a bit of a stretch. But I figured the fewer details I gave him, the better. "I don't think I can sleep, but if you want to rest first—"

"I'm not going."

"Stewart—"

"Go without me."

"Don't be stupid," I snapped. "I'm not going without you."

He didn't say anything, eyes still glued to that window.

"Look, I know this sucks," I said, "but we don't have any other option. This is it. We walk to Brighton Ranch, and the sooner we leave, the better."

"It's too far," he said, like he'd already made up his mind about that.

"It's *not* too far. I promise you, we can walk there in three days."

"Even if that were true, you think I'd show up on the Brightons' doorstep like a beggar?"

"A *beggar*? Are you kidding me, Stew? We were just robbed! The Brightons would want to help us, Jess especially. You know she would want us to go to them for help."

He shook his head. "It doesn't matter. It's too far. And I'd rather die at home than out there in the desert somewhere."

He was calm when he said it. *Completely* calm. He'd already thought it through and he'd made a decision for himself. Even though it was a *stupid* decision.

I tried to tell him that. I tried to tell him he was stupid, but I couldn't get the words out. It suddenly felt like every muscle in my chest was constricting. I couldn't take in a good breath. I couldn't breathe at *all* in that room. It was hot, stuffy without the fan, and my brother was sitting on the couch, talking about where he'd rather die.

I left him, went back to my room, put my pillow over my head. Stopped thinking about it, stopped thinking about my stupid brother. Until I could finally breathe. Until I finally fell asleep.

When I woke up, I had the worst idea ever.

I found Stew asleep on the couch. Nudged him awake. "If your plan is to just go ahead and die, then fine. I guess I'll get the whole dying thing over with too." I dropped the food pouch from my pack on the couch beside him. "I don't need this. If we aren't going to Brighton Ranch, then you can have my food and water. No way am I going to risk you dying before me and then get stuck burying your rotting corpse."

Stew called my bluff.

It was the longest I'd ever gone without eating or drinking anything. Almost two full days. The worst headache of my life, nausea, the pain in my stomach as it folded in on itself like a piece of origami. That unquenchable dry spot at the back of my throat.

All of that was easier to focus on than thinking about my stupid brother giving up. It wasn't like him. It wasn't like Stewart to give up when things got hard.

The second day, I mostly felt tired and weak. Which meant I couldn't defend myself very well when Stew finally caved.

"Fine!" he screamed, his voice cracking, pounding me with a couch cushion. "Fine, John! I'll do it, you stupid jerk!"

I drank five cups of water with Stew, slowly. I ate a half-melted chocolate bar, some trail mix, a stick of beef jerky, and an entire sleeve of saltine crackers. But before I did any of that, I had a deal with Stewart. I'd eat, he'd walk to Brighton Ranch with me, and neither one of us would bring up dying again.

"If we're going to make it, you have to trust me," I added. "No more negative thoughts. We don't need to talk about it, we don't even need to think about it. Let me make the decisions, and I promise you, I'll get us to Brighton Ranch in three days. Is that a deal?"

Flat and emotionless, he repeated, "Don't talk about it, don't think about it, you make the decisions."

Knowing Stew, I don't think he ever really intended to do all that. Especially the part about me making all the decisions.

And knowing my decisions lately, I don't exactly blame him for that.

. . .

When I reach them, the packs are untied, the tarp is lying flat on the ground, and Stew is looking at me like he expects something—arms crossed, eyebrows raised.

"I hope they at least thanked you," he says.

"For what?" I say before thinking.

"For running my canteen out to them."

I give him a hard look. As if I don't feel stupid enough about losing the canteen. "The guy had a rifle aimed at me, Stew. What did you want me to do?"

"I don't know, how about *not* taking my canteen with you in the first place?"

Cleverly comes between us, holding out my hatchet. "We can't get the stakes out of the ground."

I take it and kneel down at the corner of the tarp.

Stew sighs heavily behind me.

"Whatever," he says as I work the stake out of the packed dirt. "I don't care anymore."

I think he knows that him not caring will bother me more than his anger ever would.

"Will's gotta go," he says. "I told him I'd help him find a spot."

"Fine." I drop the first stake on the tarp and move on to the next one, resisting the urge to ask Stew if he's gotta go again too. I swear he's been peeing out more fluid than he takes in. Then I notice Will looking around nervously as they head out, like he expects some masked gunman to jump out of the brush and attack us.

Maybe I shouldn't have blurted out that stuff about the rifle.

"Hey, Will," I call, "don't pee into the wind, okay?"

"Okay," he says, but looks confused. Stew grabs his hand and I hear him say, "It's just some stupid thing my dad always says. . . ."

The wind has actually calmed down quite a bit, dying down to something just annoying now, rather than completely unbearable. When I have all the stakes out, Cleverly helps me fold the tarp tight, matching corners and bringing our ends together.

"I'm sorry about the canteen," I finally say.

"People don't usually apologize for being robbed."

"I'm not apologizing for being robbed." We bring our corners together one more time, and I take the rectangle that's left from her, hugging it to my chest and pushing out the trapped air. "I'm apologizing for generally screwing everything up."

She doesn't correct me this time, just says, "What did they say? Why did they take the canteen? And why didn't they come back here and take anything else?"

"It was a man and a pregnant woman," I say. "They wanted to know where we were headed. And they apparently wanted our canteen."

"That's weird," she says. "A pregnant lady? Don't you think that's weird? I mean, I'd think a pregnant lady would want to help kids."

"I thought so too," I say, thinking of Mrs. Yardley. "She wouldn't even look at me, though. And then I remembered Spike and Killer. Not every pregnant lady is the same."

"Spike and Killer?" she asks skeptically. "Are those a couple of pregnant ladies you know?"

"They're ducks. My grandparents up in Idaho, they have ducks that live on their property, a male and female, and Stew and I used to play with them when we were younger. Until the female had her first round of ducklings. Then she became so protective of her babies that she turned into a freaking assassin. Attacking our ankles and flapping her wings and squawking like a madwoman. So we started calling her Killer."

"Wow. I didn't realize ducks could be so vicious. And Spike was her husband?"

I laugh because she'd said it with a straight face. "I don't think they were married."

She looks thoughtful.

"Cleverly, I need to know what you have in your backpack." I'm still smiling about the duck-husband thing, so my request comes off less than serious, when it really is.

She hesitates, and then nods.

While she gets her backpack, I put the tarp away and heave my pack onto my back, adjusting the straps on my shoulders. It feels heavier than it did before, but I know that's impossible. I'm just weaker.

I watch Cleverly make her way back to me, slapping the tan dirt from the bottom of her backpack.

"Okay," she says, unzipping her backpack and holding it open for me to look inside. "We left in a hurry. Keep in mind that we didn't know . . . things would go the way they did." Her voice trails off as my eyes search inside the bag. Mostly clothes. Not exactly survival gear. Although I do see a small flashlight and the handle of that steak knife from the trailer home sticking out of a notebook pocket.

She pulls the bag back, puts her arm inside, and starts pushing things aside. "A change of clothes for me and Will, pajamas, toothbrush, deodorant, a hairbrush, my dead cell phone, some cash.

"And we do have . . . this." She pulls out a standard plastic water bottle—the kind that hold exactly 16.9 fluid ounces.

That's a little more than two cups. It's one-fourth the amount of water that Stew's canteen could hold. It's empty, of course, the label peeled off, the plastic thin and crinkled.

"This just saved the day," I say with a smile. Which I realize is kind of an overstatement. But it's something.

We get through the next couple of miles by putting one foot in front of the other and then repeating the process. And by talking about zombies.

Not my favorite topic.

"So you're saying zombies caused the blackout," Cleverly says to Stew. Will is beside her, holding her hand. Every once in a while, their hands break apart and she wipes the sweat off on her jeans.

"Yeah," Stew says. "It's just a theory at this point, but yeah."

"Why zombies?" she asks. "Couldn't it have been, like, werewolves or some other fictional creature?"

I look over at Will and he grins back—both of us thoroughly enjoying this.

"*Fictional?*" Stew says, completely frustrated. "No! Were you even listening to me? I just explained a whole theory in which a zombie pandemic could occur in today's society. The Centers for Disease Control even put out an official zombie-survival guide—"

"Right," she says like she's trying extra hard to understand, "the comic book you were talking about."

"No. I mean, yeah. It's in the form of a comic book so people would actually read it, but it's an official guide. Put out by the *CDC.*"

"Okay, so zombies exist," Cleverly says, cutting to the chase, "and they took out our power. Because why?"

"Isn't it obvious?" Will says. "To get the upper hand on us!"

"*Thank* you, Will," Stew says, waving his arm out toward

him, and Will grins in response. "Geez, this is not that complicated."

Cleverly gives me a look, her eyebrows raised, and I shrug. I notice another mile marker ahead and I pull out the Sharpie, add another tally mark to my forearm.

Cleverly says to Stew, "Do we know *how* the zombies accomplished this takeover of our power grids?"

"Well . . . there are basically a lot of them. A zombie horde."

"Seriously? How does that explain anything?"

Stew gives in with a shake of his head. "Okay, at this point, we do not know the 'hows,' only the 'whys.'"

"Hmm," Cleverly says. Then, "Let me ask you something, John."

For some reason, my heart does this little flip when she says my name. "I don't know anything about zombies."

"He's clueless," Stew adds.

". . . when it comes to zombies," I clarify. "I don't read much fiction."

I do, actually, just not the kind with zombies, and mostly I just wanted to restate that zombies are fictional.

Stew glares at me.

"It's not about zombies," she says. "Completely different topic, but just as confusing. It's kind of a 'how' question."

"Okay. What is it?"

"Can you please explain to me how school works out here in the middle of nowhere?"

"What do you want to know about it?" I say, though I'm familiar with the usual questions. We have some cousins up in Idaho, and whenever we visit, they like to gather their friends around and have us tell them about our school experience in No-man's-land, Nevada. The details seem to both fascinate and freak people out. It doesn't bother me, though. Usually.

"Do you go to a regular school?" she asks.

"What do you mean by 'regular'?"

"A building with four walls and a roof."

"Yeah," I say.

"And this building is located . . . ?"

"In Lund," Stew answers.

"We saw no such school, did we, Will?"

Stew and I exchange a look—as if we would make this up.

"It was the building with four walls and a roof," I say, and she frowns at me, so I tell her, "It's off the highway. You wouldn't have passed it on your way out to our place." Then I go ahead and volunteer the usual information that seems to amaze kids from more densely populated areas of the country. "It goes from kindergarten all the way to twelfth grade. We have nine teachers. Last year, there were forty-seven students."

There's a pause of silence; then Will squints over at me and asks, "Forty-seven students in your grade?"

"No, forty-seven students, total. At the entire school."

Cleverly is speechless. She hasn't even heard the weirdest part—or at least the part that seems to freak out kids the most. Stew's got this stupid grin on his face, so I know he can't wait to tell her.

"In John's grade," he says, "there are three boys, and he's one of them."

It takes her a few seconds to understand what this means, and then she sort of gasps in shock. "There are no *girls* in your grade?"

"Whoa," Will says, "that's awesome!"

"Yep," I agree, ignoring the heat blooming on my cheeks.

"No *girls*?" Cleverly repeats.

Stew can tell I'm getting embarrassed because his grin widens, the jerk. "No girls in John's grade," he says, "or the next grade down. But there are six girls in my grade."

"Stewart's class is the largest we've had in a decade. Ten students." I state these facts mostly to get off the subject of me. It doesn't work.

"But, John," Will says, undeterred, "is Cleverly the first girl you've ever *seen*?"

Stewart bursts out laughing.

"No, Will," I say shortly. "I've seen plenty of girls. One of my best friends—" I stop, suddenly noticing that they've all got big grins on their faces, even Will.

He's messing with me.

"Okay, Will, you got me," I say, unable to hold back a smile, though my cheeks still feel warm. "So tell me, how many girls are at your school in Las Vegas?"

"Too many," he says, and Cleverly rolls her eyes.

"You know, boys can be pretty annoying too," she says.

Will bites his lip thoughtfully. "Like Adam Leblanc."

"*Who?*" Cleverly says. And when he doesn't explain, I ask, "Will, are we supposed to know who Adam Leblanc is?"

He shakes his head. "He's just this kid who sat next to me during math last year that would snap my pencil in half every day. I'd have to get up and sharpen it, and it'd get shorter and shorter until it was just a stub and I couldn't write with it anymore—"

"Why didn't you tell your teacher this kid was taking your pencil?" Cleverly says.

"He wasn't taking it. He'd ask for it, and I'd give it to him, then he'd snap it in half—"

"Will, that doesn't even make sense. You were *giving* him your pencil?"

"You sound like Mom," Will says, dropping her hand,

wiping his palm furiously up and down his pant leg. "She kept getting mad at me for wasting her favorite kind of pencil."

"Your mom has a favorite kind of pencil?" I ask, confused.

"The Ticonderoga. You know, 'The World's Best Pencil.'"

"Will, it's not about the pencils. You shouldn't have let that kid get away with treating you like that!" Cleverly insists. "You should have told your teacher—"

"You act like it's *my* fault," he says, jerking his hand away when she reaches out to take it again. "Adam Leblanc is bad at math, and he doesn't like that I'm good at it, and he's *twice* my size!"

"Okay," she says quickly, "I shouldn't have said it like that. Don't get upset."

Will looks away from her, swipes the back of his hand under his nose. He doesn't say anything else about it, and neither do we. Although, the more I think about it, the more I'd like to meet this Adam Leblanc kid and break a few pencils myself.

Stew ends the silence, saying almost to himself, "That kid's screwed."

Will sniffs, looks over at Stew. "What do you mean?"

"Adam Leblanc. He's totally screwed. Picking on someone half his size? That means he's a coward. And cowards don't stand a chance in a zombie apocalypse."

Will sniffs again.

"Stew has a point," I say. "He's a coward *and* he's bad at math? He's screwed."

Cleverly crosses her arms and grumbles, "The zombies probably already ate his tiny brain."

A smile starts to tug at the corner of Will's mouth.

"I've got this friend, Ryan Ericson," I tell them. "He can

be kind of wimpy, but he's not a coward and he's really smart. I think he could outsmart a couple of brainless zombies."

"He'd do all right," Stew says, shrugging. "What about his little sister, Maddie? She's really brave. Remember when we slept out on their trampoline, and we kept hearing that scraping sound, and we all got freaked out and dragged our sleeping bags into the house? She slept out there the entire night by herself!"

"I think she was just too tired to get up."

"Still!" Stew says.

"The bravest kid in my class is Izzy Rodriguez," Will says. "She took on the biggest bully at my school for always cutting in line at handball. I bet she could take on some zombies."

"I think my friends would do all right," Cleverly says, "mostly because they'd stick together."

"I'll tell you who could kick butt against an entire zombie *horde,*" Stew says. "Our dad. He's really strong, and he can figure a way out of pretty much anything. Right, John?"

You're a lot more like your dad than you think.

Yeah right.

"*Right,* John?" Stew says again.

I push the thought from my mind. "Right," I mumble.

Cleverly sighs. "Our dad would probably try to reason with them."

"Yeah," Will agrees with a crooked grin.

"What about Jess?" Stew asks me.

"Oh, she'd kick butt," I say without hesitation.

"Who's Jess?" Cleverly asks.

"Jess Brighton," I say, emphasizing her last name. "She's my age," I add, still feeling weird about having no girls in my grade at school.

"Oh!" Cleverly says, her forehead creased in thought. "So there are kids at this Brighton Ranch?"

"Two," I say. "Jess and her older brother, Nate."

Stew says, "Jess is awesome. We go to the same summer camp together every year. This year's camp is supposed to start next Monday, actually."

"It's probably canceled," Will says, like he's completely serious.

Stew shakes his head. "I don't care so much about missing camp, but I do care that I won't get to hike the Narrows with my dad."

"The Narrows?" Will asks, his face scrunched up in curiosity.

"It's this gorge in southern Utah," Stew explains. "It's called 'the Narrows' because it's *really* narrow. The gorge is a thousand feet high on either side, and in some places, you can stretch out your arms and touch both sides of the canyon wall at once. And almost the whole time, you're trudging upstream through water, even wading through it at some points."

"That sounds pretty cool," Cleverly says.

"Yeah, I really wanted to see it," Stew says in a quieter voice.

"We can do the hike next summer, Stew," I say. "When things go back to normal."

He doesn't answer, just keeps his eyes straight ahead on the road, his hands gripping the straps of his pack. I notice he looks kind of pale, tiny beads of perspiration wetting his hairline.

Then he says in that same quiet voice, for my ears only, "Will you do me a favor, John?"

"Depends what it is."

"Just . . . will you tell Jess I'm sorry we couldn't all hike the Narrows together?"

"Tell her yourself," I say, and it comes out more sharply than I intended.

Stew whispers to me again, "But, if I don't get the chance to—"

"You're gonna get the chance to."

"But if I don't?"

"Fine," I say, elbowing him away, just to make him drop it.

Because really, there's no reason why Stewart can't do it himself. He's going to see her in a couple of days.

Then Cleverly says to us, "This zombie horde that took out the power . . . How come nobody smelled them coming?"

And just like that, we're back to zombies.

9

"HOW MUCH FARTHER do we have to walk today?" Cleverly asks.

I get down next to one of those yellow reflective highway markers, drop the pile of sticks I've gathered, the wind barely a breeze now. I glance at my forearm, at the fifteen black tally marks, and frown because we haven't made good time. "Eighteen miles to go," I say.

Stew groans.

Out of the corner of my eye, I see Will's shadow slump, see Cleverly's hand squeezing his a few times, as if she can pump strength back into him.

Stew collapses across from me. He leans back against his pack, like a recliner from the waist up. His legs stretched out in front of him, his arms resting limp on his lap.

"Isn't the ground hot, Stew?" Cleverly says.

"My butt is on fire," he confirms.

"Get the tarp, you can sit on it," I say, and start to arrange the larger sticks of wood into a small log cabin. It's mostly brittle tumbleweed, stuff that was easy to collect and break up as I walked—and stuff that also won't burn very long. But I did find a couple of pieces of dry wood about the width of my wrist that will make better fuel for the fire.

We're decontaminating the water now because the wind has stopped its attack. And because we can't afford to put it off any longer—we'll need water before tonight. But I can't help feeling anxious about the passing time. The sun has crossed more than half the sky. To stay on track, we'll still be walking well after it goes down.

"Can't get up," Stew says, dropping his head back, resting against his pack with his eyes shut.

I stop what I'm doing for a minute and get the tarp out of my pack so they can sit. Cleverly takes it from my hands before I even know she's there. "What do you need us to do, John?"

"Spread the tarp out over there," I say, pointing to a spot upwind. "You don't want to sit too close to the fire. It's hot enough as it is—"

"Okay. Now tell me what you need us to do."

She's looking at me, waiting for an answer. A *real* answer.

There's a trail of dirt on her forehead where she's wiped away sweat, and there are thin circles of red around her eyes because she's exhausted. But she's no worse off than me. We're *all* exhausted.

"I need some rocks, about this size." I show her with my hands. "Maybe three or four."

"Okay. Anything else?"

"I need more wood, probably twice the amount I have."

She nods. "Anything else?"

I shake my head. "No, that's it."

"Are you sure? You don't need me to rub two sticks together or strike some flint?"

I reach into my pants pocket and hold up a box of matches.

"Right. I'll go find those rocks." She gives the tarp to Will so he can lay it out, and heads out to the brush. I watch her for a second, and when I turn back to finish building my stick cabin, I catch Stew staring at me with one eye open.

"What?" I say, my smile fading.

"Nothing," he says with a shrug. "Help me up, will you? I think the asphalt has melted beneath me because I'm stuck."

I take the pot from his pack and set it aside, along with some tinder—a bundle of dryer lint that my dad kept in our packs to use as fire-starter—and then I manage to pull Stew to his feet. He and Will go about three yards up the road to spread out the tarp, while I arrange the sticks, stacking them from largest to smallest until I'm satisfied with the little structure I've built.

I'd set aside a few skinnier sticks to use as kindling, and I break them up, twisting them into a bundle. I use my knife to shave more pieces of kindling from a larger piece of wood, gathering the shavings up as I go and stuffing them under my shirt, because it's still pretty breezy.

When Cleverly comes back with the rocks cradled in her arms, she's also got a bunch of sticks with her.

"Thanks," I say.

"Is that enough to get two pots of water boiling?"

"I think so." I scratch the back of my head. "But here's the tricky part. Not only do I need to decontaminate the water, but I've also got to decontaminate the canteens holding the water, so we can use them again. And I've got to do a thorough job of it too. We can't risk anybody getting sick."

We get sick, we get dehydrated. We get dehydrated, we . . . Well, we *can't* get dehydrated. Simple as that.

She crouches down, her hands on her knees. "Can you

113

boil the water while it's inside the canteen?" she asks skeptically.

These are old-school canteens. Metal, circular in shape, with a hard plastic cap, a canvas shoulder strap, and fabric on the sides. I can remove the caps and shoulder straps, but the fabric is glued on, with crimped metal around the edges. The best I could do is prop up the canteens in the fire and let the fabric burn off. But I'm worried about damaging the canteens. Worse, if they were to topple over in the fire, I wouldn't be able to grab them and save any of the water.

"I considered it," I tell her, placing the rocks inside my structure. I move to crouch upwind, blocking the occasional gust. "But I think if I bring the water to a boil in the pot and then hurry and scoop some back into the canteens, swishing it around really well as I go, it'll do the trick."

"If you say so."

Using my hand as a shield, I strike a match and light the tinder, carefully pushing the growing flame deeper into the log cabin, feeding the fire more kindling until the larger pieces of fuel finally catch.

With a close eye on my fire, I open the first canteen and carefully pour all the water into the pot. I'll need a pot holder, so I quickly unbutton my shirt.

I'm hot enough by this fire anyway, and I've got a white undershirt on beneath this that will at least protect my back and shoulders from the sun. Wrapping my shirt around my hand and tucking in the ends, I grip the handle of the pot and carefully set it on the rocks, adding sticks to the flame to keep the fire going.

"Think the pee will boil out?" Stew says.

I jump at the sound of his voice so close, and turn to see that Stew, Cleverly, and Will have moved the tarp just inches behind me.

"I told you to sit away from the heat," I say. Turning back to the fire, I add over my shoulder, "And there's no pee in it."

"How do you know?" Stew says. "There's probably a little bit in there."

I turn my back to him and don't bother answering. I've got a fire to keep burning.

"Is it horribly disgusting that I don't even care anymore?" Cleverly says.

"Yes," Stew says. "I don't want to live in a world where I am forced to drink toilet water with a little bit of pee in it in order to survive."

"I'm okay with it," Will says, "as long as I don't have to do it every day."

"Don't worry, you won't," Cleverly says.

"Yeah, it's not like there are toilets up and down the highway that we can drink from," Stew says. "Though John would probably love that."

"It would make things a whole lot easier," I concede with a shrug.

The pot feels good and stable on the rock platform, so I go ahead and drop my tin mug into the water, using a stick to force it down to the bottom. I figure I should boil the cap as well, so I unscrew it and drop it in the pot, aiming so it lands right inside the mug. As soon as I get the water boiling, I think I'll just dunk the top of the canteen into the water and let it sit there for a while, so I'll know the rim is safe.

"We should definitely make a big deal about this," Cleverly says. "How many people can say they drank toilet water? After this, we'll be part of an exclusive club."

"I don't know if I want to be part of that club," Stew says.

"Too bad. You're one of its founding members."

Will says, "Once you drink the water, *urine* the club."

Cleverly laughs. I can't help but grin, even though I'm trying to concentrate on my fire.

"Fine," Stew says, and I can hear the smile in his voice. "We're all in the toilet water club."

"We aren't calling it that," Cleverly says.

"We could call it the Potty Patrol," Will says.

"No," Cleverly and Stew say in unison.

"Something less obvious, Will," Cleverly says.

"How about Pathetic Desperadoes?" Stew says. "Because we're pathetic and desperate."

Cleverly sighs. "You suck, Stew, you know that?"

No one comes up with anything better, so we sit in silence like the pathetic desperadoes we are, and wait for our toilet water to boil. I stay crouched on one knee, sweating over the flames, my one leg starting to feel tingly and numb, feeding kindling to the fire as the flames get too low. I'm starting to think that old saying is true, the one about a watched pot never boiling. I'm worried I'll use up all our kindling on our first pot of water, and we'll have to collect more. But then the first tiny bubbles appear on the bottom of the pot.

"It's starting to boil," I say with a relieved smile.

Stew gets to his knees and peers over my shoulder into the pot. "How about we call ourselves the Battle Born?" he says.

I go still. I don't look back at him; just stare down at the water.

"Oh yeah," Will says. "That's our state motto! I learned about it in school last year."

"Well, yeah," Stew says, sitting back. "But it's also something my dad says to us all the time. Like, if something disappointing or bad happens, or if we just totally screw up, he tells us we're Battle Born."

It'd look pretty good on your bedroom wall.

"But, what does that mean?" Cleverly asks.

"It means we can do hard things because we're made of hard-core awesomeness. If we get knocked down, he expects us to get back up and keep going. Because we're Battle Born."

Shining my flashlight at the words on the flag, my brother lying beside me.

I stay tense while Stew talks, waiting for my heart to race uncontrollably, waiting for my lungs to feel like the air is being squeezed out of them. But nothing happens. In fact, all I feel is a strange sense of optimism. Well, my eyes do water up a little, but I think it's just the smoke.

I duck my head, use the sleeve of my pot holder to wipe at them. Then I look down at those tiny bubbles at the bottom of the pot. I watch through the smoke as they grow bigger, rise to the surface, and burst.

We are boiling water to drink. We are in control of our own destiny.

That's a whole lot harder than battling some fictional zombies.

"I like it," Cleverly says.

"Me too," Will says. "The Battle Born! Made of hard-core awesomeness!"

"Are we afraid of drinking a little toilet water?" Stew says, like he's a drill sergeant. I can hear the smile in his voice, and it makes the corners of my mouth turn up, because he sounds like the old Stew.

"No!" Will shouts.

"Are we afraid of the miles of desert in front of us?"

"No!" Will and Cleverly shout together.

"Are we afraid of the snakes?"

"Wait, snakes?" Cleverly says.

"Just say no," Stew says, exasperated.

"No!" Will shouts.

"Because we . . . dramatic pause . . . are the Battle Born!"

While three of the Battle Born nap, I finish boiling the rest of our water.

But I don't mind that they fell asleep. I'm actually kind of glad. Because I need them-who-are-made-of-hard-core-awesomeness to get back up and walk another eighteen miles before we set up camp for the night.

I'm just hoping I can do the same.

During the whole boiling process, I lose only a small amount of water—I have one spill toward the end, about a tablespoon's worth—but otherwise everything goes okay. I aerate the water when I'm finished, pouring it back and forth from the canteens to the pot, allowing the water to come in contact with oxygen so it won't taste so flat once it's cool enough to drink. No burns, and I manage *not* to set my shirt on fire.

Judging by the position of the sun, I'm guessing it's about three or four in the afternoon, and that worries me. It could take us six hours to walk eighteen miles. We need to get going, but I let them sleep while I fan out my shirt and put it back on—even though it's still uncomfortably warm. I let the fire mostly die out, and stomp out the embers. I open the canteens and hold them close to my face, testing how much warmth is still radiating from the water.

The metal canteens aren't going to help the cooling process. We'll have to keep aerating the water, and maybe in a few hours it'll cool down enough to drink.

Stew is curled up on one side of the tarp, his head sandwiched between his folded arms—one acting as a pillow, one blocking the sunlight. Will is on the opposite side in a similar position, and Cleverly is in the middle.

"Hey," I whisper, touching her shoulder. She's got my hoodie bunched up under her head, her arm blocking the sunlight. She moves and squints up at me. "It's time to go."

She nods without hesitation and leans over Will, shaking him awake.

I nudge Stew a few times. "You ready to go?"

"Are you giving me a choice?" he mumbles.

I roll my eyes. "Not really, no."

I wait for him to get off the tarp, and then I fold it while he tries to lift his pack onto his shoulders.

"You okay?" I say, watching him carefully.

"If I looked okay, you probably wouldn't be asking," he says.

I hesitate, and then ask him, "Do you need to eat something?"

I had hoped we could make it to the halfway point before eating again, but if Stew needed to eat now, I wouldn't blame him. We basically skipped lunch. I don't even know if it's best to keep pushing ourselves and save the food for later, or feed ourselves now. Either choice could have bad consequences.

"Nah, I think I'm just groggy from the nap. Once I get walking, I'll be fine."

I nod and take his pack from him, lifting it so he can get his arms through the straps, and then I release the weight onto his shoulders. He wavers slightly but nods like he's got it.

The sun is off to our right as we walk now, which is both a relief and a worry. We no longer have sunlight glaring in our eyes, but it's also a reminder that the day is mostly over.

"Did the rest of the water boiling go okay?" Cleverly asks.

We're walking in what has become our usual order: Stew, me, Cleverly, and Will. I nod at her and say, "Yes. It's clean, but it won't be cool enough to drink for a while."

"How long?" Will asks. He's dragging his feet again. But I guess we're all kind of dragging.

"I don't know, maybe three or four hours?"

Nobody says anything. I guess all that Battle Born energy is gone. I try not to think about how tired I am, try to ignore that pain at the back of my throat, the emptiness in my stomach, the weakness in my legs.

Then Will says, "I have an idea. It sort of came to me in a dream, but I think it could work in real life."

"What is it?" I say.

His face is scrunched up in thought, his flop of blond hair blown back over one ear by the wind. "I was thinking, maybe when we get to Brighton Ranch, we could borrow some of their horses and ride to our house in Las Vegas."

Stew bursts out laughing, and my face breaks into a smile. But at least I don't laugh.

Will's cheeks get red. "What?" he says.

"Don't listen to him, Will," Cleverly says, glaring at Stew. "I think it's a good idea."

Will shrugs. "I just thought, horses don't need gas, we could ride home on some horses."

Stew is laughing so hard, he's walking almost doubled over now and seems to be having trouble breathing. I don't want to burst Will's bubble, so I say, still smiling, "I'll ride with you, but only if we can leave Stew at Brighton Ranch."

"We have food in the pantry at home," Will says over Stew's laughter, "stuff that wouldn't have gone bad yet. And we have a swimming pool. The horses would have plenty to drink."

"What is so funny?" Cleverly asks, because Stew can't

seem to get his laughter under control. He manages to take a breath and squeak out the word, "Horses."

I can't help it; I start laughing a little too. Stew's doubled so far over now that it looks like he's going to fall forward and face-plant on the ground. And I realize a second before it happens, that that is exactly what he's about to do.

"Stewart!" I call out, barely getting ahead of him in time to grab the straps of his pack. He goes limp in my arms, his eyes rolling back in his head. I haul him up, getting my arms underneath his and around his back.

"Stew!" I yell at his face, inches from mine, and his eyes suddenly clear.

"What—" he starts to mumble, confused, searching for footing on the ground. Cleverly helps me take off his pack and slowly lower him to a sitting position.

"Just keep your head down," Cleverly says to him, but I can barely hear her over the ringing in my ears.

I have his food pouch out of his pack in an instant. I pick a protein bar and unwrap it part of the way, putting it into his hands. They're shaking. Or maybe it's my hands that are shaking.

"You got it?" I ask, my hands gripping his until I'm sure.

"Sorry," he says with an embarrassed smile. He puts his knees up, hanging his head between them. "I guess I got a little light-headed."

Cleverly is crouched beside him, her hand on his back. "It's not a big deal, Stew. We're all feeling a bit weak."

"We need to eat," I say, standing abruptly and slipping off my pack. Because she's right. That was a stupid decision. *So stupid*, making us walk again without eating first.

I pull out my food pouch, get the can of Vienna sausages I was saving for tonight. It takes me a few tries, but I fit my thumb through the tab and pry back the lid. The tops of seven tiny sausages are visible within a pool of cloudy liquid. I dig out the sausage in the center and stuff the whole thing into my mouth. Then I hand the can to Cleverly, who is now giving me the same worried look she was giving Stew.

"Are you okay?" she says, taking a sausage and passing the can to Will. He's sitting beside my brother with his hand resting on Stew's knee.

"Me?" I say, quickly chewing and swallowing without tasting anything.

"You look pale."

"I think Stew's pack is too heavy. I bet it's heavier than mine. I'm going to move some stuff around."

I hunker down in front of our packs, gripping the zipper. But then I suddenly see Stew's limp body in my arms again. Like he was dead. For a split second, I actually thought he was dead. Out of nowhere, just *dead*.

"John," Cleverly is saying from beside me. "He's okay."

I squint down at that zipper, sweat dripping from my forehead, and concentrate on the headache that is just starting to build behind my eyes. It's only a dull ache at this point, but it's enough to distract me, to take my mind off other things.

"I can carry his pack," she says.

I glance up at her, but before I can say anything, Stewart calls out, "I don't need her to carry my stuff."

I look back at him. "Let her carry it for a while."

"She's got her own backpack to carry."

"I can take the backpack," Will volunteers. "I haven't had a turn yet."

Stewart ignores him. "I said I can carry my own pack—"

"Let her carry it." It comes out sharply, but he needs to know I'm not backing down from this one.

His eyes narrow at me. "Geez, John. Calm down."

"Believe me, I'm working on it."

For the next mile and a half, I lead out in front, getting farther ahead of the others. Until eventually, Will quickens his pace enough to keep up with me.

"There's another mile marker," he says, spotting it before me.

I take out my Sharpie, glance over my shoulder to see how far behind Cleverly and Stewart have fallen. "We'll stop at the next mile marker after this one, aerate the water, help it cool down faster," I tell him.

He nods thoughtfully. "That'll give them a chance to catch up."

I give Will a sideways look. He was supposed to be the one to slow us down. But he's staying right beside me, widening his stride to match mine. It's almost as if having that backpack to carry has given him superpowers or something. A second wind.

"There's gotta be some food out here," he says after a while. He shades his face and looks out at the miles of desert landscape. "I've seen survival shows on TV. I know there are small animals that live in the desert, but what about an eatable plant, something easy to gather and eat."

I feel him turn to look at me in question, but keep my eyes ahead. "You really want to know?"

"Yeah, of course!" he says, getting excited about the idea.

"The desert dung beetle," I answer.

He makes a face. "A *dung* beetle?"

"Yep. They're super nutritious. Packed full of protein, according to Stew. I'll help you find some when we stop for the night. That's when all the bugs come out."

His face scrunches up in thought. "All right," he finally says.

I start to laugh, but it quickly turns into a dry cough, warm air hitting the back of my parched throat.

"Wait," he says. "Are you teasing me about the dung beetle?"

I smile and shake my head, still getting my coughing fit under control. "If you ask Stew," I say, my voice coming out hoarse, "he'll tell you there are all sorts of eatable bugs out here. I'm just not *that* hungry, you know?"

He grips the straps of his backpack, admits with half a grin, "Yeah, me neither, I guess. Not yet anyway." Then he says, "What about water?"

I nod, rubbing a hand across my dry lips. "We are currently heading to the best source of water we have out here, Will. The reservoir."

"I can't wait to see it," he says, and I tamp down my guilt, knowing that I'm basically lying to him. I mean, he's not actually going to *see* it. My plan hasn't changed. I'm going to the reservoir on my own.

Every mile marker from that point on, we stop to check the water. Will holds the empty canteen while I pour it back and forth. And mile after mile, Stew and Cleverly never manage to close the gap between us completely, though stopping helps the distance from growing too far.

By the time the sun sets, I know we've gone at least nine hours without drinking water—besides each of us taking a sip of the cloudy liquid in the Vienna sausage tin. The air temperature has lowered—the sun no longer warming the backs of our necks, the sweat on our shirts. But I don't know how much longer we can go without drinking. All I can think about is the water in my canteens, the soft glugging sound it makes with each step I take.

We aerate it one last time. It's still early twilight.

"What do you think?" Will asks hopefully. His lips are cracked and dry, but he stops short of licking them—taking my advice from earlier, which kind of makes me feel proud of him.

I test the water again with my pinkie. The water will get cooler if we wait, give the air temperature a chance to drop more. But I say, "It's cool enough," and he lets out a relieved breath.

We spot a large rock a little farther ahead on the highway, where we can sit and wait for Cleverly and Stew to catch up. They aren't too far back now.

Cleverly is feeling the weight of the pack—I can tell by the heaviness in her walk, the way she pulls the straps away from her shoulders every so often, like she's trying to ease the burden on her back. Stew looks all right, considering. Definitely not dead. But I've also decided he's not going to carry that pack again. If Cleverly can manage it for one more day, then we'll ditch it when we set out on the last day.

"Ready for a drink?" Will calls out to them, holding up the canteen.

Cleverly nudges Stewart and they actually pick up their pace, Stew grinning at whatever Cleverly's said to him.

Will and I have the first mug of water already poured when they reach us.

"I think John should take the first drink," Cleverly says. She pulls off the pack awkwardly, one strap at a time, and collapses onto the rock beside me, her back soaked with sweat.

Stew squats down on his heels in the dirt, streaks of dried sweat down his temples. "You found it, John," he says, hanging his head as he works to catch his breath. "You go first."

"I agree," Will says. He holds out the mug for me.

I look down at my brother, watch his back rise and fall with each heavy breath. I take the water. I don't think too hard about where it came from. Just raise the mug to them and say, "To the Battle Born."

"To the Battle Born," they repeat, lifting invisible mugs of their own.

Then I down the first cup of toilet water.

10

"CAN YOU SHINE that down here for a minute?" I say to Cleverly.

"Sorry!" She jumps and points the flashlight back to the ground, where I'm clearing an area for our tarp.

It's not completely dark, but we're down to the last few minutes of dusk—the sky deep blue against the black silhouette of distant mountains, a blanket of stars just beginning to appear. Bugs and other desert critters are already out in full force. We hear them all around us, a nighttime chorus of clicks and chirps that I find both familiar and calming. But it makes Cleverly nervous. She's got the flashlight going everywhere, jumping at the slightest sound.

"Over here," Stew calls to Will from a few yards away, gathering up whatever they can find to make a fire—mostly sticks. Just to give us more light. Scare away snakes and small animals.

"It's a good thing we won't need a fire to keep warm through the night," I say to Cleverly, looking out at the sparse brush. "There's not much out here."

"Do you often make fires to keep warm in the desert?" she asks.

"It gets below freezing in the winter," I say. "But not this time of year. It might get down to sixty degrees tonight. Good conditions for sleeping in the open." I kick aside a few loose rocks, pry loose a few more with my hands, and chuck them out in the desert. The sound of tiny scurrying feet follow, and Cleverly's light shoots out there again.

"Those are probably just kangaroo rats," I say. "They aren't going to bother you."

"I'm not a fan of rats," she says.

"Trust me, they're probably more terrified of you right now."

She shines the light at her face so I can see what she thinks of that.

I shake my head, holding back a laugh. "They don't look like the big scary sewer rats you're imagining. They're kind of cute."

"I'll take your word for it," she says, then looks down at the flashlight's fading beam. "Hang on." She flips out the crank on the handle and starts winding it up as fast as she can.

I sigh, slapping the dirt from my palms onto my pants. "These flashlights suck."

"At least we don't have to worry about batteries dying," she says, which is a good point, considering dead batteries are the reason the flashlight in her backpack is completely worthless right now.

Both Stew's flashlight and mine are self-powered. They don't need batteries, but you have to wind them up every ten minutes or so when they start to dim. Even at full power, they don't offer much in the way of light.

Which is part of the reason I agreed to stop at dusk, two

miles short of our goal, about a mile from the turnoff to the reservoir.

The other reason being that I've decided to choose my battles carefully. At least for tonight.

Cleverly's still winding the flashlight when I drop the tarp, spreading it flat on the dirt. I don't bother to hammer stakes in at the corners, not worth the energy, just toss Stewart's and my rolled-up sleeping bags on top. I've been thinking about the different ways our sleeping arrangement could go. The obvious being that Stew and I squeeze into one sleeping bag, and Cleverly and Will take the other. But sharing a sleeping bag with Stew will complicate things. He'd definitely feel me getting up to sneak off to the reservoir.

"My feet are killing me," Cleverly says, sitting on the tarp, propping the fully charged flashlight against a sleeping bag.

I glance over my shoulder and see Stew and Will crouching on the ground not far away, getting that fire ready. "Hey," I say quietly, getting down on my heels beside her. She's gotten her shoes off, and is pushing her knuckles into the arch of one foot. "I've got to go get the water tonight," I tell her.

She stops rubbing her foot. "*Tonight?*"

"After everyone is asleep. I was thinking, I'll suggest we unzip the sleeping bags and lay them out the long way, like blankets."

"John—"

"One under the four of us, and the other on top. Then I was thinking, you could say something about not wanting to sleep on either end, because of snakes, and I'd volunteer to take one end, and Stew would have to take the other end. Then he won't feel me getting up—"

"And when are you planning to *sleep*?"

"I'm pulling an all-nighter."

"Really?" she says. "Without any Red Bull?"

"That's right." I smile at her sarcasm.

"I don't think Stew is going to be happy when he finds out you went to the reservoir on your own."

"Well, yeah." I shrug.

"Will is going to be upset too."

I feel guilty enough about lying to my own brother, without throwing in Will. He was getting pretty amped about it earlier. I say to Cleverly, "It makes sense for me to go on my own. You know that, right?"

"But in the middle of the *night*? And then walk all day tomorrow on *no* sleep?"

"This is the only way to keep us on schedule." She starts to say something else, so I quickly add, "It's just one night. It's not like I've never stayed up all night before."

She rolls her eyes. "This isn't the same as staying up all night in your room playing video games, John. Have you even thought this through?"

"Well, I'm trying not to think about it too much." I say it jokingly, but it's actually the truth.

"Stew is right," she says in a sharp whisper. "Just like when you wouldn't drink that cup of water in the tarp shelter. You think you're stronger than everybody else!"

"What?" I say, confused by her sudden anger. "No, I don't."

"Yes, you do!" she insists, her voice rising. "You're full of yourself. That's why you think you can go an entire night without sleep, and then walk thirty more miles the next day! Which is just crazy—"

I put my hand on her knee to quiet her, glance over my shoulder at the silhouettes of our brothers, hunched together and talking low, smoke already rising between them. "Just listen to me for a second, all right?"

She presses her lips into a hard line, glares down at my hand on her knee, so I quickly take it off.

"I don't want to do this," I admit, the words coming out in a desperate whisper. "My feet hurt, my legs are sore, I'm tired. All I want to do is shut my eyes and forget about how hungry I am, forget about—" I stop myself, pushing thoughts of failure from my head.

I sit back on my heels and say with resolve, "But I'm doing it. I'm walking to that reservoir and back again tonight. All I'm asking you to do is help me sneak off without my brother waking up."

"Hey," Stew calls out, the smell of burning sagebrush wafting through the air, the soft crackle of a growing campfire.

"Come see what we created!" Will says, pounding his fist on his chest.

"We're coming!" I call back, still looking to Cleverly for an answer.

"I'll think about it," she finally says. She grabs her shoes, wincing as she pulls them back onto her feet.

I get the food pouches from our packs, the last canteen of water, watching Cleverly out of the corner of my eye, trying to decide if she would actually sabotage my plan. But maybe her "thinking about it" is a good thing. Deep down, she *has* to know that my going to the reservoir tonight is our best option, crazy or not.

Will's found a good rock to sit on—flat, not too close to the warmth of the campfire. He moves over to make room for Cleverly. "It's a tepee structure on top," he says, talking about the fire. "But first we made a platform, crisscrossing sticks on the bottom like this." He shows Cleverly with his fingers. "That lets oxygen creep in from below."

"How did you know that, Will?" she says.

"I didn't. Turns out, I don't know *anything* about building a fire. Stew just showed me."

Stew stares into the flames, as if he doesn't hear Will say his name. He's got his ankles crossed with his knees up, his folded arms resting on top.

It hasn't escaped my notice that Stewart's mood has changed again. Eyes dull and emotionless. I'm just trying to ignore it. Trying to get this night over with as soon as I can.

"Don't feel too bad," I say to Will, squatting down beside my brother. "Stew's been building fires with my dad since he was five years old."

"So, to make a fire, you don't just throw down a pile of wood and light a match?" Cleverly says, joking.

At least, I think she's joking.

But then Will nods seriously. "That's what I thought too."

Stew makes a noise that almost sounds like a laugh.

I smile. "If you hold a match up to a pile of wood, the only things that are gonna burn are your fingers."

"You need tinder to light the kindling," Will says to Cleverly. "I'll show you next time we build a fire. When we boil water at the reservoir."

I feel myself tense up, unsure of what Cleverly will say. But she just presses her lips together tight, like she's annoyed.

So maybe she doesn't love what I'm planning to do tonight, but she's had a chance to think about it, and she knows I'm right.

I roll onto my knees toward the waning fire, grab a few of the bigger sticks, and carefully place them upright against the crumbling tepee, building it up again. Then I sit back and take the meal for tonight from my pouch—four sticks of generic beef jerky. I give one to Stew, hold out two pieces to Cleverly, and she passes one to Will.

"Is this the same jerky we had earlier?" she asks.

"Yep. It's the last of it."

Cleverly tears off a small piece with her fingers and examines it thoughtfully. "Best jerky I've ever had in my life," she says before putting it in her mouth.

"It's delicious," Will agrees.

I gnaw off a bite of the plain jerky, my stomach grumbling—a loud, slow grumble that seems to go on forever, no matter how hard I press down on my hollow stomach.

"John," Cleverly says, "will tonight's dinner have a second course? You know. To keep us from *sleeping* all night on an empty stomach?"

I shake my head. "It's better to save food for the morning, for the middle of the day when we need it most." But then I notice the way she's looking at me, her eyebrows raised like I'm missing her point.

She's not really talking about some of us sleeping on an empty stomach. She's talking about *one* of us walking to the reservoir on an empty stomach.

"We can split a couple of my protein bars," Stew says, as if I didn't just make a good argument for saving our food for tomorrow. He pulls them out of his pouch.

"Perfect," Cleverly says.

My stomach rumbles again.

I think about whether to let her win this one, and then give her a small shrug. At least she's accepted the fact that I am going to the reservoir tonight.

"My last one with no nuts," Stew says, breaking a protein bar in half for me.

It's chewy, sticks to the roof of my dry mouth, and has the weird aftertaste of artificial sweetener.

I savor every bite.

"I gotta pee," Stew announces.

"I gotta go too," Cleverly says. She shines the flashlight into the dark with a shiver. "I'm dreading it."

I stop my brother, picking up the canteen. "Let's drink this first, all right?"

He sits back down with an indifferent shrug.

"The whole canteen?" Will asks as I pour, like he's surprised.

"Yep." I don't explain to him that I'll need it empty so I can refill it tonight.

We drink just as slowly as we ate, the water barely cooler than it was before, slightly more refreshing.

Then we all relieve ourselves in the desert.

Cleverly goes last, takes the toilet paper, and makes Will go with her to hold the flashlight and watch out for snakes. When they get back, Stew and I have gotten the sleeping bags unzipped and laid out like I suggested.

"I don't need to sleep under a blanket," Stew says. "I'd rather have the extra padding beneath me."

I start to agree with him—it's still pretty warm—but then I think about Stew changing his mind in the middle of the night, waking up to pry the covers out from underneath him, and finding me gone. . . .

"The ground's not that hard, Stew," I say, which is kind of a dumb thing to say.

Stew gives me a look like I'm crazy, but then Will says, "I've got an idea of how we can have extra padding. It's called 'the human pillow chain.'"

"*The human pillow chain?*" Stew repeats.

"We'll sleep in a square formation," Will says, speaking over him, "with each person resting their head on the stomach of the person next to them."

"There is no way I could sleep with someone's *head* on my stomach," Stew says.

"Let's just try it," I say, mostly because Will looks like he's getting ready to dig in and *insist* we try it, and I'm anxious to hurry things along.

We form a square, with my head on Will's flat stomach, and I can tell the weight of it is crushing him.

"How's that feel, Will? Comfortable?" I say.

"Yes," he groans, and I bite back a laugh.

Cleverly's got her head on my stomach, and I lift mine to look down at her. "It's probably very hard, as far as pillows go."

"It's not that hard," she says. Then she props herself up on her elbow and punches my stomach a few times like she's fluffing a pillow.

My laugh comes out like a grunt, and it starts a chain reaction of laughing and bouncing heads. Will concedes failure, and we all sit up.

"Okay, it's been fun, but I'm going to sleep," Stew says. He pulls up his knee and starts untying his shoe.

"I'm not sleeping on the end," Cleverly blurts out self-consciously.

I have to look down to hide the smile tugging at the corner of my mouth.

"Seriously?" Stew says. I can almost hear his eyes rolling. "Snakes can crawl over people, you know."

"Thanks for informing me. I'm still not sleeping on the end."

I get up to stomp out the last of the dying embers, because it's not safe to keep them burning without a pit, and also because I can't seem to wipe the smile off my face. I'm so relieved that Cleverly is taking my plan to heart. I go back to the tarp cautiously, my eyes still adjusting to the darkness after kicking out the fire. In the moonlight, I can make out the silhouettes of Stew, Will, and Cleverly laid out like sardines in a row, their heads and feet at opposite ends. Stew has his end of the covers thrown off, but if he gets cold, I guess he could easily pull it back on without really waking up. Will and Cleverly are both under the top sleeping bag.

I pull off my shoes, putting them in line on the edge of the tarp next to the others. They're good running shoes, but still. That spot right where my arch meets the ball of my foot is so sore, like a stabbing ache. Especially on my right foot. I've got more walking to do, so I spend some time working my thumb into the muscle before lying down beside Cleverly, my head opposite hers.

The ground is hard, the tarp and sleeping bag beneath me not offering much padding, but I could be asleep in an instant if I wanted to. I crook one arm behind my head, the top cover bunched up between me and Cleverly, and stare up at the stars.

This is what zero light pollution looks like, I think, remembering the first night of the blackout. Sitting on that porch swing next to Mrs. Yardley.

All those stars are enough to make you feel like the last person on earth. Or at least one of four.

I squeeze my eyes shut, take in a deep breath, and let it out slowly.

Will's small voice cuts through the hum of desert insects. "We could do a foot-massage chain."

Stew's muffled voice replies, "I'm not rubbing anyone's feet. Go to sleep."

I try not to think about how long it's taking them to drift off, try not to count the seconds. But it isn't easy to rest my body while at the same time make myself stay awake. I make a mental list of the things I'll need to gather together before I leave, decide to move everything into Cleverly's backpack. It's less bulky, easier to carry. I don't think she'll mind.

Then I think about time. I've got one mile to go before I reach the turnoff, then another eight miles before I reach the reservoir. I'm giving myself three hours to get there. If I spend a couple of hours there boiling water, then take three hours to get back, I'd arrive back here just before sunrise. I could sleep for maybe an hour or so.

Finally, Stew's familiar snore starts up, and even though I'm dreading it, I know it's time to go.

I pull my knees up carefully, propping myself into a sitting position while keeping my sights on Stew's sleeping form. He's on his side, his back toward me. Out of the corner of my eye, I see Cleverly move and sit up.

I tilt my head and give her a look that says, *What are you doing?*

She bends close to me and whispers, "I'm going with you."

I pull back, mouth the words "No, you're not" to her. But she ignores me, reaches for her shoes.

I look over at Stew, his snore soft and even. Will looks totally out too. But I don't want to risk waking them. I grab my shoes, give them a few taps on the ground to scare out anything that might have crawled inside there, then pull them onto my aching feet. I grab the flashlight, tug on Cleverly's arm, and though she's only had a chance to slip her feet halfway into her shoes, she follows me off the tarp and into the brush.

"I thought about it," she whispers, using my shoulder for balance as she pulls on the heel of each shoe, "and there are a couple of points I'd like to make.

"First," she says, releasing a deeply held breath and standing up straight, "I don't think it's smart for you to go alone. I think it's a stupid idea, John. Not to mention reckless."

My eyes narrow at her, but she continues, "And second, if I go with you tonight, I can drink my fill at the reservoir. Then when we get back, only two of us would need water in the morning. That's more water for Stew and Will, more water for the next two days. It'll even make up for the lost canteen. You *know* I'm right, John."

Of course I know she's right. I knew she was right the moment she sat up and said she was coming with me. But I still have to ask her. "Are you sure you can do it?"

Her chin goes up. "I don't know. Like you said. I'm trying not to think about it too much."

I give her a long look, like I'm considering her answer. Then say, "Can't really argue with that. Ready to go?"

11

WE STAY QUIET until we're a good ways from camp. Me, carrying the backpack with the canteens, water bottle, pot, fire-making supplies, and our knives—just in case. Cleverly with the flashlight.

"I have a question for you, Jonathon," Cleverly says, breaking the silence.

"Okay," I say, snorting out a short laugh, "but call me John."

"Oh. You don't like three-syllable names?"

"My name is just John."

"Oh. Just John."

"Sorry to disappoint you."

"No, I like just John," she insists, even though I definitely remember her saying John is a boring name.

"What's your question?" I say.

"What was so funny about us riding horses to Las Vegas?"

I grin a little, remembering Will's idea. "Well, first, there are no horses at Brighton Ranch. It's not that kind of ranch."

"Ah," she says, but she sounds confused. "What kind of ranch is it?"

I hesitate, because I know the Brighton Ranch she is imagining is about to change. Horses on big green pastures, rolling hills, shade trees, a babbling brook. Well, the babbling brook is actually there, and some shade trees—it's all just surrounded by a lot of dirt. "It's a tortoise ranch."

"A *what*?"

"A ranch for desert tortoises."

"You're kidding."

"What, you don't have tortoise ranches in Las Vegas?"

"Pretty sure we don't."

My grin widens. "When Will was talking about horses, I kept picturing us straddling a couple of Mr. Brighton's giant sulcata rescue tortoises and slowly riding them to Las Vegas. You know how long that would take?" A laugh escapes me now, just thinking about it.

"What is the purpose of a turtle ranch?" she asks.

"Tortoise. It's part wildlife preserve, part business. Mr. Brighton ships them all over the world. Mostly to locations with desert climates."

"A mail-order turtle?"

"Tortoise."

"Are you trying to tell me that turtles and tortoises aren't basically the same thing?"

"As nicely as possible," I say. I grab the straps of the backpack, just to give my hands something to do.

"You know an awful lot about animals," she says. "Ducks, and tortoises, and rats, and cows . . ."

I look at her with a raised eyebrow. "You brought up cows. I think it's my turn to ask a question."

She clamps her mouth shut and faces forward.

"What's your last name?"

"Iverson," she says.

Cleverly Iverson, I repeat in my mind.

"What's your favorite color?" I ask.

"Green. What's yours?"

"Cobalt blue."

"That's oddly specific, John. Any other deep questions?"

She's been doing this side-to-side, back-and-forth motion with the flashlight since we left, scanning the ground while we walk. It's sort of dizzying. I don't think she even realizes she's doing it. Every once in a while, her light will fall on a big beetle or the tail end of a lizard scrambling away, and she'll make this little squeaking sound, like she can't help it.

"Do you regret coming along?" I ask a little hesitantly, because we haven't gone that far. There is still time for her to change her mind.

"No," she says. "I would have been awake most of the night worrying anyway."

"Worrying about me?" I ask, surprised.

She gives me a look. "You are the last thing I'm worried about, John."

"What are you worried about?" I ask.

"Ha ha," she says, as if that were a bad joke.

But I didn't mean it like that. Of course she's got things to worry about. We're less than halfway to Brighton Ranch, and as bad as today was, it's only going to get worse. We'll have less food, less water, less energy for walking.

But even beyond this walk to Brighton Ranch, there's so much more to worry about. I wonder if she worries as much as I do about the things she can't control. If she thinks about being on her own, without her parents, as much as I think about being without my dad.

"Why did you come out here?" I ask.

"I told you. So I can drink at the reservoir—"

"No. I mean, why did your grandparents send you and Will to our place?"

Her forehead creases, like she's trying to remember something. "Did I say that?" she asks.

My eyes widen a little. "I don't remember your words perfectly, but you said *something* like that. You said your grandparents know my dad, and that he would take you in," I say, suddenly remembering the words.

"Oh yeah," she says. "You're right. I'm sorry, John. I just made that up."

"You made it *up*?"

"I didn't know who you were. Just some boy filling up his canteen with toilet water. Was I supposed to tell you everything?"

I don't bother reminding her that she drank some of that toilet water. "So, your grandparents *didn't* send you to Jim Lockwood's place?"

She shakes her head. "We left on our own, without them knowing."

She doesn't elaborate, so I ask, "Why?"

"My grandpa had started skipping meals," she says, making a figure eight pattern on the ground with the light. "Insisting he wasn't hungry. But we knew it wasn't true. We could see the tremors in his hands."

"There wasn't enough food?"

"There wasn't enough *anything*," she says quietly. Then she quickly adds, as if she's worried how that might sound to me, "They kept a food and water storage. My grandma had chickens, a vegetable garden. But it's just the two of them, John."

I get what she means. Her grandparents hadn't planned on Cleverly and Will. Four people using the food and water storage meant for two.

"If my grandparents would have had any idea how long this would last, I think they would have done things differently in the beginning, made different choices. Rationed food and water sooner, or driven us down to Las Vegas before the gas ran out. Not that I blame them," she insists. "I would have done a lot of things differently too."

"What happened exactly?" I ask.

"I told you. My grandpa started skipping meals. He had talked about your dad, said he wished he'd had a setup like Jim Lockwood—big tanks of water, racks of food in your garage. So I filled up a bottle of water for Will and me to share. Then I wrote a note, and I left it on the fridge. My grandpa won't have to skip meals anymore."

Something about the way she says it reminds me of Stewart. A stubborn determination to do things on her own, not rely on someone to the point of breaking them. Still, I can't help but admire her and Will for deciding to leave.

Then I think back to when we first ran into them in the abandoned home. "How did you know how to get to our place?"

"Mile marker 98," she says. "I found it in my grandma's address book."

I nod in understanding. When you live off a highway in the middle of nowhere, you don't bother with street names. Going sixty-five or seventy-five down the highway, you could blink and you'd blow right past the crooked green sign on the unpaved road leading to our house. But mile markers on a highway count down the miles—or up, depending what direction you're traveling. People just know what mile marker to look for to get to our place. Mile marker 98.

"Obviously we didn't know your dad was gone," she says. "Or that everything else was gone." She pauses, then says, "Stew told me, you know."

A heat blooms in my chest before I'm even sure what she's talking about. "Told you what?"

"He didn't say much about it, but he told me what happened to your dad's food and water storage. That some men broke into your house in the night and took everything."

It doesn't bother me so much that Stew told her, just that she's brought it up. I'm not sure why—I mean, she just told me all that stuff about her grandparents, how she ended up out here. But I am bothered that she's brought up the robbery. Does she expect me to talk about it? Tell her what it felt like to wake up with my dad's gun pressed to my head?

I drop my hold on the backpack straps, stuff my hands into my pockets. "What did you think happened to it? That the two of us ate a six-month supply of food in three weeks?"

"Well, no—"

"That we *somehow* misplaced six fifty-five-gallon water tanks? You know how much water that is, Cleverly?"

"Three hundred thirty gallons," she says without missing a beat.

I roll my eyes. "That's right. I forgot you're a math genius."

"Genius? That's really simple math, John."

"Look, can we just not talk about it?"

She glances up at me, then back at the road. "Sorry," she says quietly, like she's confused or hurt.

I can't explain it to her. It doesn't even make sense to me. The way a thought can enter my head and suddenly my entire chest goes tight, my throat closing up, impossible to breathe . . .

Don't talk about it, don't think about it.

"It's fine. I'd just rather talk about something else, all right?" I say.

She nods, but neither of us comes up with anything.

Cleverly has to wind up the flashlight again, but we don't stop walking through the darkness, the shoulder of the highway flat and gravelly here. I listen to the sound of gravel crunching beneath our feet. My stride is different from hers, a bit longer, but every once in a while, our steps fall into perfect sync, an even *crunch, crunch, crunch*, before falling out again.

We're close to the turnoff, and I'm surprised at how fast the mile went by. Years back, some creeks used to extend out here, closer to the highway. There's a small ghost town near where they used to be, mostly crumbling walls and a few gravestones, but also a row of trees. I see their dark outlines getting bigger against the starlit sky.

Cleverly's done charging the flashlight, and the beam hits the ground, swinging forward and back with the movement of her arm. We approach the trees. On one of her upswings, the light flashes ahead on the road and I catch a glimpse of something on the ground. On the next swing, I see it again.

I slow and come to a stop. "Can I have the flashlight for a minute?"

"What is it?" she asks. But she hands it to me.

I wind up the light really fast to brighten it, and then walk forward about ten more steps, past the gravel, shining it directly at the soft dirt. Where the side of the highway meets the turnoff to the reservoir.

Tire tracks. Standing out in the dirt like a 3-D stamp. Wide, like they came from a truck.

I GRIP THE flashlight tighter, crouch down on my heels, and stare at the wide trail of dirt like I'm inspecting it.

I don't need to. It's obvious that the tracks are recent, the impression of tire tread crisp and clear. This morning's windstorm would have erased any tracks that were already there, would have blown the dirt road smooth.

"I guess this means there are people already at the reservoir," Cleverly says behind me. "Think it could be Spike and his pregnant wife, Killer?"

You better hope I don't see you again.

My pulse kicks up a beat, though I hate that I'm letting that stupid threat get to me.

"That would be my guess," I say, as if it's not a big deal. I push to my feet, wincing as my arches stretch, pulling at that sore spot on my right foot.

"Oh, good. We can get Stew's canteen back," she says, but I hear a nervous tremble when she speaks.

"It's a big enough reservoir," I tell her. "I think we can avoid running into anyone who's camped out there. You ready?"

We start down the road, heading west toward the far-off mountains. I hand her back the flashlight so she can continue her scanning, our path flat and dusty now.

"What do you miss most?" I ask, just to get my mind off threats from tattooed bodybuilders twice my size. "Can't be a person," I clarify. "Something that uses power."

"Listening to music," she answers after thinking about it. "With my headphones in, full blast, walking through my neighborhood—"

"You miss *walking*?" I say, bumping her with my shoulder.

"*No,*" she says, bumping me back much harder, causing me to stumble a little. "I don't know how those words even came out of my mouth. What do you miss most, John? And don't say something stupid, like your Xbox."

"But that's what I miss most," I say, throwing my hands up. Then, "Fine. My cell phone."

She gives me a look. "That's cheating."

"How is that cheating?" I ask, even though I already know.

"The only reason you miss your cell phone is because you want to use it to talk to someone," she says. "Missing a cell phone is basically missing a person."

"You can do a whole lot more with cell phones than just call people, you know," I argue. "Maybe I miss taking selfies—"

Cleverly grabs my arm to stop me. "Hang on, I'm getting kind of cold." She gives me the flashlight to hold and unties my hoodie from around her waist.

The temperature has dropped more since we left. I wonder if Stew has felt the chill and woken up to pull the sleeping bag over himself. If he's realized we're gone.

"Do you think we should have left a note for Stewart and Will?" I ask. "Just in case they wake up?"

147

"Will won't wake up," Cleverly says like she's sure. "He sleeps like the dead, even when he hasn't spent an entire day walking." She pushes her arms through the sleeves, pulls the hoodie over her head. "You would know more about how Stew sleeps, but he seemed completely exhausted to me."

"Yeah," I say, frowning. "You're probably right."

"Let me take a turn with the backpack," she insists, and I shrug and peel it off my back. She takes back the flashlight and we start walking again. I stuff my hand into my pants pocket and find that box of matches, turning it end over end.

"There's a campsite," I tell her.

"A campsite?"

"On the west side of the reservoir. It's pretty flat and rugged. Not much different from what you've seen out here. But all along the banks of the lake, there's tall grass, up to your waist in some places, and some cottonwood trees. There are twenty sites, and maybe half of those have decent fire pits and picnic tables. And then five of those also have shade enclosures. Those five sites with shade, all in a row, are really the only ones that ever get used."

"Any bathrooms?" she asks.

"No, just pit toilets. The campsite has no plumbing, no potable water."

"I don't know what you mean by 'potable,'" she admits.

"No drinkable water. You have to bring your own."

"Oh, great. We didn't bring any."

I hold back a grin. "Anyway. We can assume that whoever got there before us has set up camp at one of those five sites."

"All right. So we know what area of the reservoir to avoid."

"Actually," I say, releasing a breath, "maybe we should check out those five sites."

She gives me a quick look. "Why would we do that?"

"Just to see who's out there, check out what they've got."

"You mean *steal* from them," she says.

"They stole from us," I point out, thinking of Stew's canteen, the gas can in the bed of Spike and Killer's truck. She doesn't say anything right away, so I add, "I've never stolen anything before in my life, but I don't have a problem stealing food and water from a couple of thieves."

"It's not that, John. I mean, it does feel weird to steal stuff. But mostly, I'm worried about getting caught. Or what if they wake up tomorrow, find food and water missing, and come after us?"

"They won't come after us."

"How do you know?"

"Because," I say, "I'm not just thinking of stealing food and water. If I get the opportunity, I'll be committing grand theft auto."

She stops in her tracks. I take a few more painful steps forward before turning to look at her, putting on a confident expression.

"You can *drive*?" she says.

I shrug. "Sure. When you live in a small town in the middle of nowhere, you can get away with things like driving your dad's truck to the neighbor's house to borrow a ladder. Stuff like that."

Okay, that's not exactly true. I mean, I did that one time on some back roads with my dad earlier this year.

But I say, assuring her, "I've driven with my dad before. And I know a lot about cars. Honestly, it's not that much different from driving our riding lawn mower."

"Okay. But what if we steal food and water, and you *don't* get the opportunity to commit grand theft auto?" Cleverly says. "Then what?"

"Then I'll slash their tires," I say with another shrug.

"Either way, I will be a wanted criminal, and they won't be going anywhere."

We get to where the road curves north, leading around to the west side of the reservoir, and I know we're not too far out.

"If we stay on the road," I tell Cleverly, "we'll eventually reach the campsites at the reservoir. About two more miles. But we can also take a shortcut directly through there." I point to the brush straight ahead.

That is what I would rather do. Cut through the brush. Just saying the words *two more miles* makes my feet throb, my calf muscles ache.

We stop at the edge of the brush where the road bends, and I can tell Cleverly is hesitant to walk through there. There's less sagebrush out here; some yucca plants, with their thick, swordlike leaves; but it's mostly cheatgrass. Ankle-high grass the color of wheat—not native to Nevada. Different from the slick, tall grass around the reservoir.

"It'll save us a lot of walking," I say. "We just need to be careful where we step."

"Careful where we *step*?" Cleverly says.

Well, that was the wrong thing to say.

She aims the light so far out there, it disappears into the darkness. "What's out there? Snakes? What else?"

I lower her hand holding the flashlight, until it's shining on what looks like a footpath through the brush. A rough trail of packed dirt.

"A lot of dirt," I say. "And a lot less distance."

She still seems hesitant, so I say, "The worst thing out there is the cheatgrass. See those pokey seed pods that hang down from the top like a shepherd's crook? They stick in your shoes and socks like Velcro. It's really annoying."

"All right," she says with a groan. "I'll walk through that snake-infested cheatgrass, but you have to make me a deal. We get water from the reservoir first. *Before* we check out the campsite. Just in case."

She's still unsure about our stealing. About our getting away with it. If it's worth the risk of being caught. I'm not. But I don't mind having a backup plan.

"Deal," I say.

Before she can change her mind, I reach my hand into the dark space between us and find hers, and then lead us down the trail.

It's gritty with dirt, sticky with dried sweat—our hands together, I mean, not the trail. But when the path opens up to where we can walk side by side, I don't let go right away. I hold her hand for a little while longer for some reason. Just a little while longer. *Just* until it starts to get weird. Then I let go.

"Um, I should wind this up again," Cleverly says quickly. We stop, and I shove my gritty hands into my pockets and breathe out a puff of air while she recharges the light. Which wasn't that dim to begin with.

Then we walk again.

We'll have to leave the path and head south soon, pick our way through the uneven terrain to reach the north end of the reservoir. I stretch my height, squinting ahead into the darkness as far as I can see. I think I can tell where the cheatgrass ends, where the brush gets darker.

"John," Cleverly says.

She does that a lot. Just says my name out of the blue like that. It makes my heart do this weird little flutter every time.

"Do you ever swim in the reservoir?" she asks.

"Why? You wanna go swimming?" I joke.

"Sort of. I'm wondering if we have time for a quick washup."

"Sure," I say, suddenly positive that I smell funny.

I haven't had a proper shower in weeks. Before our water supply was stolen, Stew and I would wipe ourselves down every day with wet washcloths and a little soap, use a few cups of water to wash our hair, but that's about it. Now, after walking all day in the sun and the wind, my skin is tacky with dried sweat, and on top of that is a layer of grit and dust. Even the parts of me that were covered up are dusty. There's no way to avoid dirt in a desert basin wind.

"I know washing up isn't that important," she says, "so if you think it's a bad idea—"

"No, it'll be fine," I say. "We're going to cut across south to the reservoir, all right? Just ahead there."

She nods. When we get clear of the cheatgrass and turn off the trail, the brush is actually pretty sparse, easy to walk through, though the ground is rocky and uneven in places.

"This is way less creepy than walking through that grass," Cleverly says.

"Yeah. Can I see the flashlight again?"

She hands it to me, and I start sweeping the ground with the light as we walk.

"What are you doing?" Cleverly asks in a low voice.

"I'm looking for a good yucca plant. Something small enough to dig up."

"*Why?*"

"The reservoir water isn't the best bathing water. It's a fishing lake. It's summer, so it won't be nearly so bad as it gets in the winter, when the waterfowl make a mess along the banks. But whenever we swim at the reservoir, we usually go home and take a shower afterwards, or else smell like a lake."

"And that's the same water we've got to boil for drinking?"

"Yep," I say, hoping the idea of our stealing drinking water is sounding a little less risky to her.

I spot the plant I'm looking for, small with green sword-like leaves shooting up from the dirt.

"Here, let me see the backpack," I tell Cleverly, and she slides it off for me. I get my hunting knife, and then crouch down to dig it up, careful to pull up the whole thing.

"The root is a natural detergent," I tell her. "You just beat it between a couple of rocks, add water, and you can get a fairly decent lather going."

Standing, I hold up the entire yucca plant, gripping it where the waxy leaves meet the thick brown root. I shine my light on it and say, "There. I picked you some soap."

"Looks fancy."

"*And* it's all natural. If you're into that sort of thing."

She holds the flashlight for me while I crouch down and cut off the top of the plant. Holding the root at an angle, I chop away the outer woody fibers, like I'm peeling a stubborn potato, until I reach the white inner fibers. Then I chop off two nice chunks of it—one bar of soap for each of us.

"You're handy to have around in the desert," she says as I pass her the pieces of root.

I wipe each side of my knife across my pant leg and put it away. "Nah, Stew is the one who knows all this stuff."

She gives me a look because I sound like I'm trying to be humble, but it's the truth.

"Seriously. I hike and camp a lot, but I bring my own soap from home. Stew's the one who's into surviving in the wild, and stuff like that. He's the one who showed me this."

"Really? I can't picture Stew going to the trouble of digging up his own soap," she says, and I feel my expression fall a little.

She's right. I mean, the Stewart she knows is the one who

chugged a canteen of water to get me to agree to walk to the reservoir. The one who passed out *after* taking a nap . . .

"He's not himself lately," I say, though I wish I could say more, find the words to explain how my brother changed after kneeling on our family room rug that night. I want her to know the Stew that I know.

She says, "Maybe when we come back with the water, and he gets a good night's sleep, he'll be more like himself."

"Maybe," I say, knowing that's a long shot, to say the least.

I trade the pieces of root for the flashlight and we get on our way again. I can smell the dampness in the air now, see the trees around the reservoir and hear the strange, noisy buzz of cicadas in their branches. The volume is almost deafening. They sound like electricity, like a high-voltage electric fence.

Ironic, if you think about it.

The ground is clearer now, covered in short dry grass, and sort of slopes downward. I lead us to a spot between two trees, where a triangle of moonlight cuts through the branches, then get to one knee, motioning for Cleverly to do the same.

She keeps looking over her shoulder as she gives me the root and takes off the backpack. I don't blame her. It's pitch-black all around us beneath these trees.

"I'm trying not to freak out," she says, squinting at the tall grass along the bank, "but I'm starting to think I can't do this."

"You can do it," I say. "Just be careful—the bank can be slippery." I slide my knife into the waistband of my pants, blade down.

"What lives in that grass?"

"Nothing," I say, which is an obvious lie, so I add, "some

harmless fish." I explain what to do with the root, then say, "Use my hoodie to dry off with when you're done. It's thin enough, it'll dry in a heartbeat out here." She nods like she hears me, but I'm not sure she's listening.

"Do I have to wade out through that grass?" she asks. "How deep is it?"

"Just stay close to the bank, you don't have to get all the way in, but I am. Here, take the flashlight," I say, handing it to her. "I'll go about ten yards to your right." I point out the area. "We'll meet back here."

"All right, I'm just gonna do it," she says, but she's mostly talking to herself, like she's getting herself psyched up. Her focus is on the tall grass and the still, black water of the reservoir.

I take that as my cue to leave, grabbing my half of the yucca root. With the moonlight blocked out under these trees, it's ridiculously dark. I might as well be blindfolded. Keeping my steps small and careful, I find a good place to stop along the bank. Then I sit and pull off my shoes and socks. I'm getting all the way in, so I stand up and strip down to my underwear, slip the knife into my waistband, the cool metal pressing against my hip.

There is something really eerie about walking into a dark lake in the middle of the night with only the moon for light. At least half a dozen horror movies start out this way.

The edge of the bank is abrupt along the north side. You have to step down into it. The water is colder than I remember it being, but it feels good. The grass is thick and sharp; the ground is hard and slimy. The noisy cicadas cancel out the sound of my legs dragging through the water. I push aside tall blades of grass, reach down and find two rocks about the size of my fist, and bring them to the edge of the bank. Then I use them to break up the root and get a lather going.

I make quick work of washing up, drawing the suds up my arms and shoulders, my neck and face, my chest and armpits and stomach. The tally marks, marking the miles we walked with Stew and Will today, fade from my forearm, leaving behind faint lines, but it's all right. I'll start fresh tomorrow.

At first I try to keep my underwear dry, but then realize it's pointless. After some hesitation, I dunk my head, getting my hair wet, and then work the suds into it. Moving out farther into the water, I pick up big scoops of water with my hands and rinse, dunking my head again and then pushing the water and suds out of my hair, away from my face.

Maybe it's standing water, and maybe it isn't the cleanest, but I already feel better than I did before, more awake and alert, and I probably smell better too. I have to resist the urge to lick the cool water from my lips, resist the urge to scoop up a handful and take a nice long drink.

Once clean, I do what I had intended to do next: I wade out past the grass and try to catch sight of the campsite in the distance. The water is up to my stomach now. Hard and slimy things brush against my legs, and something drifts along my back. I cringe away and turn in place. It's just a stick. I shove it away and wade out a little farther. The ground suddenly drops, the water going up to my chest, so I take a step back and instead move down the bank. There are still some trees blocking my view, but I catch the whiff of campfire.

I keep trudging along the edge of the grass until my view of the campsite starts to open up. I see the first shade enclosure. I see firelight reflected against metal. The cab of a silver truck. And a white truck parked next to it. And another truck parked beside a second shade enclosure. And a fourth truck.

And between the campsites, under one of the shade enclosures, I see all six of our fifty-five-gallon cylindrical water tanks.

13

I PLOD BACK to shore, and I know I should be quieter, but the sight of those water tanks has my pulse racing. Clayton Presley is here. *Here* at the reservoir.

This is why Spike cared what direction we were walking. Why he wanted us to go north for help instead of south. It had nothing to do with Brighton Ranch. But I don't quite get it. Why are they *here*? And hadn't Spike just come from our house with that empty gas can? Or was he also there with Clayton Presley the night we were robbed?

It takes me a while to find my clothes, not only because it's dark but because I'm distracted. I eventually spot my crumpled-up white undershirt sitting on top of my shoes. I grab my long-sleeve shirt and use it to wipe down my face and chest, my arms and legs. I yank my jeans on over a pair of soaking wet boxer briefs.

"Ugh," I groan, regretting now that I got my underwear wet.

I've been gone long enough, so I don't bother putting on my socks or shoes. Just pull my undershirt over my head, and then carry everything else back to that triangle of moonlight.

"Finally," Cleverly says. "What took you so long? Okay, that was freaky, walking into the water in the dark. Remind me never to do that again." She stops talking and her light hits me in the face. "John, what's wrong?"

I squint and shield my eyes from the flashlight. "Nothing." I sit down and brush the dirt from my feet before putting on my socks and shoes.

"I can tell something's wrong. Just tell me. You're making me nervous."

"It's good news, actually," I say without looking up at her. "We for sure won't be boiling reservoir water tonight."

"What do you mean?" She kneels down next to me, tucking a loose piece of damp hair behind her ear.

"I got a look at the campsite. It's not just Spike and Killer. The people who robbed us are there—"

"You *saw* them?" she asks.

"I saw my dad's water tanks. The ones they stole from us." I grab the backpack and sling it over one shoulder. "You ready?"

She doesn't get up. "Wait. What are we going to do? What's the plan?"

"That's our water, Cleverly. And our food. I'm not just gonna let those jerks get away with taking everything from us."

"Okay, but—" Her eyes move to my waistband, where the handle of my hunting knife is visible. "John, maybe we should wait a minute. Just calm down and think—"

"Why, because of this?" I say, gripping the handle of my knife. "It's for tire slashing, Cleverly. Did you think I was gonna use it on the guys who robbed us?"

She doesn't say anything.

"Why are you looking at me like that?" I ask, sounding overly defensive even to my own ears.

She stands up slowly, her eyes not leaving my face. "I think you're not as calm as you're pretending to be."

I laugh like she doesn't know what she's talking about, but I swear, my heart wants out of my rib cage. It's pounding like a victim trapped in a closet, and it's exhausting me, making me breathless. "I'm fine, really." My voice sounds echoey, like it's coming from far away. My jaw muscle is twitching, my skin is on fire . . .

"John, I think we should slow down and come up with a plan."

"If you're scared—"

"That's not what I'm saying," she says, eyes narrowed. "I just don't want to go barging into the camp without being prepared with a plan!"

I roll my eyes. "Don't talk to me about being prepared."

Her eyes sort of tighten; her voice changes. "What do you mean?"

"I mean, if your grandparents had been a little more prepared, you wouldn't be out here right now, would you?"

I've hurt her; I can see it in her eyes. But I keep going for some reason. "Not that you're any better at being prepared. You left their house without even taking a jacket or anything to protect you from the sun and wind." I stop and shake my head. "Look, it doesn't matter. I just want to get to the campsite, okay?"

"It matters to me," she says quietly.

"What?" I say in a tight voice.

"What you just said. Maybe it doesn't matter to you, but it matters to me." She takes my damp hoodie from where it's tied around her waist and holds it out to me.

I shake my head, confused. "I don't want it."

She gives me a hard look. "I guess that makes two of us." She drops it in the dirt.

I don't pick it up. "That's not what I meant—"

"First of all, John," she says, her voice shaking. "My grandparents are generous people. Maybe *too* generous. The reason we started running out of food and water is because from the very first day, they shared everything they had with neighbors who were *less prepared* than them."

My eyes drop, unable to meet hers.

"Chickens, vegetables, dry food storage, water, gas. They shared everything. My grandma said that's how it's done out here. That's the *point* of being self-reliant. It's not so you can keep everything for yourself. It's so you can help yourself *and* others. Both."

A new rush of warmth washes through me. *Dad would do both.*

"And second of all," she says, "not that I owe an explanation to some judgmental boy with a backpack full of empty canteens, but I didn't leave without a hoodie. My little brother is wearing it."

Will's oversized hoodie.

I look up, my cheeks flushed with heat. "Listen, I'm sorry I said—"

"Go by yourself," she says, cutting me off. She thrusts the flashlight into my hands. "Since you Lockwoods know everything, I'm sure you'll be fine rushing into a camp of armed robbers without a plan. I'll wait here with my fingers crossed that you come back alive."

She sits in the triangle of moonlight, arms folded on her knees. "Though don't expect me to care if you don't."

Some of that anger comes flaring back. "Fine," I bite out. I turn and leave without her. If she's not going to accept my apology, there's nothing I can do about it. I'm not going to beg her to forgive me.

The cicadas are buzzing in full force, a piercing electric current, and I feel the vibration in my eardrums.

I know what her problem is. She doesn't get it. She doesn't get why I'm so angry. She doesn't know what it feels like to kneel next to your brother and feel his shoulders shake. Hear him cry, when he *never* cries—not even when he broke his wrist in gym class last year. She doesn't understand that Clayton Presley may not have pulled the trigger that night, but he might as well have.

Before I know it, my breathing has become rapid, labored like I've been running for miles even though I've barely walked the length of two basketball courts. I know I need to slow down my heart rate, force these thoughts from my mind before I reach the point of no return. I fill my lungs with as much air as they can take, letting it out through my nose until my chest deflates. I shut my eyes and just keep doing it over and over.

It smells like yucca and summer campouts with Stew and my dad at the reservoir.

My dad. What would he say if he were here now? What would he say about my leaving Cleverly behind like that, to fend for herself in the dark with no flashlight? Knowing she's probably freaked out about snakes right now. What would he say about the things I said to her?

I've already stopped walking, gripping the flashlight so tightly it hurts. I know exactly what Dad would say. I know what he'd say to me. And I know what he'd say about Cleverly and her grandparents.

It takes me only a few minutes to get back to her, to hunker down in front of her.

"Hey," I say, and it comes out kind of breathless. Her eyes narrow at me, so I talk fast. "I don't know why I said that stuff. It was mean, and you didn't deserve any of it. I know your grandparents, and you're right. They are generous people. They didn't deserve what I said about them either."

She's still kind of giving me that look, but her eyes have softened.

"Also, I should have told you this earlier, but your grandpa skipping meals so you and Will can eat? And you and Will leaving so he won't have to? *That* is what it means to be Battle Born."

Her cheeks are pink in the moonlight.

She stands and dusts the dry grass from her palms, and I stand up in front of her.

"Apology accepted, John," she says, holding out her hand. I start to take it, but she says, "Flashlight, please."

I smile another apology and hand it to her. "I won't leave you in the dark again."

"It did give me a minute to think about something," Cleverly says. "When I was trying not to imagine being surrounded by snakes in the dark." She shudders a little, shines the light on the ground around us until she spots my discarded hoodie, grabs it, and ties it back around her waist—much to my relief. Then she asks, "If you were to commit grand theft auto, how would you go about getting the truck started?"

"Keys would be nice," I say.

She frowns. "That's what I thought. The odds of us finding keys lying around aren't very good."

"I said keys would be *nice*. But not necessary."

"Are you telling me you can start a car without keys?"

"Yeah. I watched a video online—"

She sighs and starts off in the direction I just came from, heading toward the campsites.

"It was a video about hot-wiring cars," I say, walking beside her. "Anyway, it's a long story, but I can do it."

"I guess we can *try* to look for keys," she says to herself, as if she didn't hear anything I just said.

"My dad drives this old truck that you can literally start up with a screwdriver," I explain, "or just about anything else you can shove into the ignition—"

"So your plan is to find a screwdriver and shove it in the ignition?"

"Cleverly?"

"What?"

"Will you just let me tell the whole story without interrupting?"

"All right, sorry," she says, stopping to face me, her arms crossed, the beam of light hitting the wild grass at our feet.

"The ignition switch in my dad's truck is broken. That's the only reason you can start it up with a screwdriver. A friend of my dad's thinks it's hilarious to play this prank on him. He likes to jump in my dad's truck after he's parked it, and move it to another parking spot, so my dad can't find it and has to hunt it down."

The corner of her mouth tugs up, like she appreciates the prank. But she doesn't interrupt.

"Anyway, this one time, we'd gone up to Stew's basketball tournament in Ely, and when we went out to the parking lot after the game, the truck was gone. It took us over an hour to find it, because Davis Yardley—that's my dad's friend—had driven it half a mile down the road and parked it at the McDonald's. We had to get him back. So we looked up 'how to hot-wire a car' on the internet. It took Mr. Yardley two days to find his piece-of-crap Corolla."

The smile on Cleverly's face is so wide, I somehow don't think it has much to do with our pranking Mr. Yardley back, epic as it was.

"You can hot-wire a car," she says as if I hadn't told her that already. "That changes things."

"Changes what things?"

"The plan!" she says, her excitement contagious, though I'm still not sure what has changed. "We forget about the food, forget about the water tanks."

My smile fades a little, and I start to say something, but she speaks before me.

"If you can steal a truck, then nothing else matters. A truck changes everything, John. Who cares about the water when we can pick up our brothers and drive to Brighton Ranch in less than an hour."

We get to the place where the trees end, and Cleverly turns off the flashlight. It's got to be late, nearing 1:00 A.M. by my guess. Everyone at the campsite might be asleep by now, but that's doubtful. We can smell the campfire.

For another fifty yards, we walk in the open, with only the darkness of the night for cover. Moving slow and careful through the dry grass. Hoping it's dark enough. Hoping we're far enough away that we can't be seen. Then I see the short gravel access road ahead that leads to the campsite.

It's easy to spot because the gravel is white, reflecting an unfortunate amount of moonlight.

My heart is pounding again. But this time, it's adrenaline. We've got one goal: steal a truck. Leave the water tanks untouched. A trade. Six water tanks for one truck. That's how I'll think of it. That's how I'll let my dad's stolen water tanks go.

On the side of the road closest to us is a huge flat rock, about waist high, engraved with two mallard ducks taking flight from a lake, and the name of the campsite: WILSON RESERVOIR.

I point to it, and Cleverly nods in understanding. *Stop there.*

Once we're crouched behind it, I take off the backpack, set it on the ground between my knees, and take out Cleverly's steak knife.

There's one thing we've got to do before we steal the truck. Slash the tires on the other three trucks. Make sure they can't come after us.

Silently, I demonstrate to Cleverly how she should hold the knife, in a reverse grip with the blade opposite her thumb, and swing outward. She'll have more force behind her swings this way, making it easier to puncture tires and pull the blade out. She takes the knife and shows me she understands. Then she looks down at her hip and carefully slips the knife blade-down into the waist of her jeans.

I raise myself up high on my knees, peer past the edge of the rock. Look at each truck carefully, all of them backed in, ready to drive straight out of there.

I kneel back down. Cleverly lifts her eyebrows in question.

"I can only hot-wire one of them," I say quietly. "Spike and Killer's silver truck. The other three are too new."

Newer models have complicated wiring and the components are hidden. Even if I could figure all that out, most of them have kill switches that cut the engine if you even try to mess with it.

"Okay," she says, and doesn't ask me to explain.

"How about," I say, slinging on the backpack, "I jump in the truck and start working on it while you slash the tires on the other trucks. When you're done, you can meet me at Spike's truck."

"You mean split up?" she asks in a whisper.

"Is that okay?" I ask, remembering the promise I just made to her. Not to leave her in the dark again.

But splitting up would mean getting out of there faster, which would mean less chance of getting caught.

She agrees with a nod.

"You're sure?"

"Yes."

I move to peer over the top of the rock again, getting one more look at the trucks. Left to right, it goes: piece-of-crap silver truck, white truck, wide gap of about thirty feet, red truck, and another silver truck—that one's Presley's. They are backed up against the roots of three tall cottonwood trees, which cast a lot of shadow around the area, so we'd have decent cover once we reach the trucks. We just have to cross a length of white gravel in direct moonlight to get there.

I'm still not sure if we should creep across it slowly, careful to not make noise, or just full-out book it across before we're seen.

I turn back to Cleverly on the balls of my feet, thinking of how dark it looks around those trucks. "Actually," I say as if reconsidering things, "I think we should stay together."

"Yeah?"

"Yeah. That way . . . Well, yeah, let's stay together." She looks relieved, so I go on, working out the new plan aloud. "We'll slash the tires on the farthest truck first," I whisper. *Presley's.* "Take care of the other tires, making our way to Spike's truck. Then you can keep a lookout while I'm working with the wires under the steering wheel," I add, already warming up to this new plan.

"I like that plan. Let's get it over with."

I move to crouch beside her, taking her hand in a firm grip. "Slow and quiet?" I say, and she nods in agreement.

Then, staying as low to the ground as possible, we start out across the gravel road.

14

THE SOUND OUR soles make on the road is like the first few mouthfuls of Cap'n Crunch before the milk makes it soggy. Or like fireworks exploding beneath our feet. And I realize there's no possible way to get across this gravel road quietly. We're better off sprinting.

Cleverly must've realized the same thing, because I barely have to tug on her hand. Then we're making a run for it, heading for the farthest truck, Presley's. Wind rustles through the sagebrush. Night critters scrape and skitter across the packed desert earth. The cicadas in the cottonwood trees sharpen up their dull hum to a piercing buzz. I can only hope all that noise is enough to mask the crunch of our feet hitting gravel.

My sights are locked on the front bumper of the truck, and we're almost there when I see something out of the corner of my eye. A glint of metal in the wide gap between the two sets of trucks. I squint into the darkened space, and see two dirt bikes and a four-wheeler. Panic hits me, because we missed those, and what if there are *other* vehicles parked around camp that we didn't know about?

We reach Presley's truck and hunker down between it and the red truck parked next to it.

"Did you see . . . ?" Cleverly whispers.

I don't have to ask what she means. "Yes." I drop her hand and crouch next to the front passenger tire on Presley's truck. Pull the handle of my knife from my waistband and stab the blade hard into the sidewall of the tire.

I don't know what to expect, but when I yank it out, there's a big hiss, a whoosh of air, and then it's over. The front passenger side of the truck sinks maybe three or four inches lower, but without close inspection, the difference isn't noticeable.

Cleverly stabs her knife into the front driver-side tire of the truck next to Spike's, just like I showed her, but the serrated blade of her knife gets stuck. I help her wiggle it out. *Hiss, whoosh,* and the truck settles lower to the ground.

We move to the rear set of tires, and I'm aware that we are making too much noise, our feet scurrying and slipping on the gravel. My pulse pounds in my ears, and I catch a glance of Cleverly's widened eyes. If we don't calm down and at least try to be quiet, we're gonna get caught.

Before we slash the rear tires, I trade knives with Cleverly. The blade of my hunting knife is smooth, stronger, and easier to use. *Hiss-hiss, whoosh-whoosh,* and the two trucks sink toward each other.

We start to scramble back to the rear bumpers, but I stop Cleverly before she goes any farther, holding her arm. She leans in close.

"We gotta slow down," I say next to her cheek. "Slow down." She jerks her head in agreement.

We're still for a minute, just listening. Listening for the sound of footsteps, or voices in the distance. But I don't hear anything besides the desert, besides our combined heavy breathing and pounding hearts.

I'd almost rather hear something else. Then I'd at least know whether someone was coming. I hate being surprised.

"Okay," I whisper, and we move away from each other. I've got Cleverly's arm still, and I start to pull her right, taking us around the other side of Presley's truck, but she pulls in the opposite direction.

She motions that she's going to go around the other side of the red truck, to take care of those tires on her own, so I guess she's feeling okay with splitting up. Or maybe she's still terrified, but she's going to do it anyway. Either way, it's pretty Battle Born of her, if you ask me.

I nod, but tug her to the right, trading places with her because even though I'd like the pleasure of slashing all of Presley's tires, I'd rather be closer to the camp. I want to know if anyone is there waiting for us, if anyone has seen or heard us.

I move quietly around the rear bumper, and as the distance between us grows, Cleverly's crunching footfalls fade until all I hear are my own. I stop to listen. Nothing. Maybe we're okay. Maybe we weren't as loud as we thought.

I get to the rear tire and turn around so I can puncture it with my right hand, all the while scanning the area. The smell of campfire is stronger, the bright glow visible through the scattering of tree trunks.

I slash the tire at my side, and then the front one, and the red truck is all one level now, a couple of inches closer to the ground.

Cleverly comes around the front of the bumper just as I'm slashing the last tire on the four-wheeler. I motion toward the dirt bikes, like I'm asking a question, and she nods in understanding.

Then I hear a sound. The creak of canvas stretching over metal. A camping chair. And my eyes dart to the lighted space between the tree trunks.

Someone's sitting by the fire. And I don't know how I know this, but I know that that someone is Clayton Presley.

Standing, I move toward the cottonwood tree in my line of sight. Its trunk is wide—wide enough to stand behind it unseen and then some—and I put myself close, the soles of my shoes slipping on a root bulging up from the ground. I rest my knuckles against the dry bark, knife still clutched in my fist, and I see him.

Clayton Presley's not ten yards away from me. He's alone, sitting in one of several camp chairs by the fire, slouched low in his seat. His ankles are crossed and balanced on an upright quarter of firewood, arms slung out over the armrests. His face is expressionless, eyes staring unblinkingly into the flames. On the ground by his chair is what looks like an old shortwave radio with a long antenna. I can just make out the crackle of static, but nothing else.

I thought seeing Clayton Presley would trigger the rage I'd felt earlier. I'd been tense, expecting it, knowing I'd need to find some way to control it before I did something stupid. But anger isn't the emotion I'm feeling right now.

There's something about the way he's staring into that fire, listening to static. Like he's lost. Like he doesn't remember where he's headed or what his purpose is anymore. Like he doesn't care if those flames eat him up. And he reminds me of someone. Stewart, the night we were robbed, and almost every moment since. Stew walks around with that same look on his face, as if there's no reason to be here anymore, and he's just going through the motions, waiting for everything to end.

I watch Clayton Presley, unmoving, and I don't like the resemblance of him to my brother. I don't like it . . . but I can't pretend it's not there. And it's not as if this makes me feel one shred of pity for him, or that I forgive what he's done. Not even close. It's just that I know confronting him would no longer give me any satisfaction. Sucker-punching him in the face, sure. But I don't need any answers from him anymore. I'm not interested in hearing one thing that comes out of his pathetic mouth. Unless it's *Help yourself to those water tanks over there.*

Not that I need his permission. It's our freaking water, every last drop of it.

My eyes move to the tanks, set up in the open grassy space between where I stand and he sits, all six of them, under a shade enclosure.

It's not part of the plan. I know it. But our water is *right there.*

I tuck the knife into my waistband and unzip the backpack, taking out the water bottle on top and leaving the bag halfway open.

Then I do something that might seem stupid, but I know it's okay. And I've got to do it anyway.

I step out in the open and walk straight in the direction of Clayton Presley, slowly, until I reach that first tank. His eyes never leave the fire.

I drop down behind it, knees up with the backpack between them, back against the cool plastic. I know these tanks well. I know how they work. I don't need to look. Just reach my hand behind me to the front of the tank and find the short hose where it latches against the side. I pry it loose and bring it around. Then I unscrew the water bottle, palming the lid, and position the hose over its opening. I turn the brass valve halfway, letting it catch so it pours slower. Watching it fill, inch by inch, with clear water.

Hands shaking, I raise the bottle to my mouth.

I don't think I even realized how much I needed water until it hits my cracked lips and floods my dry mouth. Then I do what I've been dying to do for so many days. Guzzle the water in long, dragging gulps.

It tastes a little like iodine—the geniuses have overdone the purification—but I don't care. The first bottle goes down fast. The second, I swallow with a hefty dose of guilt. Not because I'm taking anything that doesn't already belong to me. But because this is as much my brother's water as it is mine, and he's ten miles away, and he thinks I'm there with him, camped on the side of the road, but here I am, drinking from a water tank that we both thought was long gone.

And the thing is, every drop I swallow now means less water I'll take from Stewart later. I know that. I get how critical that is. But that's not my only thought as I drink. I've got the plastic rim pressed to my lips, eyes shut, water leaking out the edges and dribbling down my chin, my throat working as fast as I can guzzle . . . because every dried-up cell in my body is crying out for it.

And then my eyes fly open and I come up for air, swiping my chin across my shoulder. *Shoot,* Cleverly. I search the line of trees, looking for her between glimpses of tailgate and chrome bumper, but there's no sign of her. Does she know where I am? Did she see me walk out here?

This wasn't part of the plan. What was the plan?

She's waiting for me at Spike's truck! Either really freaked out or really annoyed. But now that I'm here with the water tank, there's no way I'm leaving without getting water for her. For Stew and Will. Three canteens, one for each of them to guzzle.

I fill the water bottle for the third time, screw on the lid, and set it aside. I plan to drink that one, too, but I'm forcing myself to take a break. I'll make myself sick, drinking water at this pace after going without for so long.

I start filling the first of the three canteens. Occasionally, the tank glugs softly behind me, and I know it's too quiet for Clayton Presley to hear, but I cringe every time—

"... *an unprecedented national emergency* . . ."

I shut off the valve, my entire body going still.

It's the radio.

I strain to hear the voice over the static. The sound quality is bad, but I can tell pretty quickly that it isn't a real news station; it's just some guy talking. But it's someone who's out *there, not* surrounded by miles of desert and silence.

"... *and these people who are still whining, still waiting around for their government to step in and save them ... they're simply dim-witted. People, you will* not *survive this blackout unless or until you come to the conclusion that only you* have the power to save yourself."

The words jolt me back into action. I turn the valve on, carefully filling the canteens while listening to the voice on the radio.

"... *Here's your first clue. We are twenty-two days, going on twenty-three, into probably the* worst *crisis our nation has ever seen, with no end in sight, and still no FEMA to the rescue? At least not in my town, or any town that I have been in contact with. Mind you, this is a federal agency that has an eleven-billion-dollar annual budget, funded by our tax dollars. You'd think they could manage to transport drinking water, maybe some MREs. Because the basic needs of the citizens of our nation are not being met. I'm not even bringing up all that other stuff—and believe me, it's a mess out here and we'll be dealing with the consequences of this blackout for years to come. I'm just talking about the most basic things people need to survive right now. Food, water, suitable shelter . . .*

"*So what do they do? How do they decide to solve this problem? FEMA is overwhelmed, we have a devastating lack of resources, and they decide to close the state borders! People are dying, they need food, they need water, and they close the state borders so no one can get in—*"

A crackle of static interrupts the voice, and I'm kind of glad. I don't know what I was expecting to hear, but it wasn't that. People can't get in? *My dad* can't get in? But the static lasts only a moment, and then the voice is back.

"*—yet manage to place military at state borders and around our power stations? Is this use of resources not highly suspect? No one is leaping to hasty conclusions here. All of these things are leading intelligent people to suspect deliberate sabotage on the part of our government.*

"*So, what's the lesson, kids? The lesson is if you're still sitting around, twiddling your thumbs, and waiting for someone to swoop in and save you, then maybe you weren't cut out for life. Because maybe this isn't something you planned for, but this is life as we know it now. It's 'survival of the fittest' time. And the question you should be asking yourself is: 'Do I want to be a survivor, or—?'*"

The radio goes silent. It's not the static this time. He shut it off.

I go completely still.

Does he know I'm here?

I don't breathe.

Ten seconds pass. Twenty seconds. Enough time for him to get to me.

Nothing happens.

Quietly, I pack up, placing the full canteens in the backpack. I drink one last bottle of water. I try to take it slow, but my hand is shaking so hard. I guzzle it. A queasy feeling pulls at the back of my throat.

My body wants more water, but I couldn't swallow more if I tried. My gag reflex would send it right back up.

I fill up the bottle one last time—for later. Screw on the cap and put it in the bag with the other canteens.

I don't bother to latch the hose back in place, just leave it on the ground. My back pressed to the water tank, I inch my way up, but stay down on one knee. I'm much taller than these tanks. They aren't very wide either, maybe twenty inches.

I listen one last time, strain to hear anything. A creaking camp chair. Footsteps in the dry grass.

Nothing.

Maybe he's gone? Or maybe he turned off the radio, slouched down in that camping chair, and went to sleep. I can't kneel here all night. I've got to get back to Cleverly. I've got to meet her at the truck.

Letting out a shaky breath, I rise to my feet, glance over my shoulder.

Clayton Presley's emotionless eyes are no longer staring into the flames. They're staring directly at me.

15

I DON'T MOVE. I *can't* move. My brain won't send the necessary signal to my legs, or maybe my brain has sent the signal but my legs are ignoring it. Or maybe Clayton Presley's eyes have me pinned in place, like a moth to a corkboard. Because he's not moving either. He's just staring at me.

There's no expression on his face, no shock, no anger. I think for a second that maybe he can't see me. Maybe his eyes are still adjusting to the darkness, and if I stay still long enough, he'll go back to staring at the flames.

"J-*Dog*!" a voice suddenly calls out, and Clayton Presley's eyes unpin me, his head jerking toward the tents beyond the campfire. I'm down on one knee before I even know what I'm doing, scrambling back behind the water tank, breathing hard.

As soon as I'm out of sight, I wonder what the heck I'm thinking. It's a little late to be hiding. Clayton Presley has seen me. He *knows* I'm here.

"You tired or what, man? Ready for a break?"

The same voice asks these questions, and I can tell he's

closer. I can also tell that the voice belongs to my old pal, Spike. *Great.*

I tense, ready to bolt. But all Presley says is, "I told you I'd be fine tonight." He sounds annoyed. I wait for more, crouched on the balls of my feet.

"Don't bite my head off, Jer. I'm not in the mood for your crap."

This comes from Spike, and I can only assume "Jer" is Presley's actual name. Or at least a portion of it.

It's quiet for a moment, and I hear the sound of a log hitting the fire, followed by crackles and pops. I'm itching to run, but something is holding me back.

"I can't sleep anyway," Spike says.

There's a hesitation, and then Presley says, "How's Steph doing?"

"She's eight months' pregnant. Gonna give birth in a tent at this crap-hole campsite. How do you think she's doing?"

"I can't say I've been in her position," Presley says.

"You're a chump, Jer."

There's another stretch of silence. I don't like the silences. I can't help imagining that Presley is miming my where-abouts to Spike. Any second now, they could surprise me, catch me off guard.

I pull the steak knife from my waistband and cringe. It's such a pathetic excuse for a knife. It probably wouldn't even cut steak. My hunting knife, on the other hand—you could do some serious damage with that knife. Not that I regret giving it to Cleverly.

I'm taking too long to get back to her. Is she still waiting at the truck? Is she searching for me in the dark now?

"I've been staring into this fire too long," Presley says. *Good.*

"Remember that game we used to play when we were

kids?" Spike says, and the genuine humor in his voice kind of throws me off. "Fire tag." He laughs. "Stare into the campfire for a count of twenty, then stumble around like a blind man, trying to tag as many kids around camp as you can."

"Isn't that how you broke your arm?" Presley says.

"Oh yeah. The first time I broke it. And you made fun of me for crying before we found out it was fractured—"

"You were always such a baby."

"And you were always such a jerk."

"Well, you know me. I get off on tormenting kids."

There's a pointed silence. Then Spike says, "You still feeling bad about Jim's kid? The one that was crying?"

I go completely still. Except for my hands. I squeeze them into fists, pressing my knuckles hard against the ground, my pulse throbbing in my ears. I don't want to hear them talk about this. I don't want to hear my brother's name leave their mouths. If I do, it's all over. I don't care if all I'm armed with is a knife that's not worthy of cutting a piece of cake—I'll use it to cut Clayton Presley.

"I traded most of that stuff for things Steph and I need for the baby. You know how hard it is to get diapers right now?"

Silence, just crackling fire.

"Besides," Spike continues, "I told you, I saw them. They're fine. They're going up to Ely for help. Resilient little—"

A loud crash from across camp cuts him off, the thunder of metal cans colliding. My whole body jolts in alarm. There's cursing—I hear Presley and Spike jump up from their chairs and run off in the direction of the crash. I force myself to wait until the count of three; then I push myself off the ground, my soles slipping on the grass before I get a grip and sprint for the trucks.

When I reach the open space where I left Cleverly, she isn't there. And I'm not really surprised, but I kind of need her to be there, as stupid as that sounds. I skid around the front bumper of one truck, heading for the silver one, and notice that the remaining tires have been slashed on the last truck. Cleverly took care of it.

I want to race off in the direction of that crash, find her now. I messed everything up. I was supposed to forget about the water tanks.

But I can't go look for her. I know she'd want me to go back to the plan. Meet at Spike's truck. Hot-wire Spike's truck. Commit grand theft auto.

The windows are down on the truck. There are no running boards along the side, nothing to step up on. But I can't open the door—the cab light would come on. So I grip the frame and hoist myself in through the driver's side. My shoulder hits the vinyl first, and I use the wheel as leverage to haul the rest of myself inside. The steering wheel locks, and I cringe at my own carelessness, but I guess I'd need to bust the lock either way.

Lying low across the bench, I twist, slinging my backpack onto the floor. I'm gonna need the flashlight, there's no way around it, but I can keep it dim, make sure it's not putting off too much light. I pull it out, wind it. Then I grab the steering wheel and use it to yank myself around.

Headfirst under the column, first thing I do is look for the parking lights and manually switch them off. I pull myself upright, staying as low as possible, keeping my light aimed downward.

A flathead screwdriver would come in handy right about now. I can make do without it, but breaking the steering lock and prying open the panel on the steering column would be so much easier with something like a screwdriver.

I scan the floor of the cab, looking for anything I can use. I yank open the glove box. A bunch of crap falls out, mostly folded-up papers and receipts. I shuffle through the mess blindly, throwing stuff aside, until I find what I'm looking for.

A screwdriver. *Thanks, Spike!*

Gripping the wheel, I jam the screwdriver between the steering wheel and the top of the steering column, forcing it back and forth and working the wheel left and right until I feel the snap of the lock breaking. Then I work the edge of the screwdriver into the side seam of the lower panel, prying it upward. It's harder to pry off than I expected.

After a little investigating, I find where it's screwed on and confirm that the screwdriver is too thick to fit into the holes. I drive it back into the seam and apply more pressure. I can get it separated about half an inch, but it's not budging.

I check the glove box for a smaller screwdriver, check under the bench for a toolbox or something, but find nothing. So I try prying it off again, and the seconds start adding up into minutes.

I'm starting to panic. I can feel myself losing focus. I'm thinking about backup plans, and ditching this truck to find Cleverly, and getting the heck out of here before something else goes wrong.

But then I think about what would come next. Sixty-six more miles on foot, not enough water, not enough food. I imagine the look on everyone's face when I explain that I couldn't get the freaking panel off the freaking steering column.

I forget about staying low. I get up on my knees and put all my weight onto the screwdriver, bouncing on it until a chunk of the plastic *finally* snaps off, hitting me in the chest.

It's not enough to get to the wires, but it's enough to fit four fingers inside.

I grip the opening and apply the same bouncing pressure, pushing straight down from my shoulder. The sharp plastic cuts into my flesh, but that's okay. Because I can feel it breaking, and when it snaps off, I have to hold back a yell of triumph.

I chuck the broken panel aside and grab the flashlight, vaguely aware that my hand is bleeding. I pull myself under the steering column headfirst, holding the flashlight between my teeth, and check out the wires. The two red wires control the truck's battery, and the two brown ones are for the starter.

I barely register the sound of running footsteps and look up in time to see Cleverly collide with the passenger-side door.

"Hi," she says breathlessly, and I am extremely glad to see her.

I take the flashlight out of my mouth, unable to suppress my relieved grin. "Perfect timing. I need my knife back."

"No problem," she says, still out of breath. She tosses something heavy into the cab before climbing in. I wipe off my bleeding hand on my jeans and she quickly passes me my hunting knife. With the flashlight back between my teeth, I return my focus to the wires. I separate them with shaking fingers, and then cut the two red wires.

"Hurry, they'll be back soon," she says, peering out the back window, the window at her side.

"I am," I mumble, flashlight still clenched between my teeth.

"Let me hold that," Cleverly says, taking it from my mouth, giving it a quick winding.

Laying one wire against a piece of broken plastic left behind, I use my knife to carefully strip about a half inch of insulation from it, and then do the same to the other red wire. I test the wires, touching the exposed ends together and watching the dashboard lights flicker on.

"Power's working," Cleverly says with a quick smile.

"Still gotta do the tricky part," I say. Because I've got to twist two live wires together without electrocuting myself.

I lay them side by side against the same piece of jagged plastic, wishing my fingers were steadier, wishing my hand weren't bleeding. Then I carefully keep the exposed ends in place with the flat of my knife. I take a second to wipe more blood from my hand, and then I pinch the insulated part of the two wires together between my fingers, twisting from behind. It takes a little patience, sweat gathers at my temples, but I finally get them twisted together. The dashboard is lit.

"Almost there," I say, catching a breath. The stressful part is over. No more twisting live wires. The brown starter wires carry a strong current as well, but I've only got to strip them. I cut the wires, and my hands are shaking more than ever. Not so much because I'm stripping live wires, but because this engine is about to start up.

I palm the knife when I'm done, taking a starter wire in each hand with the ends out—

"John," Cleverly says urgently.

"Hang on—"

"John!" she shouts, and just as I touch the exposed ends together, just as I hear the engine rumble and start up, I feel a yank on my upper right arm, pulling me out from under the column, and Cleverly screams.

"What in the—" Spike growls. I don't hear what comes next, because his fist connects with the side of my face.

The hit is absolutely stunning. So stunning that I think

I'm out of consciousness for a second, but I can't be sure. I do know I'm halfway out the window without even realizing it happened, and I've dropped my knife on the floor of the cab somewhere along the way.

I feel Cleverly's fingers latch on to the waist of my jeans, feel her pulling back, and though it feels like my head is underwater, I brace against the doorframe before Spike yanks me all the way out.

"Get out of my truck, you little—"

I yank back hard, manage to twist and get my legs and feet between the door and me. I push against it until I'm back in the cab, facing the side window with my feet planted against the door, my left hand holding the headrest.

Spike's got my other arm in both his hands, but lets go with one hand and uses it to try to leverage against the doorframe. Then puts a knee up against the door for more leverage, cursing for me to get out of his truck.

I blink hard, shaking my head a little because my vision is still swimming. I'm trying to think through the buzzing in my head.

The engine is running. I can't move. I can't get my feet to the pedals.

"Cleverly," I say, winded. She's behind me, still clutching the top of my jeans. "Put your foot on the brake."

Spike's eyes jump to meet mine. "Don't," he says, a low warning.

"Which is the brake?" she shouts, but Spike is squeezing my upper arm, yanking it so hard I can think of nothing but the pain of it.

"Do it!" I call, getting my whole arm around the headrest.

Cleverly slides down the bench, stomps her foot on the pedal.

The engine revs, a deafening roar, the truck still in park.

"Wrong one!" I shout over the noise.

"Sorry!" Cleverly says to me, stomping the other pedal.

I hear shouts from the other side of the camp.

Spike calls back over his shoulder, "Hey! I need help over here!"

I stretch across and grab the gearshift on the steering column, just like in my dad's truck.

"I'm serious, kid—"

I pull it into drive, twist forward to grab the top of the steering wheel.

"You're not gonna get far," Spike says through gritted teeth.

"Let your foot off the brake," I tell Cleverly, ignoring him. The truck starts to roll forward.

"I'm warning you, kid." He stumbles sideways alongside the cab, still gripping my arm with one hand and the doorframe with the other.

"Too bad your piece-of-crap truck has no running boards," I say.

He shakes his head. "You picked the wrong truck to steal!"

"You picked the wrong kids to rob," I say back, then to Cleverly, "Foot on the gas, *now*!"

Spike curses, takes a few running steps as the truck accelerates, and then finally has to let go.

I fall back the second he does, the truck swerving a little as I adjust my hold on the wheel and shake out my right arm. I turn in place, get my legs down, quickly reach around the column, and find the headlight switch, flipping them on.

"I got it!" I say to Cleverly, and she moves her foot off the gas.

The truck lurches back.

And right before I floor the gas pedal, I glance at the side mirror, see Spike illuminated by the red taillights. I see him jogging to a stop, cupping his hands around his mouth, yelling out at the top of his lungs.

"You picked the truck with no gas, *moron*! The truck has no gas!"

16

I HIT THE brake hard as we take the first turn onto the narrow road. The tires skid in the gravel, the front end of the truck almost plowing through the wooden sign that says NO FACILITIES PROVIDED. PLEASE CARRY OUT *ALL* YOU CARRY IN.

"*Holy crap,*" I say on an exhale of breath, correcting the turn.

"You've done this before, right?" Cleverly shouts, gripping the passenger armrest.

"Yeah, one time!"

"*One time?*"

"I don't remember it feeling this weird," I say.

I am in control of a big hunk of metal that is somehow attached to my body.

I squeeze the steering wheel with my good hand, my injured hand braced against the opposite side in a fist, elbows out. My heart is pounding, my whole body jittery.

We just committed grand theft auto! I am driving a *freaking truck*!

A freaking truck with no gas in the tank.

"I forgot the first rule of committing grand theft auto," I say, the sinking feeling in my stomach worse than my jitters. "Check the gas gauge."

"*We* forgot," Cleverly says. "I should have thought of it too. But the truck started. That means there's some gas in it, right?"

I take my eyes off the road for a second, lean forward, and squint at the gas gauge.

"The line is all the way on red," I say. My eyes jump back to the road. It looks like the truck is straying to the side a little, so I quickly jerk it back to the left, then jerk to the right.

"Sorry," I say, gasping.

Cleverly leans back and reaches for the seat belt—which is probably a good idea, but no way am I taking my hands off the wheel to get a seat belt on.

I've got to relax, got to remember what my dad said about driving.

Ease off the gas. And the trick to keeping the vehicle steady is, focus your eyes farther ahead down the road.

I do that. I ease my foot off the gas, just as we bounce over a dip in the narrow road.

I don't know if it's the bouncing, the sucker punch to the head, or the fact that it smells like old dust and sun-cooked vinyl seats in here, but that nauseous feeling starts to build at the back of my throat again. I try to swallow it down.

Cleverly asks, "How much gas do we have if the line is on red?"

I shake my head. Then cringe, because the movement makes me sick. "I don't know. A few gallons? We'll see how far we get."

But that sinking feeling is back. Because for a split second back there, right when I touched those two tiny wires together and the engine roared to life, my brain sent a quick message to the rest of my body. It said, "*Guess what? We're done walking! We've got a ride all the way to Brighton Ranch!*"

From where we left Stewart and Will, it's another sixty-six miles to Brighton Ranch. There's no way there's enough gas in this truck to make it all the way. But if we can make it five, even ten miles on fumes . . . that's better than nothing, right?

After a few miles of successfully keeping the truck on the road, the weirdness starts to wear off. I relax my shoulders a little, let my elbows drop.

"Hey," I say to Cleverly, swallowing hard, "I'm sorry I didn't stick with the plan."

"I'm not," she says. "If you had, we'd be in trouble right now."

That's right. We'd have a truck with no gas, an empty water bottle, and three empty canteens. We'd be back to where we were when we left for the reservoir—no water, two days away from Brighton Ranch.

"Are you thirsty?" I say. *Stupid question.* "I mean, you want to grab the water bottle from the backpack?"

"Maybe we should save it," she says hesitantly. "That was the reason I came with you to begin with. I was supposed to drink at the reservoir so we could bring back full canteens, and the water bottle, back to Stew and Will."

"I think the reason you came is so I'd have someone to save me when I got stuck behind that water tank," I joke.

She still doesn't move to get the backpack, so I say, "I drank three bottles of water. Help me get over the guilt."

"All right," she says, and takes off her seat belt long enough to grab the backpack off the floor. "That guy by the fire," she says, clicking her seat belt back into place. "Why do you think he didn't go after you, anyway?"

She's talking about Clayton Presley. My good hand squeezes the wheel.

"I mean, when he caught you getting water. I'm not gonna lie, it freaked me out. I thought we were both dead."

I have to admit, it's a little embarrassing, knowing she saw me stand up from behind the water tank like an idiot.

Still, I tell her, "He didn't know I was there."

"Yeah he did."

I shake my head. "It probably seemed like he saw me," I explain. "That's what I thought at first too. But his vision was all screwed up from staring into that fire. That's the only reason he—"

"John," she says like I'm being dense, "he knew you were there the whole time, even before you stood up."

Heat travels up the back of my neck. "How do you know that?" I say, the truck slowing as my foot slips off the accelerator, then jolting forward when I find it again.

"I could see you both from where I was," she says, "behind one of those big tree trunks. When you didn't meet me at Spike's truck, I knew you probably went for the water. Anyway, he kept watching the tank you were sitting behind."

The heat floods my face. "Yeah, well, he's kind of a creepy guy."

"Maybe, but that's not my point."

You still feeling bad about Jim's kid? The one that was crying?

I don't ask what her point is, just shut my mouth. I don't want to think about Clayton Presley. I don't want to think about him staring at the water tank with me behind it. He's not a good guy. He's the kind of guy who robs kids and leaves them to die.

If my jaw were clenched any tighter, my back molars would be pulverized. I'd be choking on the dust.

Cleverly takes a long drink of water, and then holds out the bottle to look at it. "It tastes funny."

Relieved at the change of subject, I say, "That's just iodine. Our water storage has been around for a while, so it had to be purified to make it potable again. They dropped in too much iodine, and didn't add the vitamin C tablets to counter the taste. I guess the idiots didn't read the instructions in the water-purification kit they stole from us."

"Idiots," Cleverly agrees, taking another drink.

Then I ask, "Did you hear what that guy said on the radio?"

She comes up for air, wipes the water from her mouth. "The part about the borders being closed?"

"Yeah," I say, though that wasn't the only crazy thing he said.

It's "survival of the fittest" time.

"Do you think it's true?" I ask about the state borders. As if she knows whether some random guy on a radio was telling the truth.

She doesn't answer.

"Almost to the highway," I say a moment later, seeing the dark strip of asphalt ahead, our headlights flashing on the small reflective markers.

I slow at the end of the road, bringing the truck to a stop with a sudden jerk. The dust settles around us, billowing in through the open windows.

I reach for my seat belt while we're stopped—kind of awkward to do with my injured hand. Cleverly takes off her seat belt and slides over to help.

"Here." She takes the buckle and pulls it out and around me. "Is your hand okay?" She's eyeing my balled-up fist.

I say, "It's fine," even though it's throbbing like crazy.

"It's bleeding a lot," she says, clicking the buckle into place and sliding back.

I don't need to look. I can feel the trail of blood down my arm, all the way to my elbow. I squeeze my hand tighter. "I've got a first aid kit in my pack."

"The side of your face looks all red and swollen too," she adds.

I grit my teeth at that. I don't really want the visual reminder of Spike's stupid fist connecting with my face. "I'll be all right," I say, taking a breath. I flip on the blinker for some reason, then carefully press the gas and turn onto the highway, using mostly my good hand.

I'm not going too fast, because I'm kind of new at this whole driving thing. But also because Stewart and Will aren't that far up the road. I've got the high beams on, watching for that mile marker on the side of the road where we left them. If the clock on the dashboard is right, it's exactly three in the morning, and it feels like it. The glowing yellow reflectors in the middle of the highway blink past us. They're mesmerizing, swaying back and forth, my vision starting to double.

A jackrabbit dashes across the highway, narrowly missing our front tires, and I adjust my grip on the wheel, shake my head a little, and force my eyes wider.

My hand is throbbing. I've got a skull-splitting headache at my left temple, where Spike punched me. But it's the exhaustion that's hitting me hardest.

"I'm not asleep, by the way," Cleverly mumbles. I glance over and see her head resting against the doorframe, wind scattering pieces of her hair, eyes closed.

"It would be all right if you were," I say.

"No, it wouldn't."

I turn back to the road, slam my foot on the brake with a curse, tires skidding. Cleverly gasps. The brakes lock, the truck slides, jolting to a stop.

Eyes wide. Deep breaths.

"Did I mention your brother is crazy?" Cleverly says, staring straight ahead, her hands braced against the glove box.

Stewart is standing not ten feet from the front bumper, arms out to his sides, fists balled, chest heaving. I sit back against the seat and breathe out another curse, willing my pulse to slow down.

I don't defend him this time. *Stewart is crazy.*

But my initial shock of almost running over Stewart with a truck is suddenly replaced with a strange sense of relief, seeing him standing in the middle of the highway, angry. I guess a part of me had been wondering, worrying about the state I'd find him in when we got back. Standing on two feet, looking like he might murder me? I could think of worse things.

Cleverly jumps out the second I put the gearshift into park. "Will?" she calls, running in front of the high beams toward the side of the road. "Hey, Stew," she says as she passes, her shadow darkening his figure for an instant. But he doesn't even look at her.

I decide to leave the truck running, and hop out. I'm giving up a little bit of gas, letting the truck idle like this, but with the light of the headlamps, we can throw everything in the bed of the truck and get out of here quicker. Plus, with the truck on empty, maybe running on fumes, I might not even be able to get it started again.

"You all right?" I say to Stew, shutting the door behind me. His cheeks are flushed and he's breathing pretty heavily, but I'm not sure if it's a side effect of anger, or if he's actually experiencing shortness of breath.

"Where were you?" he says through clenched teeth, his voice cracking.

I don't think he needs me to answer that, but I do anyway.

"We left for the reservoir after you fell asleep. We've got some water for you and Will. And a truck. There's not much gas, but—"

Stew hauls back and shoves my shoulders, pushing me back a step. I stare at him, uneasy. Not because I'm surprised he pushed me, but because he'd gathered all his strength to manage it, and the push was still pretty pathetic.

I may be bigger than him, his older brother, but Stew is no wimp.

"Stewart," I say as calmly as possible, "you have every right to be mad. But we need to get our stuff and go, all right? I'll tell you everything that happened once we get going."

I don't wait for an answer. I head to the side of the road to help Cleverly, who is already rolling up the sleeping bags as fast as she can. Will is on his feet at her side, but he seems to be in a confused stupor, gazing sleepily at the truck idling in the middle of the highway, his hair flattened to his skull on one side and a ratted-up bird's nest on the other.

Just as I reach the brush, Stew shoves me again, this time from behind. I turn and face him, my patience already dwindling. "Listen, Stew, I'm sorry—"

"No, you're not," he says. He looks like he's going to shove me again, so I take a step back.

I say with forced calmness, "The longer the truck idles, the farther we have to walk. So I officially apologize for going to the reservoir without you, okay? I knew you'd be mad, and I don't blame you. But right now, we need to pack up and get out of here. We're wasting gas."

"I'm not going anywhere with you," he says, his chest

rising and falling faster. "You're the biggest liar, John. You lie, and it makes me sick."

"Get in the truck, Stewart."

"I'm not going."

"Get in."

"Just leave me behind!"

"No."

"What difference does it make? Just go without me!"

"I won't, and you know it."

"What about what *I* want, John? It's *my* life, not yours! I *hate* it when you do this. You're so selfish. You act like I was put on this planet to be your brother."

"Because you were, Stew! You were put here to be my brother, and I was put here to be yours."

"Well, one of us got the short end of the deal!"

"Believe me, I know. Get in the truck."

"I don't want to be here anymore!"

"Get in the truck."

His frustration brimming over, Stewart stalks away from me, swiping the back of his hand across his eyes. I watch him, my heart hammering against my chest. He gets as far as the front bumper, and then stops and turns back to the cab. He yanks open the driver's-side door and climbs in. The heavy metal door slams shut with a loud clunk.

I take a deep breath and turn around, my quaking hands in two fists.

Cleverly is standing beside Will, one arm around a sleeping bag. They're both staring at me, probably wondering what that was about, but they don't ask. I pass them without a word.

We make quick work of packing up, Cleverly and me hurrying back and forth to the bed of the truck. I run back for my pack last, and Will is still rooted in place.

"C'mon," I say, taking him by the back of the neck, steering him toward the truck.

"Where'd the truck come from?" he asks.

"We . . . found it at the reservoir."

"You *stole* it?"

"Pretty much, yeah."

"That's cool."

Through the rear window of the cab, I see Stew slumped against the passenger door, sleeping, or at least pretending to sleep. Getting him into the truck was a small win, I know. But I'm already past it, already worrying about the bigger battle ahead. Because when the time comes, I've got to figure out how to get him *out*.

"Cleverly said there's not enough gas," Will says.

That sinking feeling again. But I just say, "How Battle Born would we be if we *drove* all the way to Brighton Ranch?"

Cleverly's throwing the last sleeping bag over the side, and Will goes around to the back bumper and climbs in.

Leaning my pack against the rear tire, I get down in front of it, quickly unzipping pockets, trying to remember where I moved that first aid kit. . . .

"You got a flashlight?" Will calls, thumping around in the bed of the truck. "There's a lot of stuff back here."

Nowhere near the amount of stuff Spike had when he stopped this morning.

"There's one in Stew's pack. Front left pocket," I call back. I finally locate the first aid kit and pass it up to Cleverly. "Can you help me with my hand really fast?" I ask, zipping up various pockets before getting to my feet.

"Of course," she says.

"Found it!" Will says. A soft light bobs around the bed of the truck. "Looks like a lot of junk . . ."

Cleverly takes out a roll of gauze and a tiny pair of scissors, a small bottle of rubbing alcohol, and a tube of liquid bandage—superglue, basically—and lines it up along the bed of the truck. She takes my hand.

"Bring that light over here for a minute, Will," she says.

"Hang on," he says.

"Will, come on!"

He stomps over and collapses against the side, knocking the gauze to the ground in the process.

"Will!"

"Sorry!"

Cleverly grabs the flashlight from him and crouches down, looking for the gauze.

While all this is going on, I am painfully aware of each passing second. Every so often, the engine sort of lulls before picking up a steady rumble again, and every time that happens, my anxiety level goes up a notch.

We don't have time for this.

"Just forget it," I say, but Cleverly's already on her feet again, gauze in hand.

"Don't worry, I'll be quick about it."

I believe her—she seems nearly as anxious to leave as I am.

Will's kneeling in the bed of the truck, holding the flashlight for us, and Cleverly's holding my hand. I uncurl my fingers and we get our first look at the cut. It's not so deep as I thought it was going to be, but it still needs to be glued shut.

It's in a really bad spot. Right across my palm where my fingers bend, getting deeper as it reaches the outside of my hand, which is probably why it bled so much. Keeping my hand closed has helped it clot up, but just opening my fingers produces fresh blood.

"Gross. What *happened*?" Will asks, his nose scrunched up in disgust.

Before I can answer, Cleverly splashes a bunch of rubbing alcohol across my palm, and my eyes fill with tears.

"Ahh!" I suck in a breath, yanking my hand back.

"Sorry!" Cleverly says.

I pace a few feet away, cradle my injured hand against my chest, squat low to the ground.

"Does it hurt?" Will asks.

"*Seriously,* Will?"

"No, Will," I snap through clenched teeth. "It feels great." I stand up, shake out my hand, blow on it. Then force myself to walk back, a sheen of sweat across my brow. "Just glue it shut," I say to Cleverly. "Hurry."

She cuts off a few pieces of gauze, hands me one so I can wipe some of the drying blood from my arm, my elbow. She dabs at the fresh blood on my hand, clearing the cut. Then, using her index finger and thumb to hold the wound closed, she squeezes an even bead of glue across my palm.

"Hang on," she says when I start to pull it away, "it's still drying." She raises my hand to her mouth, gently blows back and forth across my palm, the pain magically disappearing . . .

"There's a gas can back here," Will says in a whisper, like he's trying not to disturb us.

Cleverly looks up at him sharply. "A *gas* can?"

He nods.

"Does it have the letter *L* spray-painted on the front?" I ask.

He nods again.

"Is there gas in it?" Cleverly asks.

"I was gonna check, but then you yelled at me to bring you the flashlight."

"Okay, whatever, go get it!"

Will clomps off to retrieve the gas can.

"That's one of ours," I tell Cleverly. "It's gotta be bone dry."

"How do you know that?" she says.

I frown for a second, realizing that I don't actually know. I don't know if Spike took the can this morning, when for sure all the gas cans at our place were empty. Or if he took it the night we were robbed, when we still had full cans of gas in the shed.

Cleverly climbs up on the back bumper to watch Will. "Hurry up!"

"Just a minute, it's on here tight," he says, trying to unhook the can from where Spike had bungeed it into place.

I can't watch. I don't want to get my hopes up, but I can't help it.

I finish taking care of my wound, hands shaking with nervous energy as I wrap the gauze around my palm a bunch of times, tucking the end under. I get down in front of my pack to put away my first aid kit, find my black Sharpie—I'm gonna need it to keep track of miles again. I'm just lifting my pack into the darkened truck bed when Will's shadowy form comes toward us in a crouch, five-gallon gas can in his hand.

He passes it over. "There's gas in it."

It's not until I take the can and feel the liquid sloshing around inside that his words register in my mind.

"He's right," I say, grinning.

Cleverly breathes out a relieved laugh. "Will!" she says, leaning over the side to grab him in a quick hug. She twists back to look at me. "How much is in there?"

I test the weight. "Maybe half full?"

Still, we all have the biggest smiles on our faces.

I turn toward the cab. "Hey, Stew!" I call, but my smile fades when I see him slumped against that window. Resting. Exhausted.

I look back at Cleverly and Will, force my smile back in place. "I think the tank's on the other side."

I go around the back bumper and Cleverly hops down and trails after me. Will tromps across the bed of the truck to meet us on the other side.

"Can you put gas in the tank without turning off the engine?" he asks, one hand planted on the side of the truck, the other shining the flashlight at the gas cap for me. "Won't it, like, explode or something?"

"That kind of stuff only happens in movies," Cleverly says. "Right, John?"

"Um . . ." I hesitate, my hand on the gas cap. "Yeah, I'm like eighty-five percent sure we won't die in a fiery explosion."

But just then, the engine sort of lulls again, rumbles softly for a few seconds, and then dies.

My heart sinks. Not just because the gas in the truck is gone. But because I'm gonna have to mess with those stupid wires and get it started again.

I say to Will, "Good news! Our odds just improved to a one hundred percent chance of not exploding."

I pull off the nozzle attached to the top of the gas can, screw it in place, and upend the gas into the tank. It doesn't take long, but then I shake the can for a good thirty seconds, making sure we get every last drop of it.

"Let's get out of here."

17

THERE'S A WEIRD buzzing in the cab of the truck. Like a dying fly trapped where the dashboard meets the windshield.

"John."

I flinch at the sound of my brother's voice, scrunch my eyelids tighter against the bright light seeping through . . .

"John."

I let them crack open. Sunlight glares off the windshield. Clusters of dead bugs splattering the glass like constellations.

"Where are we?" he asks.

A groan comes from deep in my chest. I start to sit up, peeling my sweat-soaked back away from the vinyl bench. My neck cramped from where my head was resting— between the seat and the hard doorframe. Arm stiff, hand throbbing, an ache at my temple—all reminders of last night at the reservoir. Then I try to swallow.

"Oh no," I rasp out, wincing at the dryness in my throat. "I think I slept with my mouth open."

"You did," Stew says matter-of-factly.

I glance over at him on the passenger side. He looks small in this space, for some reason. He's looking back at me with dark eyes, the cowlick at his hairline fanning his hair back, his dry skin dusted with pale desert dirt. An unreadable expression on his face.

He's not angry, though—at least, not so angry as he was last night.

"How long you been awake?" I rasp. I try to work up enough saliva to wet my throat.

"A while."

"Cleverly and Will?" I ask, lifting myself up higher on the bench to look out the back window.

"Still asleep."

I see them on top of the sleeping bags in the bed of the truck—same place they were when the truck rolled to a stop last night. Will, crowded against Cleverly in the last remaining triangle of shade. Both of them completely out.

"Where are we?" Stew asks again.

I drop back against the bench, getting my first look at where the truck stopped in the light of day. Though, when I pulled apart the power wires at 3:52 in the morning, I was too exhausted to look around anyway. Too exhausted to do anything but shut my heavy eyelids and collapse against this seat.

There's nothing around us but the same desert landscape. Although ahead, I can see where the mountains stretch to the highway. Where the road curves.

I try to remember the math I did last night, the tally marks on my arm.

"Twenty-three miles from Brighton Ranch," I tell him, rounding down a mile to make it sound better.

"That far?"

"It's not that far."

"Not that far for you," he says, staring out at the highway.

He's got something halfway unwrapped in his hand, one of his protein bars. He brings it to his mouth and gnaws off a bite.

"It's a miracle we got as far as we did on that gas," I tell him. "I think we rolled for a mile at least after the engine died."

"We're not supposed to talk about dying, remember?"

His words stop me short, but I don't let myself react. "Good one, Stew," I say with no humor in my voice.

He's holding something in his other hand. A piece of junk mail. One of those glossy half-sheet ads that had fallen out of the glove box last night.

"What do you have?" I say.

He looks down at it, then gives it to me.

TAKE A DRIVE DOWN THE EXTRATERRESTRIAL HIGHWAY! it reads. UFO SIGHTINGS AHEAD. EARTHLINGS WELCOME! AREA 51 SOUVENIRS! ALIEN FRESH JERKY! ICE-COLD DRINKS!

"Ice-cold drinks—I wish. Or wait, are you considering a new theory? Aliens instead of zombies? Or maybe the zombies and aliens are working together—"

"Flip it over."

"What?" I say, frowning. But I do what he says.

The other side of the ad is blank, except for a mailing address printed in the center. TO THE RESIDENT OF, followed by a street address in Ely, Nevada.

But that's not what he's talking about. He's talking about what's handwritten in the upper right corner.

HWY 318, MM 98.

"It's directions to our place," Stew says, gnawing off another bite of his protein bar.

He's right. I'm holding evidence of their plan to rob us in my hand.

I already know the robbery wasn't something Clayton Presley and the others just decided in the heat of the moment. But seeing the handwriting, seeing proof of what I already know, *here* in Spike's truck, sparks that warm feeling in my chest again.

A trickle of sweat runs down the center of my back and I tug at my shirt, tossing the ad on the seat between us.

Then I look over at my brother, suddenly bothered that he's not as angry as I am. *Why* isn't he angry? Why isn't his pulse pounding and blood burning? Why isn't he feeling what I'm feeling?

"They *knew* Dad was on a work trip," I say, biting the words out. "Clayton Presley knocked on our door just to make sure we were still alone. Just the two of us alone. Then they came back."

There is still no spark of anger from him. Not even a flicker.

I feel a pinch between my eyes and look out at the road, far ahead, where the asphalt meets the sky in broken waves, like a swimming pool stretched across the highway.

"They were at the reservoir, Stew. All of them. Who would do something like that? Take everything from us, and then set up camp forty miles down the road? It's like they knew they could take what they wanted, and we couldn't do *anything* about it. But they also didn't expect we'd go south. They didn't expect us to show up at the reservoir, slash their tires, and take this truck. But we did. I put my knife through the tires of that stupid truck Presley paid cash for—"

I stop myself, take in a few steadying breaths, push them out. Look over at my brother again.

Nothing. I know he was listening. He *had* to have been listening. But he just looks at the protein bar in his hand and brings it up to his mouth for another bite.

"What *is* that?" I say, squinting at the wrapper, because now that I think of it, his food pouch is in his pack, and his pack is in the bed of the truck. He doesn't answer immediately, so I reach over and snatch it out of his hand. He pretty much lets me have it without a fight.

"Where'd you get this?" I say, yanking the wrapper back to see what it is.

"There's a whole box of them on the floor."

It takes me a second to remember Cleverly tossing something through the open window of the cab before she got in at the campsite last night—something from Clayton Presley's stash of stolen food.

I crouch to look under the console, where a bulk-sized, opened box of peanut butter bars is wedged between the floorboard and the underside of the dash. It's from our food storage, a favorite snack of my dad's—peanut butter layered with granola and nuts and coated in a shiny glaze of corn syrup.

"I hate nuts," I snap, pulling the wrapper flat to read the ingredients. "Oh, good. Loaded with sodium, carbs, and sugar."

"I don't care what's in it. I'm hungry."

He tries to grab it back, but I hold it out of reach. I'm tempted to chuck it out the window.

There are shadows under his eyes. The corners of his mouth are cracked and dry, the skin on his arms chalky with dirt. His shirt is dry, too, I notice. Not wet with perspiration, like mine.

He's stopped sweating.

"Did you find the canteens?" I ask him, leaning forward and spotting the backpack at his feet, unzipped.

"Yes."

"You need to drink more water. Grab the bag."

Stewart hesitates, like he's thinking about something. Then his words come out like a confession. "Before you woke up, I drank a canteen."

It takes me half a second to get his meaning, and then I can't stop my eyes from going wide. "A *canteen*? As in, half a gallon of water?"

He looks back at me with nervous eyes, like he's waiting for me to freak out, waiting for me to blow up at him.

But I don't. I *can't*. I want to get mad at him, I do. I'd rather my pulse be racing with anger right now than racing with fear.

"John." He says my name in a rush, and I feel that pinch between my eyes again. "I'm gonna throw up."

Something he says all the time.

But this time he gags. His shoulders thrust forward, hand clamped over his mouth. He shoves the lever down and the door open in one motion. Feet on the ground, hands braced on his knees, back hunched.

In the dirt on the side of the road, my brother vomits up half a gallon of water.

18

DAD ALWAYS SAID, if you want to have a productive day, get out of the clothes you slept in.

I want to have a productive day. I *need* to have a productive day.

I stand behind the truck and peel off my bloodstained pants, my underwear that's still slightly damp with reservoir water and sweat. I change my filthy undershirt and socks. Then I calm my nerves, crouched down on my heels, deep breaths, willing my hands to stop shaking.

I've got to focus on one thing, and one thing only. Get my brother to Brighton Ranch.

I'm giving us seven hours to walk it. Twenty-three miles, seven hours.

I stand and heave my pack onto my back, lifting the straps and rolling my shoulders under the weight. Everything we need is in here. The rest we can ditch.

On the shoulder of the road just ahead of the truck, Cleverly's got Stew sitting with his head between his knees.

"Take deep breaths through your nose, Stew," she says, fanning his neck with that stupid Extraterrestrial Highway ad.

I press my lips hard when I see it. I don't tell her that she's cooling my brother down with evidence to the robbery that put us here in the first place.

She's wearing a faded blue T-shirt and a pair of light gray jeans that she cut off above the knee with my hunting knife a few minutes ago. Will's changed too—a light blue T-shirt with a cartoon taco on the front.

The only one of us who didn't is Stew. He's still wearing the clothes he slept in, the clothes he puked in. . . .

"You think it was the toilet water?" Will asks me, squinting up from Stew's other side.

I ignore the tight feeling in my chest.

"No." I shade my eyes against the midmorning sun. "It's getting late. We need to head out."

"If it was the toilet water, we'd all be sick," Cleverly explains to Will.

"Was it something he ate?"

"Maybe you guys didn't hear me," I interrupt. "It's time to get going."

Cleverly squints up at me—or maybe she's glaring. "We heard you," she assures me. "Maybe you didn't *notice,* but Stew is in no condition to walk yet."

I let out a hard sigh but stop short of rolling my eyes at her.

I already feel sweat accumulating where the pack rests against my back. The heat is going to be bad today. Unlike yesterday, the air is completely still. Which is normal around here. One day, a windstorm that can steal your breath, and the next day, not even a breeze . . .

"Think it's heatstroke, John?" Will asks, shading his eyes with both hands.

I wish he'd just stop talking about it.

"No." I crouch in front of my brother, put my hand on his sun-warmed shoulder. The gesture is automatic, and it makes me think of my dad, makes me feel this weird catch in the back of my throat, so I pull my hand away. "Stew, we've got to walk. I know you can do it."

I slip my pack off one shoulder so I can unclip one of the full canteens for him.

"Here," I say, holding it out to him, the canvas strap dangling on the asphalt between his feet. "You're going to wear this across your chest while we walk. Take small sips, *tiny* sips, every few minutes."

He doesn't take the canteen. He slides his feet up, folds his arms across his knees, drops his forehead there.

"Stew?" I say firmly, and he lifts his head enough to look me in the eyes, his expression flat.

The shadows around his eyes are a deep pink color, and I feel a pang of guilt, pushing him like this. I know he's dehydrated. I know he needs water badly. But I'm not going to let him give up. *I'm* not going to give up. I'm getting my brother to Brighton Ranch.

"Try standing up," I say, hardening my resolve.

His forehead falls back to his arms, bridging his knees. "I can't," he mumbles.

"On your feet, Stewart. Now."

"John—" Cleverly starts to say, but I cut her off with a shake of my head, my eyes never leaving Stew.

"The longer you sit here," I say to him, "the harder it's going to be for you to work up the momentum to walk. You just have to stand up. That's all you gotta do. Once you're in motion, you'll be fine."

"No, I won't," he says, his voice muffled.

Before I can tell him that he doesn't have a freaking say

in the matter and he needs to get on his freaking feet now, Cleverly interrupts again. "He just needs a break, John."

I turn to her and snap, "He's my brother. Let me handle this."

Her eyebrows shoot up. I know she's only trying to reassure me that everything is fine, because she can probably tell that I'm about to lose it, but she's actually making it worse.

"He just puked his guts out," Will says, eyes wide, aiming his thumb back toward the truck in case I forgot where Stew's vomit is.

"I *know* that, Will. I was *there*. I *saw* it." I motion between the two of them. "*Both* of you need to let me handle this."

Cleverly stops fanning and gives me a look. She doesn't think I'm handling it well is the thing.

"I know what's best for my brother."

"Really?" she says. "Because from what Will and I can tell, it's pretty obvious that Stew needs to rest—"

"Sitting on the side of the road isn't going to do him any good!"

"Neither is forcing him to walk before he's ready!"

I drop the canteen and push to my feet, let the pack fall to the ground with a clunk.

"You gonna say anything, Stew?" I say, staring hard at the top of my brother's head.

Nothing. He doesn't even look up. Cleverly and Will do, though. They look at me like I'm some kind of crazy drill sergeant, and Stew is just sitting there with his head down, because, let's face it, he really doesn't care anymore.

And then I realize that the person who really needs a break around here is me. So I leave. I start walking south down the highway rumble strip. Because it's either that or I yank Stew up by the collar of his shirt and let him have it.

"John, wait!"

I ignore Cleverly's call, but it doesn't take long for her to catch up to me. And when she does, I turn on her, pointing my finger. "You don't trust me."

She looks surprised by my anger. "I do," she insists.

"You just don't trust me to decide what's best for my brother."

A small crease appears between her eyes. "No, that's not it."

"*I'm* the one responsible for Stewart." I jab at my chest. "*I* know what's best for him, not you."

"Okay, but—"

"And I *need* you to back me up," I say, my voice cracking in frustration, the words barely coming out, squeezing through the tight muscles in my throat, "not take his side against me!"

She takes a breath, stares at me for what seems like minutes, and I'm struggling to keep it together. . . .

"Okay," she says slowly. "I'll back you up, John. But Stew is sick—"

"I *know*! I know he's sick, all right—"

I can't fight it anymore. The words break through the wall in my mind, bringing up all the thoughts I've been keeping away. Overwhelming thoughts made worse by flooding my mind all at once. My chest goes tight, and I can't catch my breath.

Cleverly is saying something, but the only thing I understand right now is that I *can't breathe*.

I'm trying to take in air, but nothing happens. My lungs have stopped working. They've seized up, like an elephant is sitting on my chest.

I lean forward, hands on my knees, head dropped, and manage to suck in a small wheeze of air. Followed by another wheeze. And another.

I stare at the ground between my feet. Blink my eyes, confused that my vision isn't clearing, until I see drops of water hit the asphalt. Tears or sweat or both. I squeeze my eyes shut tight, trying to pull everything back inside, because I swear I'm having a nervous breakdown or something.

I try the tricks that have worked for me before. I try wiping every thought from my mind, but it's far too late for that. So I try channeling my dad, try thinking about what he would do in this situation, but that doesn't work either. Instead I have this thought of seeing my dad again and having to tell him that Stewart is dead, that I couldn't save him. That I failed at the most important job he's ever given me, and now Stew is gone.

Why did you leave that weekend? Why do you always have to leave?

My breathing gets harder, thin wheezes of air, like I'm trying to suck air into my lungs through a coffee straw.

My mind screams. *Come on! Think of something else. No thinking about dying.*

I try. I try to replace thoughts of death with something positive. A good memory. But instead, it's the morning my dad left. It's that Battle Born flag hanging on my window. My room a shade of blue.

What is that doing up there?

No. That's not the last thing he said.

It'd look pretty good on your bedroom wall.

I repeat these words in my mind, again and again.

And then I think of lying beside my brother in my room in the dark, flashlight in my hand, shining it on the emblem, lighting the words on the flag. BATTLE BORN.

We're going to be on our own for a while.

Yeah, I know. But we're not completely alone, John. We have each other.

A breath comes through. Less like a wheeze, more like a gasp. I push myself up straight, grab the bottom of my shirt, pulling it up to cover my face, my eyes. It takes more concentration, it takes replacing the same negative revolving thoughts with good thoughts, but warm, stale air eventually filters through my shirt, fills my lungs.

I push it back out. In and out again. And again.

We're not completely alone, John.

My chest still aches with tightness, but my heart rate has calmed, my lungs have opened up. When I wipe my shirt down my face and open my eyes, Cleverly is still standing in front of me. I can't read her expression, can't tell what she is thinking.

I sniff, wipe the back of my hand across my nose and mouth.

"Your brother is sick," she finally says. And it doesn't sound like she's trying to inform me of something this time. She says it like something has clicked into place in her mind.

"Yes," I say, forcing the words out. Stewart is sick, and I wish it were the toilet water, or the desert heat, or exhaustion.

"Rest isn't going to make him better," she says.

"No," I say. Neither will protein bars or an endless supply of water.

"What does he need?" she asks, studying me carefully.

I look back down the road to where we left Stew and Will, see my brother still sitting on the ground.

Don't talk about it, don't think about it, you make the decisions.

I turn to Cleverly, and I know I can't go back to holding it all in. It's too late, and it's not helping me anymore. I need her help. I need her to understand my brother.

"Insulin," I tell her, and I'm surprised by the weight that

leaves my chest when I say it aloud. "He's been out of insulin for almost two days."

Cleverly's only reaction is the reappearance of that tiny crease between her eyes. At first I think she still doesn't understand what I'm telling her. She doesn't understand that my brother has type 1 diabetes, that he actually can't *survive* without daily injections of insulin. And his insulin is gone. It's all gone.

Clayton Presley might not have pulled the trigger that night, but he may as well have.

But it's not that she doesn't get what I'm saying, I realize. It's just that she'd already guessed it was something bad. It had to be something bad, right? The way I've been acting. The way *Stew's* been acting. Like this journey through the desert is pointless, like he's going to die anyway . . . it's starting to make sense to her now.

"I have a friend from school who's diabetic," she says, not really to me, but to herself. Because she's still putting it all together in her mind.

It doesn't take her long. She looks at me with sudden understanding. "I assume there's insulin at Brighton Ranch."

WE'D GOTTEN USED to the rumble of the generator, like a lawn mower engine humming in the distance, running at regular intervals. Keeping the refrigerator cold, keeping Stew's insulin from spoiling in the constant heat of a house with no air-conditioning.

But the rumble had stopped a long time ago. That complete silence. Except for our short breaths. The side of my forehead sweating into the rough fibers of our family room rug, face turned toward my brother. Knees tucked beneath us. He'd gone still beside me in the dark.

I listened for the sound of tires rolling over gravel, even though it had long ago faded into the distance. They were gone. There was no reason for them to come back. They'd already taken everything. We'd heard the conversation, the argument over the generator, over Stew's insulin.

"Stewart," I whispered into the rug, breathing in my own stale oxygen. I started to tell him again that it was going to be okay. But the words got stuck in my throat. Everything I'd been feeling for the last few hours—scared, angry, still—stopped. And without even meaning to, I suddenly felt myself in my brother's position, felt the things he might be feeling. My chest constricted with the pain of it, with the overwhelming sense that they'd taken something more than his insulin. His humanity? His worth?

I squeezed my eyes tight to stop the tears. To force the thoughts from my mind. I wasn't as strong as Stewart. I couldn't take kneeling there and putting myself in his position for longer than a few minutes.

I got up, wiped my face with my shirt. I tried to remember when Stew had last changed his insulin cartridge. One night ago? He'd be completely out in a few days. There wasn't really much of a debate in my mind about what we should do next, where we should go.

We always spent summers with the Brightons, when Jess and her older brother, Nate, were with their dad. Camping trips, weekend sleepovers that my dad said we were getting too old for, back-and-forth drives down State Route 318. This summer had been weird, not seeing Jess, losing all communication during the blackout.

It was last summer, a year ago, when Stew and I sat on the edge of Jess's bed and watched her go through the steps of changing both her infusion set and the cartridge in her insulin pump. I was just curious, but Stewart was learning how to do it. Jess was older than him, my age, and had been doing this for two years. But Stew had switched to using an insulin pump only a few weeks before, and he wanted to start doing all this stuff on his own, without any help from Dad.

"You can do it, Stew. It's easy," Jess said, her smile encouraging. She was excited that Stewart had gotten a pump—the same one as hers. Her light brown hair was smoothed back in a ponytail. She sat across from us in the white chair that matched her desk, her back straight, swiveling back and forth while she talked, all her supplies laid out in perfect order. Insulin, syringe, new cartridge, new infusion set, alcohol swabs.

She talked with her hands a lot, just like always. Every other word emphasized with an opened motion, palms out. But this time, for some reason, her hands were kind of mesmerizing to watch. She held up her insulin pump in one hand—smaller than a cell phone, about the size of a deck of cards—motioned to the display, carefully selected options on the screen with her index finger. Her fingernail polish chipped, light blue.

She showed how to open the infusion set, how to get it ready. Then she turned and lifted her shirt a little to show us a spot just below her hip, where she was about to start her new site—the place where the thin cannula would insert through her flesh, allowing the pump to deliver insulin to her body when she needed it. We both leaned close to watch her clean the area with an alcohol wipe, and place the infusion set against her skin.

"It doesn't hurt, John," Stewart assured me, noticing my expression.

"Well, sometimes it hurts a little," Jess added, her chin tucked against her shoulder so she could see what she was doing. "But Stew's right. It's not that bad."

But I wasn't thinking about it hurting. Stewart had already told me that this part wasn't so bad, that, if he distracted himself, he sometimes didn't even feel the needle inserting the cannula into his skin. I was thinking that there were *so* many steps to remember. So many little things that they had to get right. It was overwhelming. They had to do this, change the cartridge and infusion set, every three days.

And they acted like it was no big deal.

Watching Jess explain all this . . . I felt this weird swelling inside my chest, and I couldn't even talk. All I could do was watch her hands.

I guess I was just impressed. And a little envious of how brave they were, how they didn't complain about any of it.

I'm mean, *some*times Stewart complained. But it wasn't about this stuff. He didn't complain about the needles or having to prick his fingertips and test his blood sugar all the time. Or even the fact that he had to think about everything he ate, which I think would be the hardest thing for me. Keeping track of carbohydrates, keeping track of sugar. No, the thing that bothered Stew was the questions he sometimes got from people. *Did you get diabetes from eating too much sugar?* Or, *Maybe if you stopped eating junk food, your diabetes would go away.*

Jess was really patient with this kind of stuff, though. In fact, she loved explaining type 1 diabetes to people who didn't understand it, kids and adults. And she was a lot of fun to be around too.

Sometimes, I thought about how, if Stewart hadn't been diagnosed with diabetes, we might not ever have met Jess.

Our dad and her dad had actually known each other years ago. Our moms had grown up together, gone to school together. But when we were just babies, after our mom passed away, and Mr. Brighton got divorced, our dads lost touch. Then five years ago, Stewart was diagnosed with diabetes, and my dad signed him up to go to a summer camp for kids with diabetes. The same camp that Jess went to. The same camp where she's now a junior counselor.

"John," Jess said, her insulin pump back in her pocket, her eyes wide like she had just thought of something, "I forgot to tell you what happened with Nate right before school got out! He asked out that girl I was telling you about."

Stew made a face. I grinned. "The one who's deathly afraid of tortoises?"

"I'll show you her picture," Jess said, turning to grab her phone off her desk. "She's really nice, actually. Except for the whole tortoise thing. How could anyone be afraid of Herman? His cute little face!"

Stew and I shared a look. Herman was Jess's favorite rescue tortoise, a sulcata that weighed about eighty-five pounds. He was harmless, and definitely not cute.

Eventually, Jess's brother, Nate, came in to get us. He stood in the doorway and yelled at the top of his lungs, because he hadn't bothered to take out his earbuds, and his music was blaring. "Dad wants me to tell you we're having tinfoil meals out back." He looked at us—sitting on the floor by Jess's desk, almost crying from laughing so hard—looked at Jess's old infusion set on the desk, the used alcohol wipes, and walked out.

We busted up laughing again.

There's a question Cleverly wants to ask. I can see it on her face. It's the same question a lot of people want to ask when they find out Stewart is insulin dependent. Every once in a while, somebody actually *does* ask it: "How long can you survive without your insulin?"

Stew usually shrugs and gives himself about three or four days, tops. And that seems to be the standard answer among the diabetics I know. Three or four days. But I've never heard a doctor say that. And believe me, we've asked. They usually just start listing a bunch of outside factors involved—which can either speed up the process or slow it down. The food you eat, how much water you drink, your physical activity, hormones, stress.

They never actually tell you the number of days.

Cleverly tucks a stray piece of hair behind her ear, starts to ask, "How long can . . . ?" as we walk back, but she doesn't finish the question.

I've been assuming he has three days. Three days to get to Brighton Ranch. And we're only on the start of day two. I want to tell her that I know he'll be fine for two more days. Instead, I tell her what I do know.

"Without insulin, Stew's blood sugar levels are too high." I look down as I talk, frowning because it's still hard to say this stuff out loud. To admit it's really happening. "It's called hyperglycemia. It makes him weak, tired. It gives him stomach pains, an unquenchable thirst. It makes him pee a lot."

"It makes him pee a lot?" she says, like she almost thinks I'm kidding.

"It has to do with the extra sugar building up in his bloodstream," I try to explain. "His body is desperate to get rid of it. But it can't. So instead, it starts taking all the water in his body, and getting rid of that. Expelling it all in the form of urine. It's why he can chug a half gallon of water, and it's still not enough—"

"John," Cleverly says, cutting me off, and I look up in time to see Stew throw up for a second time—just lean over and throw up right where he's sitting.

She runs ahead of me. I watch her help Stew get to his feet; watch Will make a face and kick dirt over the vomit Stew left behind. It takes every ounce of control I have left not to pick up the first big rock I see and chuck it through the windshield of that stupid truck with no freaking gas left in the tank.

Stew's on his feet now. Hunched over, hands on his knees, head down, like he's at a game and his coach just called timeout. He's tired, but he can push through this. I've seen him do it before.

"We have to get going," I say right when I reach them. As if nothing has happened, as if my brother doesn't look like he's one vomit away from collapsing on the spot.

I grab my pack off the ground where I'd left it and sling it over my shoulder. Standing up straight again, I notice Cleverly is squinting at me like I'm crazy or something.

"What?" I ask a little too sharply.

She just shakes her head and turns away. "Come on, Will," she says, taking Stew's arm, helping him stand up-right. "We've got to get Stew back to the truck."

"Wait a minute—" I start, but Will rushes to Stew's other side and they start heading back.

"Hang on," I say, getting ahead of them, blocking the way. "I know things look bad, but we can't give up now—"

"Stew can't go any farther, John." Cleverly explains this to me like she's surprised I didn't know. "He has to stop here."

"We *can't* stop here, Cleverly. I'm telling you, if we stop now—"

"*We* aren't stopping here," she corrects me. "Just us." She motions side to side, meaning herself, Will, and Stew.

My heart drops a little, warmth rushing my skin. I speak through the dryness at the back of my throat. "If you think I'm going to leave my brother behind . . ."

She's giving me this patient look that makes me feel like I'm losing it again. My eyes move to Stew for a second, then right past him. Will shifts his feet, a hundred questions that he's too afraid to ask running across his face.

Finally, Cleverly says, "It's not like he'll be alone, John." *We're not completely alone, John.*

"This is what has to happen," she says. "You have to go

to Brighton Ranch on your own. You have to get . . . what Stew needs, and you have to bring it back here."

My head starts shaking halfway through her plan. "Leaving my brother now is not an option."

"It's the *only* option."

"That's not true—"

"Hey," Stewart's voice cuts me off, cuts us both off. My eyes move back to him. "Stop talking about me as if I'm not here." He doesn't say it like he's mad. I wish he'd said it like he's mad. "John, ask me how I feel."

I can't. I can't get the words out. But he waits for me to say it. So I ask, "How do you feel?"

He takes in a few short breaths. "Like that day we were playing basketball on the driveway, and I could barely bounce the ball, and I had to keep sitting down, and I crawled over and threw up Dad's spaghetti in that bush."

Dad, scooping Stewart up off the driveway, putting him in the front seat of his truck, rushing him to the hospital in Ely.

I turn my head away, face tight, eyes wet.

"I wish I could forget about it. I wish I could pretend I'm not diabetic the way you can," he says. "But I can't. Because it's happening to my body."

I lift the bottom of my shirt, cover my face, wipe away the sweat. Squeeze my eyes tight. Then I drop my shirt and look out at the highway with mostly clear eyes.

I know what the truth is. I just don't want to admit it. Stewart isn't telling me he can't go on because he *wants* to give up. It isn't because he *wants* to die. He's telling me that he doesn't really have a choice in the matter. We aren't in the same situation. We aren't fighting the same battle.

I finally agree to do what he's been asking me to do all along.

"All right," I say, "I'll go alone."

"Thank you, John," he says, his chest deflating in relief.

My dad always said, if we ever find ourselves in a situation like this, stranded in the middle of nowhere, stay together. Wait for help to come to us. But the scenario my dad had imagined wasn't anything like this. Who in their right mind would imagine something like this?

I'm going to Brighton Ranch on my own. I'm getting help. I'm bringing insulin and water back to Stewart. There is no other option.

Could it get any worse?

Most of the time, physical activity is a good thing for diabetics. It helps lower your blood sugar. But if you aren't getting any insulin at all, there comes a point when physical activity is dangerous. . . .

That day on our driveway. Stew had been struggling to get his blood sugar down. He thought more physical activity would help. He didn't know he wasn't getting any insulin through his pump. He didn't know he'd inserted the cannula incorrectly and the tubing was kinked.

The nurse in the emergency room, starting an IV on Stewart's arm, patiently explained to us that Stewart wasn't just experiencing hyperglycemia, but something much worse. "It's called diabetic ketoacidosis, or DKA. To keep up with all his physical activity, his body starts converting fat into energy. Which sounds great, but it's actually not. Because the process in which *his* body converts fat to energy happens to produce toxic acids. They build up in his bloodstream, which is as bad as it sounds. The symptoms you want to watch for next time include weakness, confusion, fruity-scented breath, vomiting . . .

"Stewart will be fine. But you need to know that DKA is very dangerous. If not treated, it's fatal."

I'm not taking my pack. I'm not carrying anything that will slow me down. I've got my Sharpie to keep track of miles. And I'm taking only what food I can fit in my pockets. Two individual packs of trail mix, two pieces of fruit leather, four of those peanut butter bars that make my mouth itch. I'm leaving the rest of the food for them.

I don't take a flashlight. I'll be back before dark. Without a pack, without anything to slow me down, I'm giving myself six hours to get to Brighton Ranch. Twenty-three miles in six hours.

I'm just hoping Mr. Brighton can drive me back. I'm hoping he has some gas left in his truck.

Will keeps sniffing, wiping his nose on his shoulder, but I pretend like I don't notice. I don't stay to help them set up the tarp. Just tell them they can close one corner of it in the passenger door, and tie the opposite end to the bumper, creating a triangle of shade in the bed of the truck, where Stew is lying down.

Then I stare out at the highway again, walk forward a little. It's long and straight for miles, but I notice again where it starts to curve to the right in the distance. The *actual* loneliest road in America.

"Hey," Cleverly says.

I turn around and she's got the second canteen. "Take it," she says.

"I can't."

"We won't drink Stew's water," she says, shaking her head. "Will and I already agreed."

Will's standing on the bumper, holding on to the tailgate. He nods. No hesitation, like he's sure.

"I can't leave you without any water."

"Will and I each drank a cup of water from this canteen," she says. "There are six cups left for you."

My lips start to part, dry and cracked, but Cleverly puts a wry smile on her face. "Trust me, we're only thinking of ourselves. See, we're all kind of betting on you coming back with ice-cold sodas and cheeseburgers and fries and whatever else they have at Brighton Ranch. And we figure if you try to walk twenty-three miles in this heat with no water, then our odds will dramatically decrease. What did we decide the odds were again?" she asks Will.

"Um, zero percent chance if you don't take the water, one hundred percent chance if you do."

"Did you calculate the cheeseburger and fries into those odds?"

Cleverly smiles but says, quite seriously, "You're not superhuman, John. Take the water." She holds out the canteen to me.

I take it. I put my head and right arm through the strap, and then pull it around until the canteen rests against my shoulder blade. Cleverly's eyes are on the strap the whole time.

I look past her, to the truck bed where my brother is lying down. "I better get going," I say.

"Don't you want to say goodbye to Stewart?" Cleverly asks.

I shake my head, start walking backwards down the highway a few steps. "No, I'll see him soon."

She nods, her brow furrowed. I smile at Will one last time, and he lifts his hand to wave goodbye. Then I turn and start walking at my full pace. I don't look back.

20

THERE'S A SHARP pain high up in my chest, almost to my throat, and it's worse than the soreness in my thighs, my feet, worse than the stabbing pain in my right heel, worse than my skull-splitting headache. In fact, I think it's almost worse than the aching thirst, that stupid dry spot at the back of my throat.

Okay, maybe not worse than the thirst. But it's equal, at least. It feels like my chest might implode.

I force air in and out of my lungs. The sweat that was once dripping down my forehead has dried, but my hair is still damp. I yank my shirt off over my head, not caring that the sun is beating down on my back, and use it to wipe the sweat from my scalp, and then my chest and back. Just because it's bugging the heck out of me. Then I force myself to walk some more, no matter how pathetically slow, my shirt balled up in my good fist.

I started out my solo journey with a strategy—whether it's a good one is still up for debate. I walked as far as the first mile marker at a good pace, just so I could be sure I was out of sight. Then for the second mile, I pushed myself into a jog, and then into a full-on run.

After walking all day yesterday, it kind of felt good to run. Using different muscles in my legs, muscles I haven't already worn out. Pushing myself, releasing all that pent-up anger. Like a silent scream.

But when I got to that third mile, I forced myself to stop running and slowed back down to a walk, letting my breathing go back to normal, my hands linked behind my sweat-soaked neck. Then as soon as I hit that next mile marker, I broke out in a run again, letting the scream out this time, because I needed the extra push.

Walk one mile, run one mile, walk one mile, run one mile. For fourteen miles straight. Right up until this pain started in my chest.

I wince at an especially hard inhale, the pain finally forcing me to stop—my walk had become more of a slow shuffle anyway. I hunker down on the side of the road, grimacing at my sore muscles, the pain in my heel, and then collapse to my backside. I'm not sure how long I sit there in the dirt, my head between my knees, just focusing on the air coming in and out of my lungs in painful drags, fresh drops of sweat hitting the ground. Eventually the chest pain eases up enough to convince me that I'm not having a heart attack. Still, I have to rest a little longer.

I take my shirt and drape it over my head, my shoulders, my knees, like it's my own personal shelter from the sun. Then I reach to the side pocket on my pants and take out my lunch: a pouch of trail mix—I swear, the packaging dates back two decades at least—and one of my dad's peanut butter bars.

Itching mouth aside, nothing triggers my gag reflex like peanut butter. I've always hated it. I can stomach most other kinds of smashed nuts, even if it makes my tongue itch. Just not peanut butter.

The bar has kind of melted and then re-formed itself in the wrapper. I open it carefully and take the first bite, holding back a gag. The sticky granola, the sweet and salty corn syrup–coated peanuts gumming up in my dry mouth like molasses.

My canteen is empty. It's somewhere out there in the desert. Six cups is not that much water. It's not enough. I drank the last of it over a mile ago. And I have to say, chucking that stupid canteen as far out into the sagebrush as I could was a whole lot more satisfying than drinking the warm, iodine-infused water inside it.

One hundred percent chance if you take the water.

I stop thinking about water. And when I'm done eating, done getting it all down my throat, I take off my shirt-shelter and pull it back over my head, pushing my arms through the sleeves and yanking it down my chest. The sweat-soaked cotton cools me down a little, but the back of my neck feels tight and tingly. A small sting, like the start of a sunburn. The sunscreen I put on before I left has worn off, and I've been sloppy about keeping my neck covered.

I squint back at the sun behind me, guess that it's late afternoon, maybe three thirty or four o'clock. I'm more than halfway there.

The landscape has slowly changed in the last several miles. The distant mountains are closer to the highway now, crops of slate-gray and burnt-red rock jut up through the earth, creating narrows for the highway to snake through. I've veered off the winding road more than once, taking shortcuts through the wild grass that now fills the gaps between sagebrush.

It's all a good sign, the change in scenery. Just the sight of more green quickens my pulse, because it tells me that I'm getting closer to the Brightons'.

I need to get back on my feet again, but instead, I look at my shoes. They were good running shoes up until this walk, have never given me a problem. My right heel, though . . . I'm dreading it, but I have to look. I have to take off my shoe. It feels wet back there.

I pull my foot toward me, take the laces in my hand, but just as I do, the bottom of my pants pulls up a little. I see the blood. The back of my sock is soaked up to my ankle, dried around the edges.

It started with the pain in my right arch yesterday, making me put more weight on my heel, the edge of my shoe rubbing against the back of my foot.

I sigh and shut my eyes for a minute. If I had my first aid kit with me, this would be an easy fix. I could have bandaged it up a long time ago, made it so every step I take doesn't feel like I'm being stabbed in the heel.

It's probably not a good idea to take off my shoe at this point. So I just roll back the edge of it, flexing my foot to see where it's rubbing. I look at the gauze bandage around my hand—dirty with dried blood and wet with sweat. I think about taking it off, using it to wrap up my heel, but decide against that. Instead I just fold down the top of my sock and tuck it under the edge of my shoe, pushing it down deep, flexing my foot again.

I get to my feet and the extra padding gives me a little relief, but not much. I still have to baby that foot. Walk kind of funny. Like a zombie.

The zombie apocalypse.

Besides my heel, the rest of my body feels worse after getting back up. I don't understand why, but I'm weaker, shaky, every muscle in my body telling me to stop and rest again.

I force breath in through my nose and out through my parched lips, filling my lungs, and start looking ahead for any road markings. A highway sign, a larger-than-average rock. I challenge myself to go that much farther, just as far as that shimmer of light ahead, the sunlight reflecting off a piece of broken glass. And when I get there, I give myself another goal.

But when I get to the next mile marker, the one that means I'm supposed to run, I can't make my legs move any faster, can't lift them up any higher. My muscles are starting to twitch. Tiny jolts through my thighs, my calves.

Ask me how I feel.

I ignore the twitching, the painful drags of air, that dull ache that still sits in my chest. I'm almost to one of the narrows that brackets the highway, burnt rock shooting up toward the sky. Shade. And suddenly I hear that tennis ball thumping. *Thump, thump, thump.* Against my bedroom wall. The wall I share with Stew. And I know it doesn't make sense, but I try to figure out where it's coming from.

Thump, thump, thump.

My feet? My chest? My heart?

My knees are in the rough grass. Blinking, swaying. Sagebrush scratching my arms, the side of my face. Breathing in the dirt. The taste of it in my mouth.

I forgot to say goodbye to Stewart.

The air is cooler. That's the first thing I notice. Then the noise around me fills my consciousness. The collective hum and chatter and click of a million tiny insects.

I roll to my side, push myself up with a jolt. It's dark. Completely dark.

I wipe the dirt from the side of my face, from my mouth.

I get to my feet, ignoring the stab in my heel, looking up at the sky in a panic, trying to wrap my head around the shift in time.

How long have I been out?

I pick my way through the grass blindly, tripping over rocks, bumping into low bushes and spiky branches, repeating the same curse over and over in my mind.

What did I just let happen? How much time has passed?

My muscles are cramped and weak, my feet are like two throbbing blocks of cement, but I get through the grass and onto the flat gravel that stretches along the highway, and it hurts, *everything* hurts, but I push myself into a jog.

What did I just let happen? What have I done?

I've messed up. I've messed everything up.

I search the night sky for the moon, but it's nowhere. Can it be that late? Is it past midnight already? But I see a change in the darkness ahead. It's a shade lighter. When I get through the narrows, get a couple of hundred feet past it, I finally spot the moon. It's hanging low among the stars, but it's still there. It's 9:00 P.M. It's gotta be around 9:00 P.M. I should already have been back to them by now. Even at my slowest pace, I should have been back to my brother hours ago.

I push my jog into a run, keeping my mouth clamped shut this time, saving any shred of moisture that remains, and forcing air in and out through my nose. My tongue feels swollen, and I don't know if it's even possible for your throat to turn into a cracked, dry lake bed, but that's what it feels like. It's useless to try to work up any saliva at this point. There's nothing left and it'll only make the pain worse. I'm not even sure I'm able to speak. And I'm too afraid to test it.

I've lost track of distance, completely unaware of how far away I am. And I let myself lose track of time as well, let my mind go foggy. Because I can't think about what I've

231

done. I can't think about it. Soon, the physical pain becomes my only relief from the pain of what I'm feeling inside. I've got to make up for this massive mistake. I've got to feel as terrible on the outside as I do on the inside. I keep running, keep feeling the pain, letting my vision cloud, and not seeing anything beyond the faded black asphalt winding before me.

So I almost miss the sign.

A painted wooden sign with two thick, square posts. No power going to the spotlight beneath it. BRIGHTON RANCH, 1.8 MILES AHEAD, it says, the message coming from a cartoon tortoise waving its scaly reptile arm.

One point eight miles. Depending on your perspective, that's either very close, or incredibly far.

But the next thing I know, I'm running beside the barbwire fence that lines the Brightons' property, counting the posts as I go. There's nearly a mile of it that follows this highway. And then I hear a dog barking in the distance. I slow to a jog and then to a walk, my chest still heaving.

Sammie, the Brightons' golden retriever, is walking alongside me on the other side of the barbwire now, his tail wagging double time. He gets ahead of me at one point, but then looks over his shoulder, slows his pace, and waits for me to catch up.

Right before I turn up the drive to the house, I stop and Sammie doubles back to me, sitting in the weeds along the fence line, his tail beating back and forth like a distress signal. I crouch down and rub him behind the ears. He stops panting and scoots himself a little closer, as close to the barbwire as he dares, lifting his chin so I can get under his neck. "Hey, Sammie," I croak out, testing my voice. I swallow, wincing at the pain. "Anybody home, boy?"

I glance up at the house. It's so dark; I can barely make it out. Not that I expected the lights to be on, of course. It's just that I've never seen it like this. So dark and lifeless. But if the situation were reversed, and they showed up at our place in the middle of this mess, they'd probably be just as weirded out.

"All right," I say, pushing the words past my throat, patting Sammie's head one last time. "Let's go."

The drive is mostly gravel with a strip of uneven asphalt near the center, just wide enough for one-way traffic. Sammie starts barking again, and as I get closer, the outline of the Brightons' ranch-style house starts to come into relief against the night sky. The wraparound porch is the darkest part, like a band of black through the center of the house, like a reverse Oreo cookie.

I notice the carport that Mr. Brighton built last year, to give him more space in the garage. His truck isn't parked there. It's always parked there, but maybe he moved it. Cleaned out the garage, parked it in there. I know they're home. They've got to be home. No way would they leave Sammie behind.

Then I see a flashlight through a window, moving along the front rooms, shining out at me. It stops. Disappears for a while, and then I hear the front door open, the screen door slamming shut on its hinges, muffled by the distance between it and me.

I keep walking forward, squinting when the strong beam hits me directly in the face. And then the light moves, and I blink away the dark spots left floating in my vision, and I see Nate Brighton halfway down the front porch steps. He greets me with a .33 Winchester rifle. Pointed straight at me.

I'm confused. Or maybe *he's* confused. I take a breath, start to call out to him that it's just me, but then I hear the click of the hammer being pulled back, hear Nate instruct me to "Stop right there, John."

21

I DON'T KNOW what Nate Brighton is doing with that rifle. I don't know why he's got it aimed at me. He's wearing only a T-shirt and boxer shorts, his hair disheveled, sleepy. And he's got a freaking rifle aimed at me.

"Where's your dad?" I say, my voice hoarse and gravelly. "His truck is gone." I take a few steps forward.

"I said stop, John."

I do what he says, still confused, my hands automatically going up so he can see them. I don't want to get too close to him with that gun anyway. I don't think he actually intends to shoot me point-blank—I'm used to seeing Nate with earbuds, listening to his weird music on full blast, not with a rifle in his hands—but he's got the hammer pulled back, the barrel aimed in my direction.

I'm not stupid enough to test somebody with a loaded gun—assuming it's loaded.

"Where's Jess?" I ask.

He doesn't answer, but my eyes have adjusted to the soft moonlight, and I see him start to turn his chin, as if to look over his shoulder. I look past him to the house, but it's completely dark, no other flashlights bobbing around.

I lower my arms, because they are starting to shake. "I'm here to get insulin for Stew. He needs it badly—"

"You're not taking any of Jess's insulin."

I shake my head, because he doesn't understand me. "Stew is out of insulin."

He sighs. "I'm sorry if you weren't prepared for this kind of thing, but you're not taking any of Jess's."

My eyes tighten at his words. "Not *prepared*—" I start to say.

Don't talk to me about being prepared.

I shake my head again. "It was *stolen* from us, Nate. *Everything* was stolen from us."

He shifts uneasily. "Well, I'm sorry, but that doesn't mean you can come steal ours."

"*Steal?*" I'm thrown off by his words, by the way he's twisting things around. I didn't come all this way to *steal* anything. I'm standing here with nothing. *Nothing*. Asking for help. Stewart *needs* insulin. He needs it, or he'll die.

Maybe it's the anger, or maybe it's just exhaustion, but my whole body starts to quake. I clutch my hands into tight fists, willing them to stop shaking. I can't talk to him while he's got that stupid rifle pointed at me. So I ask him as calmly as possible, "Is the rifle really necessary?"

He tips his head to the side a little. "I'm just being cautious."

"It's *me*, Nate. Why do you need to be cautious with me?"

"I've got to protect Jess."

My eyes widen, because he's got to be kidding. "From *me*?"

As if to make my point, Sammie, having gone around the

fence line, comes trotting around the front porch. He walks down the steps, goes about halfway between Nate and me, and lies down.

Nate adjusts his grip on the rifle. "From anyone who isn't in this family."

My anger surges again. As long as we've known each other, we've referred to the Brightons as family. And suddenly, because of this blackout, because Stewart needs help, we're *not*?

"I'm not a threat to Jess!" I say, my voice dry and raspy, barely sounding like myself.

"You just said you want her insulin."

"*What?* No—" He's twisting things around again. And I try not to let it get to me, try to stay focused, try to figure out what I need to say to get through to him.

But then he says, "I need you to leave, John," and something in me completely snaps.

"Do I *look* like I can just leave?" I yell, my throat closing up as my voice rises, edging out in a raspy shout. "*Look* at me!" I hold out my arms. "*Look* at me! I *walked* here, you—!" I stop myself from saying something I'll regret.

I drag a breath through my tight throat, trying to calm myself down, trying to breathe.

"My brother," I say, "*Stewart* . . . is twenty-three miles down that highway. That's as far as he made it. And I don't even know if he's still alive."

I stop again, my voice breaking on the last word.

Even though he's still got that rifle aimed at me, I sense hesitation from Nate for the first time. And I think maybe Nate Brighton has not completely lost it. Maybe I can reason with him. But then he says, his voice low, "I don't want to shoot anyone. But I will if I have to."

A high ringing starts in my left ear, like a warning bell.

236

And I know Nate's out of his mind. I know I'm not going to talk him into anything.

Then a sound breaks through the ringing. The screen door opening. Jess's voice. "*John?*"

Nate looks over his shoulder for the quickest second. And I bolt, using adrenaline to propel me. I run past the gravel for the cottonwood trees on the right side of their property, a quarter acre of shade.

A round goes off. Sammie barks.

It's pitch-dark beneath the trees. I hear Nate following, swearing, his bare feet on the gravel, calling my name. His flashlight cuts through the darkness. I hear Jess calling out, confused.

I trip over roots, stumble around tree trunks, and run into the five-foot wooden fence that surrounds the tortoise enclosure. Sliding my hand along the upright planks, I look for the gate to get inside.

It's locked. I ram it with my shoulder, and it doesn't budge. So I grab the top of the fence, ignoring the pain as it cuts into my injured hand, and pull myself up with a groan, my muscles shaking. My feet scramble desperately against the fence until I find the ledge of the wooden sign nailed to the gate.

BEWARE OF TORTOISES, it reads, with the same cartoon tortoise grinning and waving its arm. I use it to push myself higher, enough to swing my leg over, and then my strength gives out and I drop to the ground on the other side, landing hard on my shoulder.

I wince and roll over onto my stomach, push myself up, my shoes slipping in the loose dirt. I hear Nate coming, and I don't know whether to keep running or to find someplace to hide. I get about five feet in the dark and trip hard over something smooth and round, falling flat on my stomach with my arms caught beneath, the wind knocked out of my lungs, the side of my head hitting the packed dirt.

A pain pulses through my temple and a long panic-filled moment passes before my chest finally inflates with air. And then Nate is kneeling beside me, yanking my arm, flipping me over, my head rolling to the side.

My vision is blurred for an instant before coming into focus on a battery-powered metal flashlight clinched in Nate's fist against the ground, the light reflecting off clouds of dust, the dirt around me glowing. No rifle, must have dropped it. He straddles me, gripping the front of my shirt in one fist, breath heavy.

Blinded by the flashlight, I can't make out Nate's face. He's just a dark outline above me. I hear something collide against the fence, hear Jess beating on the gate, calling both our names, pleading for us to stop.

I try pushing him off me, but he just drags me back, pinning me down with his knees on either side. "I don't want to hurt you, all right?" he says, breathing hard. "I just want you to leave. Just agree to leave and not come back, and I'll let you go."

"I'll leave," I say, breathless, "as soon as I get insulin for Stewart—"

"You're not getting the insulin. And don't look at me like that, John. You're no different from me."

"Yeah, we're exactly the same," I say, pushing against him, chest heaving, "practically twins. Except, you're deranged."

"If it came down to Stewart or Jess, who would you choose?"

I don't know what he's talking about. "I don't have to choose between them—"

"Yes, you do. Because if you take Jess's insulin and give

it to Stew, that hurts Jess. She'll have less insulin to survive with."

I stop short for a second, trying to make sense of what he's saying. "No, Stewart just needs some of it to get him through this. We'll get more as soon as—"

"And what are you willing to do to get more, John?" he says, "Kill me? Take Jess's insulin and shorten her life like your brother's?"

"What? *No,*" I rasp out, horrified.

"Then leave."

I stare up at his dark silhouette, completely caught off guard by the fact that *he* is trying to reason with *me,* as if *I'm* the one who's nuts.

"You have to leave," he says again.

I grit my teeth. He's underestimating me if he thinks that's going to happen. He doesn't have a clue about what I've already done to get here. And that's my advantage.

He's bigger than me, outweighs me by a good thirty pounds. There's no way I can overpower him from this position. So I do the only thing I can do. I play up my physical weakness, making myself deadweight to him, my arms staying lax at my side, wincing as he attempts to pull me upright. He only manages to drag me another few inches. I sort of groan, let my eyes drift shut, and play like I'm trying to force them back open.

I don't hear Jess banging on the gate anymore.

"I'm sorry if the world we live in isn't exactly how you imagined it," Nate says, dropping the flashlight to get a better grip on my shirt, getting my shoulders off the ground, "but it's your own fault. Sure, you were probably prepared, in the physical sense," he concedes. "You had a lot of food and water, maybe even had a decent insulin supply for

Stewart. But the reason that stuff was stolen from you is because you were an easy target."

Oh yeah. It's nearly impossible to keep my mouth shut after he says that. Seriously, I deserve a freaking medal.

I let out a groan and allow my head to roll to the side a little, like I can't hold it up any longer. My shoulder bumps the flashlight as he scoots me back, the beam of light spinning away. I move my elbow the slightest bit. I can almost reach it. . . .

"If you really want to survive a societal change of this magnitude," Nate continues, trying to drag my shoulders up again, get me up off the dirt, "you can't be an easy target. Which means you need more than just food storage and supplies. *Mental* preparedness is more important than any stockpile of prepackaged food or jugs of distilled water. . . ."

He thinks this blackout is the freaking zombie apocalypse, I realize, listening to his lecture. Or the end of the world, or at least the end of life as we know it.

Just like Stewart.

But there's a big difference between my brother and Nate. I mean, I thought, after we were robbed, that Stew had changed. I thought he was a different person because he was angry and scared, and maybe even acted a little irrational.

But hearing Nate go on like this . . . I know Stewart didn't change at all. He stayed *exactly* the same. His *character* stayed exactly the same.

The last thing Stewart wanted to do was take insulin from Jess. That's one of the reasons why he fought me so hard, why it took me starving myself to get him to walk to Brighton Ranch with me. And in that shack house, the choice between getting me and Stew to Brighton Ranch alive or helping two complete strangers . . . *Dad would do both.*

240

Yeah, my brother and Nate Brighton are nothing alike.

I know. I get it. People do crazy things when their own survival is at stake, things they never thought they'd do. Like rob kids at gunpoint. Or drink toilet water. Or commit grand theft auto. Or deny lifesaving help to the kid you've called family for the last five years. But the thing is, if you *do* survive, when it's all said and done, you still have to live with yourself.

So now I have to decide. If I bash Nate over the head with that metal flashlight, seriously injure him, knock him out cold . . . can I live with that?

Yeah, I think so.

I twist my wrist, my fingers scrambling to find the cool metal handle of the flashlight. *Got it.*

I swing for his head, using all my strength. I'd shout if I could get the air out. He ducks, the heavy metal baton hitting his shoulder at the last second. Crying out in pain, he grabs for the flashlight, his hands on either side of mine, and we wrestle for it.

But I'm still weak, my muscles shaking from the effort. I feel my hold on the flashlight slipping.

I change tactics. I use the momentum from our struggle to roll out from beneath him. I twist my hips, kick my legs, lifting my torso.

His weight is too much. His hold is too strong. Through the scuffle, the gasps, and the heavy breathing, I realize with disbelief that I'm about to lose this fight in a bad way. I'm about to lose my grip—on the flashlight, on everything. I'm about to be bludgeoned.

And in the shock of that thought, I hear a sound. Like the hum cicadas make just before they begin their static buzz. Like the sound of electricity . . .

The sound of electricity!

A loud pop. Then the floodlights in the tortoise enclosure burst to life, like a spotlight on a stage. And I'm too shocked to move.

The first thing I see in the light is Nate's face. His dark eyelashes are coated in dust, and I watch his eyes go from hard determination to soft confusion, his pupils shrinking against his blue, invading irises.

But almost as soon as my mind registers the fact that the power is back—*the power is back!*—the lights dim, fading in and out before completely blacking out again. And everything is dark. Everything back to the way it was.

Only it seems darker now. And stiller. Like the world is stunned. Not just me and Nate, but every insect and animal and creature in a ten-mile radius . . . is stunned.

Nate's weight leaves me. I lie on my back, breathing, staring up at the night sky, listening to Nate's footfalls until they fade away.

22

SOMETHING HARD IS bumping against my ear, nudging me.

I roll my head toward it, my forehead creased in confusion as it scoots off. Then a stream of water hits me in the face. I choke and cough, my shoulders arching off the ground.

I press the heels of my hands into my eye sockets.

"Sorry," Jess says. "That's tortoise water, pretty gross, so I wouldn't lick your lips if I were you." She drops the wide, rock-shaped water dish in the dirt. "I couldn't wake you up. You were mumbling things. I've got you some drinking water, if you can sit up."

Her warm, familiar voice makes the corners of my eyes tighten with emotion. I press my heels back into my eye sockets. It's been months since I've heard Jess's voice.

I wipe the water from my face. She kneels in the dirt beside me. She has the flashlight, and between the light and shade of her movements, I see parts of her at a time. Her light brown hair in two smooth braids. A sprinkling of freckles across the bridge of her nose. Her hazel eyes. Concerned.

I roll onto my shoulder—the one that feels the least sore right now—propping myself up on my elbow. Then I reach back and explore the side of my head that hit the ground with my fingertips, flinching when I find the tender spot.

Jess takes my wrist, pulls my hand around, and places tiny things in the center of my palm. She cradles the back of my hand so I don't drop them.

"For the pain," she says, shining her light at the tan and white pills.

I push myself into a sitting position, my feet sliding up and my knees bending stiffly. I'm still a little confused, wondering where the pills came from. How'd she get these?

But when she puts the water bottle in my other hand and I feel the coldness of it, I'm shocked back into reality. *Cold water. Running generator. Insulin. Stewart!*

I immediately try getting to my feet, but Jess stops me. "Drink first," she says, twisting the lid off the water bottle for me.

"What time is it?" I croak out.

"Drink first," she says again.

I put the cool plastic to my lips, tip it back. When the water hits my throat, it's both agony and relief, but I keep swallowing.

"Don't forget the pills," she says.

I pull the bottle back, take a breath, toss all the pills into my mouth at once. Water floods my mouth, pushing the pills toward my throat. I shut my eyes as they go down, moisture leaking from the corners of them.

It feels like I've swallowed a handful of sharp rocks.

I ask again, "What time is it?"

She takes out her insulin pump, checks the time. "It's ten forty-eight," she says.

Heart in my throat, I get up as far as my knees. I should

244

have been back hours ago. I was *supposed* to be back hours ago.

Jess gets up with me, slides her arm beneath mine. She's always been tall, taller than me, but when she helps me stand up, I'm kind of surprised that our eyes are at the same level. We're the same height now.

"Stewart needs help," I say, and looking into her sympathetic eyes, I can't get anything else out after that.

I can't let this sinking feeling overwhelm me. I can't let emotion get in the way of my getting back to him. . . .

"Don't worry," Jess says, responding to the fear in my voice. "I heard what you said to Nate. I heard you say that Stew needs insulin. And I didn't wait around for you guys to stop wrestling in the dirt. I went and got this." She holds up her diabetes bag, the small shoulder bag she takes everywhere she goes. Stew's got one just like it, but without the paisley pattern printed on the outside.

It's cool to the touch, like she's been storing her whole bag in the fridge. And I'm telling you, Jess is so good with this diabetes stuff. It makes me feel the smallest bit of relief in my chest that I've got her with me, helping me. And I use that to push down other things I'm feeling, because I need to tell her more. I need her to know what state he was in when I left him.

Making our way out of the enclosure, I say, "Stew and I have been on our own. Dad never came back from his last trip." I don't look at her when I say this, because . . . I don't know, Jess has this way of being really sympathetic when you tell her things, and I don't want it to get to me. I just say the rest as bluntly as I can. "We were robbed. Stew's been without insulin for two days—almost three days now."

I walk with her as fast as I can, going easy on my right foot. And she stays calm, but asks a lot of questions.

"When did he last test his blood sugar?"

"I don't know." I didn't want to know. Didn't want to know how high it is.

"Has he had enough water? How has he been acting? Did he say how he feels?"

Ask me how I feel, John.

"He said he feels like he did that day we took him to the ER. Remember when he threw up Dad's spaghetti in the bush?"

"He threw up?" she says, not asking about then, but now. Those concerned eyes.

"Twice," I say, pushing back the emotion, the moisture building in my eyes. "I had to leave him behind. He's about twenty-three miles back—"

"It's good you left him," Jess says encouragingly when my voice breaks, like she's trying to think of something positive to say. "Physical activity will only make it worse. And he needs water. Just as much as insulin now."

She says that last part almost to herself. She starts walking ahead of me, leading the way through the last part of the enclosure, stepping around the occasional tortoise—just the ones we've disturbed, most of them are in their burrows for the night.

She has to know I'm exhausted, in pain, but she's pushing me to keep her pace, to walk a little faster. When we get to the back gate of the tortoise enclosure, she opens it, waits for me. And I get there soon after.

"Your dad's not here, is he?" I say, out of breath. Already knowing the answer, already thinking of other ways to get back to Stew quickly, without Mr. Brighton's truck. . . .

"No, he went to Las Vegas the day before yesterday. To check on our mom."

I look at her, a little surprised, since Jess's parents do not get along at all. But then again, survival situations make people do crazy things, things they never thought they'd do, right?

"My dad wouldn't let us go with him. And Nate's been acting weird ever since he left," she says, "paranoid. You know how he gets. The smallest thing goes wrong in his life, and he acts like people are out to get him. Failing geometry again. Getting suspended from school for fighting. As if he had no control over any of that." She shakes her head. "Well, now *a lot* of things have gone wrong. *Everyone* is out to get him."

"Yeah, I noticed," I say dryly, gritting my teeth as we cross their back lawn. "'Wrestling in the dirt.' That's an interesting way to describe your brother almost bludgeoning me to death."

Her eyes go wide. "You don't think he was actually going to *kill* you?"

"I don't know. That rifle was pretty convincing."

"I am really sorry," she says, her voice so sincere. "I'm not sure what he was thinking."

"You don't have to apologize for him. And anyway, he got off me when the power came back on." I look over at her. I guess to make sure that really happened, that I wasn't imagining those lights. Nate's washed-out face, his wide blue eyes . . .

She nods. "It came on in the house too. For just a few seconds. Then it went out again."

I feel something new stir in my chest. Hope? Jess feels it too. I can tell.

"Do you have gas storage left?" I ask. "Can we take your dad's four-wheeler or something?"

"The engine's out on his four-wheeler right now. He was working on it." My heart starts to drop, but then she says, "We can take Nate's truck, though."

247

I almost stop walking. "*Nate* has a *truck*?"

She nods and rolls her eyes. "My mom bought it for him for his birthday. Big sixteen. Dad was so mad. He wanted Nate to earn the money and buy his own truck. Anyway, he can drive us—"

"No," I say, shaking my head. She gives me a confused look, because I'm grinning.

Guess what? my body is saying. *We don't have to walk anymore! We've got a ride all the way back to Stew. . . .*

"I can drive us," I tell her. Then I move ahead, taking those back porch steps two at a time, wincing only a little bit.

Sammie's waiting on the wraparound porch, looking up at us with his tongue hanging out, his tail wagging. I get to the back sliding door, and he slips in alongside Jess and me as I open it.

I slide the door shut behind us, just as we hear a door close upstairs. We look up at the ceiling. Nate's up there.

"I can force him to drive us," she says quietly, "threaten to tell Dad if he doesn't."

"No, really. I can do it."

"You've driven *one time*—"

"Twice! I drove part of the way here, Jess. Before we ran out of gas."

She looks unsure about that, but doesn't ask me to explain. "All right. I'll get his keys."

My heart rate starts to pick up. "Is it in the garage?"

She nods and veers off toward the kitchen with the flashlight to get the keys.

I know my way through the Brightons' house like I know my way through my own, so I don't have a problem getting around in the dark. I cut across the family room quietly, past the sagging plaid couches where Stew and I sometimes crash when we stay over, past the breakfast bar where we eat pretty much every meal we have at the Brightons', and head down the long hallway that leads to the garage.

I grab the doorknob, try to turn it, yank on it, but it sticks. I yank again.

Time is passing by. Time we don't have. I grab hold of the knob with both hands, jiggling it, twisting it as hard as I can.

Soon, the beam of Jess's flashlight comes bouncing down the hallway toward me, lighting the family portraits on the wall.

"Are you guys ever gonna fix this stupid doorknob?"

"It's okay," she says, her voice calming. She takes the doorknob, does some little trick to get it to turn, and pushes the door open for me.

Okay, I tell myself, taking a breath. *I knew that trick. Calm down. Stay calm like Jess.*

I take the steps down into the garage and notice the sound of the generator right away. They've got it set up outside, an extension cord running to the large storage fridge in the garage, between racks of bottled water. Jess goes out the side door and around to open the garage manually from outside. And I go straight to the fridge, barely glancing at the shadowy outline of Nate's truck, parked in the second bay.

The light comes on when I open it. Jess's insulin, but also rows and rows of more water bottles. I grab one, twist off the lid, and start gulping it down—it doesn't help the pain in my throat, but otherwise, it's the best drink of water I've ever had in my life.

I come up for air and notice there's Gatorade down on a lower shelf. I reach down to grab one—and freeze. There's a case of Coke behind the Gatorade. *Ice-cold soda.*

The garage door rumbles, starts to roll up the tracks, and I put the water bottle down in the fridge for a minute, shut the door, and go help Jess. We get it all the way open after a few shoves. It makes a lot of noise, and we both hesitate, listening for the sounds of Nate.

Nothing.

I check out Nate's truck in the dim moonlight, walking alongside it. It's massive compared to Spike's piece of crap. Extended cab, midnight blue.

"Hey," I say quietly, swallowing down my second thoughts about driving something like that, "mind if I take a couple of those Cokes?"

"Of course not. Take anything you want."

Jess has already grabbed a plastic crate and is on her way to the fridge. She puts a bunch of non-refrigerated water in there first; then we quickly throw in some cold waters and Gatorades, and I grab two Cokes from the case.

"We need food too," I say quickly. "Do you have anything resembling a cheeseburger or fries?"

She squints at me funny, but says, "Potato chips?"

"That'll have to do," I say to myself, picking up one side of the heavy crate. Jess takes the other side, and we carry it around to the back of the truck.

She shakes her head. "Potato chips aren't the best thing for Stew right now."

I agree, but the chips aren't for Stew, I start to tell her. But then she says, "I keep thinking about him being on his own out there, in the dark."

Feelings rush back to me. Will standing up on the bumper of that truck. Cleverly holding out the canteen, insisting I take it. Neither of them had to stay behind. But both of them did.

We set down the crate, and I look at Jess, reassuring her. "He's not alone."

I start the truck, and the cab is filled with Nate's weird music—screaming metal blasting out of the speakers. We both cringe and Jess grabs the volume knob, turning it all the way down. I throw the gear in reverse, turn to watch out the rear window as I back up, and immediately bump the passenger side-view mirror against the side of the garage, bending it back.

I brake hard. Look at Jess.

She shrugs. "It's fine."

I turn around to look behind me again, give it some gas. But I'm really close to that side of the garage, for some reason. The front wheel cover scrapes along the garage door rail, metal on metal, and the bumper sort of catches at the end, prying back. It makes a terrible sound—kind of like Nate's music.

I brake again. "Sorry."

"You're sure you can drive?" Jess asks, gripping her seat belt and looking up at the house for any signs of Nate.

"Yeah, I got this. I mean, now that I'm out of the garage, I got this."

I give it more gas and reverse all the way down the long drive. And I keep it pretty straight, too, except for at the end, when the back tires go off-road. I back it out onto the highway, turning too late and going off-road again. After braking hard, I throw it into drive and floor the gas pedal without really meaning to. The tires slip a little in the dirt before gaining traction.

"Don't worry, now I got this," I say to Jess again, because

she's either really freaked out about my driving or I'm making her sick. "Not bad for a new driver, though, right?" I add just as the wheels hit the rumble strip on the right side of the road. It's like rolling thunder in the cab. I quickly correct it.

"I'm just going to keep holding on, if that's okay," she says.

I grip the steering wheel tighter, the pain in my hand not too bad now.

The road is really dark, so I take one hand off, reach around the steering wheel, and find the brights. I flip them on and it's like the whole road opens up in front of me, the whole road is lit. And I think I can take it a little faster, faster than I took Spike's piece-of-crap truck. Glancing at the speedometer, I bring the truck up to fifty-five miles an hour, then sixty-five, then seventy-five, then eighty.

The clock on the dashboard says it's 11:19.

"What did you say their names were again?" Jess asks, I guess to either get her mind off my driving or to get her mind off Stewart. Probably both.

"Cleverly and Will. You'll like them," I say confidently.

I start to explain why, but Jess says, "They stayed behind with Stew. I already do like them. Where did you meet them?"

I think about that one for a second, and I know Jess wouldn't hold the whole toilet-water thing against us, but I just say, "It's kind of a long story. And you didn't finish telling me about your dad. He went to check on your mom?"

"Yeah. He'd already checked on my mom once before. But he heard from someone in Alamo that they drove down to Vegas and were able to get cell service. It was worth the gas to see if it was true."

If Mr. Brighton got cell service, one of the first people he'd try calling is my dad.

"When is he coming back?" I ask.

"He was supposed to be back this morning."

I can hear the frown in her voice, the uncertainty. Feelings come back, of the night my dad didn't come home, when Stew and I first realized we would be on our own.

"Are you worried about him?" I ask.

She shakes her head. "I'm not. How could I be? Nate is *worried* enough for the both of us." Then she says, "I just think, something caused my dad to stay away longer than he planned. But I know him, and I know he can figure a way out of anything. And as soon as he does, he'll be back.

"What about you?" she says. "Are you worried about your dad?"

I think about what I heard on the shortwave radio, about the borders being closed. Then I think about the floodlights coming on in the tortoise enclosure, the possibility of cell service in Las Vegas.

Like Jess said. Something kept him from coming home. But he'll figure a way out of it. "No," I answer.

We're coming out of a bend, onto a straight stretch of road. I glance at the clock—11:38.

"We should be getting close," I say. Close to where Spike's truck died. Close to where I left them behind.

That pain starts up in my chest again. The one that makes it hard for me to get in a good breath.

"Your dad and my dad are a lot alike," I say, repeating the words Jess and I always say when we're together. Just to keep us talking.

"They could be brothers," she says.

"We could be cousins," I say, slowing down, starting to brake.

"We *are* cousins," she teases, though I can hear in her voice that she's as nervous as I am. "We decided that last summer, remember?"

"Yeah, I remember," I mumble, bringing the truck to a stop at an angle.

Our headlights shine through the empty cab of Spike's old piece of crap. Glint off the big dent in the driver's-side door. There's no movement around it. No bob of dim flashlight in the bed of the truck. No sign of life.

Just a dead truck, alone in the middle of nowhere.

23

"THIS IS WHERE you left them?" Jess says, frowning at the abandoned truck.

"Yes," I say, my foot still on the brake, my hands still on the wheel.

"They left the truck?" she says. "Why would they leave the truck?"

I feel that pinch between my eyes.

I should have been back by now. I should have been back before the sun even went down. It was supposed to take me only six hours to walk there, plus the drive back in Mr. Brighton's truck. That's it.

"They must have thought I didn't make it," I say, barely above a whisper.

Then I see a shadow! Movement along the edge of the truck bed. Will up on his knees, blocking our headlights with his forearm, his expression unsure.

"Will!"

I shift the gear into park, throw open the door, and stand

up on the running board by the doorframe, my heart pounding as if I'd run all the way back.

"Will!" I call out louder, reassuring him it's me.

His eyes grow big and he turns, disappearing from view.

"It's John!" I hear him say as my feet hit the highway.

I race to the back of the old silver truck, calling out my brother's name. Haul myself up on the back bumper, headlights blinding me. "Stew!" I call again.

"I knew it," his quiet voice answers from the bed of the truck. "I knew he could do it."

"We *all* knew he could do it," Cleverly says, up on her heels now, blocking those headlights.

"One hundred percent," Will agrees.

I breathe out something between a gasp and a laugh, climb over the tailgate. I collapse against the side of it, sitting at my brother's feet with my knees up.

I know I should assure them right away that Jess is here, that we've got everything we need. But I hear her coming anyway. So instead, I drop my face to my knees, squeeze my eyes shut. So glad to be back with them in this stupid truck.

The first thing Jess does is give Stew water—not cold water but room-temperature water.

Stew slides his knees up, and I move in closer, filling the space he's made. He's got one arm tucked beneath his head, his eyes shut tightly, guzzling water while Jess pricks one of his fingers and tests his blood.

"Slow down with that water," she tells him, and he listens to her.

I try to catch her expression as she reads the meter, but she gives nothing away. Just gets an insulin pen ready, screwing on the needle while Will holds the light. She swipes an alcohol wipe on the side of his stomach. "Ready?" she says, and waits for his nod. Jess pinches the skin, piercing it with the needle.

Stew doesn't even flinch.

Will watches it all with his eyes wide.

I am telling you, my brother and Jess are impressive with this stuff.

"How fast will it work?" Will says.

Jess shakes her head. "It's not something you can rush, or try to fix quickly."

Stew finishes one water bottle, and Jess puts another bottle in his hand. "Keep drinking. You've got ketones to flush out," she says.

"What are ketones?" Will asks.

"Something your body produces when you start burning fat for energy."

He's still confused, so Jess starts to explain in her usual patient way, "His body is burning fat, which *sounds* like a good thing. . . ."

I only half listen to Jess and Will, too aware of my brother's swaying knee. I drop my hand there. I know he's really uncomfortable, I recognize the small movements he tends to make when he feels sick. It'll be a while before he doesn't feel that way anymore.

I clear the lump in my throat and ask him, "Why were you waiting in the dark? When we got here, it looked like you'd abandoned the truck."

He pulls the water bottle away from his mouth. "Not in the dark," he says, taking a breath. "We've got all those stars."

I raise my eyebrows, look up at the sky. "Oh," I say softly. "You're right."

I hear Cleverly come back around the bumper with that

crate of stuff from Nate's truck, and I squeeze Stew's knee, jump up to help her lift it over the tailgate.

"How you feeling, Stew?" she asks anxiously, pulling herself up and over.

"Better," he says, which I know is not true yet, but Cleverly's shoulders drop a little, like she's breathing a sigh of relief.

"He's just gotta flush out ketones," Will says, passing me the flashlight and quickly kneeling by the crate.

"Flush out what?" Cleverly says.

"*Ketones,*" Will says. He grabs two waters—one for him and one for Stew. "Wait," he says to Jess. "How exactly does he flush them out?"

"Well . . . ," Jess says with a smile.

I sit back at my brother's feet, hand on his knee again, while Cleverly grabs a water bottle and shifts through the other stuff Jess and I put in the crate. Her hand suddenly goes still, her mouth opening in surprise, but I don't say anything.

I make room for her to sit next to me in the corner of the truck bed, and she stares at me with this funny look on her face.

"What?" I say.

"You know what," she says, cracking open that ice-cold Coke. I watch her take a nice long drink, a stupid grin on my face.

A while later, Stewart has to pee. This time, it's a good thing—he's gotta flush out those ketones—and I put down the tailgate and help him out of the truck, help him get back in when he's done.

". . . but we're from Las Vegas," Cleverly is saying to Jess when we get back.

"I live in Las Vegas too!" Jess says. "With my mom during the school year."

"John didn't tell me you live in Las Vegas! What school do you go to?"

"Hey, Jess," I interrupt, realizing I never even introduced them to each other. "This is Cleverly and Will. Cleverly and Will, this is Jess."

"Really, John?" Cleverly says.

"We figured it out, but thanks," Jess says.

Will says to Jess, "Oh! You should also know that we're two of the four founding members of the Battle Born, with John and Stew."

"The Battle Born?"

"Yeah. See, we all drank toilet water, and that's how we got in the club—"

"You drank *what*?"

I give Will a look and start to explain, "We boiled it first, Jess," but realize that doesn't actually sound much better.

Cleverly sighs. "You guys are making our club sound really lame."

Then Stew suddenly starts laughing. And his smile is more of a grimace, his voice a little strained, but he says, "John found toilet water in that old abandoned mobile home." He tucks his knees up to his stomach, laughing so hard. "And Cleverly and Will, they walked in right when we were scooping it into our canteens."

Jess's mouth is wide open in shock, and maybe we're all a little delirious with exhaustion, but the rest of us start laughing too. So hard, my stomach muscles actually start to ache.

"Okay," Jess says, wiping tears of laughter from her eyes, "so what do I have to do to get in this club? Drink toilet water?"

"Would you do it?" Cleverly asks, her chin up like it's a challenge, but she's still sort of laughing.

Jess thinks for a second. "Yes. If I had to, I'd do it."

"Then good news!" Will says. "*Urine* the club!"

We all agree. Because drinking toilet water or not, Jess is pretty Battle Born.

Then I remember something that I should have told them right away. I can't even believe I forgot it! "Stew, I have some bad news for you," I say, pushing myself up straighter. "About your whole zombie-apocalypse theory."

His forehead creases. "What do you mean?"

I look at Jess and her smile perks up, like she just remembered too. "Well, a few hours ago at the Brightons', the floodlights in the tortoise enclosure came on."

I don't mention it happened while I was wrestling Nate for control over that flashlight.

Stew, Cleverly, and Will don't exactly give me the reaction I was expecting. They just sort of look at me, confused, so I say, exasperated, "The power came back on!"

"*What?*"

"John!" Cleverly says, shoving my shoulder. "The power came back on, and you're *just* now telling us?"

Then they lose it, like we've won the freaking lottery or something. Will dives at me, puts his arms around my stomach in a tight hug. The second he lets go, Cleverly's got her arms around my neck.

It all feels pretty amazing.

Stew starts to prop himself up, but Jess pushes him back down. "It only came on for a few seconds," she says, laughing, "but it means *something* is happening."

"It means there's an end to this stupid blackout," I say.

Stew says, like he's serious, "It means the zombies are losing."

I roll my eyes. "Okay, the zombies are losing. Can we get out of this stupid truck now?"

"Yeah!" Stew says.

"Hang on a second," Jess says, pushing him back down once more. "We should test your blood again."

"I can do it myself this time," Stew says, and he sounds so much like himself, like the old Stew, that a grin tugs at the corner of my mouth.

I know he'll be all right.

Jess holds the flashlight for him while he tests his blood, reads the meter. And I'm suddenly more anxious than ever to pack up so we can get out of here. "Where's our stuff?" I ask.

"We dumped everything out on the side of the road to make space back here," Will admits.

I start to get up. "I'll move it to the other truck—"

Both Jess and Cleverly stop me.

"John, we got it," Cleverly says.

"Take a break. Wait here with Stew."

Cleverly jumps out of the truck, and Jess passes her the crate.

"Yeah, we got this!" Will says, hopping out after them.

To be honest, I'm still pretty pumped with adrenaline. But I'm also not ready to leave my brother's side.

I hesitate, then turn on my backside and lie down beside him, my legs stretched out and crossed at the ankles, my arm behind my neck.

We can hear them walking around the truck, kicking up gravel, their muffled voices, laughter, but it's all pretty hushed within our metal cocoon. I can also feel every ridge of the truck bed beneath us through the sleeping bags. "This is really uncomfortable," I say, and he sort of laughs.

Then Stew asks, "What do you think Dad is doing right now?"

I don't have to give it much thought; I know what he's doing.

"Trying to figure out how to get back to us," I say. Then I look at Stew. "I know one reason why he hasn't come back." I tell him what we heard on that shortwave radio at the reservoir, about the state borders being closed.

I'm not sure how Stew feels about this, because he's quiet for a while. Then he says, "I just want to talk to him. Even if he's stuck somewhere and can't get home. I just want to hear his voice."

"Yeah, me too," I say.

I look back up at all those stars, thinking of all the nights we've been on our own, without our dad. All the nights we've only had each other.

"I'm sorry," I tell my brother in a whisper, saying what I should have said before I left him. "I'm sorry I didn't listen to you more. I should have listened to you more."

Stew shakes his head. "You don't have anything to be sorry for," he says, his voice sure. "I've just been lying here, thinking about how lucky I am . . ."

His words fall away at the end but I know he's talking about me. Lucky he has me. And I'm kind of surprised to hear him say that, and I want to tell him if anyone is lucky around here, it's me. But I'm finding it hard to speak right now.

Stew's lying down in the backseat of Nate's extended-cab truck. Jess, Cleverly, and Will are all squished beside me in the front. I turn the key in the ignition, the engine starts up, and I've got my hand on the gearshift when I notice what Will's got in his hand. It's that stupid Extraterrestrial Highway ad from Spike's glove box. The one with directions to our place written on the back. Bent up around the edges now.

"John, what are we waiting for?" Cleverly says.

"Just thinking," I say.

I stare out at the piece-of-crap truck for a minute, and my heart starts to pound. But in a good way.

I turn to Will. "Why do you have that?"

He looks down at the glossy ad and shrugs. "It's my fan," he says, showing me, waving it in front of his face a few times.

"Can I have it?"

He hesitates, but shrugs again and hands it to me. "I guess."

"Thanks! I'll be right back," I say to all of them. I jump out, run to the cab of that old silver truck.

We know something about this blackout that Spike probably doesn't. We know it's going to end. Maybe even soon. Life will slowly move back toward normal. Borders will open up, gas won't be so scarce, cars and trucks will travel down this highway. And eventually, Spike will get his piece-of-crap truck back.

When he does, I want to make sure he knows something.

I get in the cab, lit by the headlights of Nate's truck. I take the Sharpie from my pocket, turn over the Extraterrestrial Highway ad, and write the message in big letters, just to the side of that *HWY 318, MM 98* scrawled in the upper right corner. Then I sort through the papers in his glove box, throwing them aside until I find the one with the information I want. I fold it a few times and stuff it in my pocket. I crank both windows up so wind won't blow through the cab. Then I slide the ad onto the dashboard, wedge it right beneath the glass so it won't move, my message faceup.

I slam the door of that truck for the last time.

Back behind the wheel of Nate's truck, I look over at them, a little breathless. I've got a big grin on my face, I know.

"Well?" Stew asks from the backseat.

"What did you write?" Will asks.

"I kept it short and sweet," I say, putting the gear in drive.

Hey Moron,

    Got your address.

                  Sincerely,
                  The Battle Born

THE END

EPILOGUE

"John, it's Dad again. I keep leaving these messages, I don't know if you're even getting them. Promise this time not to get choked up. Just wanted to say I made it through the state line. I'm back in Nevada. First thing that went through my mind was that song they teach you in school. '*Home means Nevada, / Home means the hills, / Home means the sage and the pines.*'

"Never been so happy in my life to see all that sage.

"Anyway, I'm calling from Mesquite, almost to Las Vegas, and from there I've got a ride lined up to take me all the way home up the 318. Chris Brighton, if you can believe the luck. He's been waiting for me to get through. Told him you've been on your own all this time, and he reminded me that you've gotta be okay because you're together. Stew's okay because he has you, and you're okay because you've got him. I know he's right about that.

"Stew, if you're listening, I love and miss both you boys more than I can say.

"All right, they're telling me we've gotta get going—

"Oh, John! One more thing. I was thinking about the morning I left town when we crossed the state line. Your bedroom lit up the color of our state flag. And it just made me smile, remembering the looks on our faces.

"Hope by now you got that Battle Born flag up on your wall, where it belongs."

AUTHOR'S NOTE

The places I mention in this book are real—Lund, Ely, Alamo, the reservoir, and, of course, Nevada State Route 318. (And yes, Las Vegas is real too!) Because these are real places, I should note that I did take some creative liberties. How I depicted Lund, and the community of people in and around Lund, came from both my imagination and from what I thought would make the most interesting story. Much of the layout and description of the reservoir came from my memory and imagination, and may not be exact. Distances between places also may not be exact.

There are a lot of long lonely highways in Nevada to choose from. I chose highway 318 for a reason. I've driven this highway for years, passing through Lund, as it's the route I take when traveling from my home in Las Vegas to visit my family in Idaho—a shortcut that saves me forty-five minutes. You can sometimes go miles on highway 318 without even seeing another car in the distance, and it really feels like you're alone out there, surrounded by nothing but desert and big blue sky.

That is the feeling I hoped to capture when I chose this highway for the setting of John's story.

All that said, it takes a long time to write a book, and an even longer time to get that book through the publishing process and into the hands of readers. Sometimes, while all that time is passing, public rest areas with bathroom facilities are constructed right in the middle of long desolate highways.

But just to be clear, when John, Stew, Cleverly, and Will set out to walk down the 318 without nearly enough water, there were no toilets up and down the highway to drink from. Though John would probably love that.

ACKNOWLEDGMENTS

The first sentence of this story is true, so I guess I should start by thanking my dad. If he hadn't gathered my siblings and me into the bathroom of our childhood home to tell us that, in the case of an emergency, we could drink the water in the toilet, this book wouldn't exist. I should also thank the great state of Nevada, particularly the desolate middle part, for sparking my imagination during long drives down lonely highways. And while on the subject of inspiration, this story of two brothers surviving in the Nevada desert without their dad also wouldn't exist without the music of a local band here in Las Vegas called The Killers—I only had the first sentence, then I listened to the Battle Born album. Thanks for that!

Thank you to my first reader, Cord Esplin, who read every scene in this book as I wrote it, and whose facial expressions let me know whether I was on the right track. Gus Esplin read the next draft, then Homer—how handy to have you three clever boys around!

Thank you to my favorite critique partner, Chase Baldwin, for your genius-level feedback, always. I couldn't have stumbled upon a better random person on the internet with which to navigate this world of publishing.

Thank you to all of my early beta readers for your totally unbiased feedback, even though we're family and friends: Mary Morgan, Sara Strasser, Amy Thurston, Memzy Waite, and Landee Anderson (aka crickets). My round-two beta readers, who were just as unbiased, I'm sure: Michelle Esplin, Ally Adams, Stacia Henderson, and Mandy Abbott. If I ever need friends to survive a blackout with, I choose you people. Even though you have no survival skills.

It was important to me that I get things right with my characters Stew and Jess. I spent a lot of time watching YouTube videos of kids just like them, and I wish I had a better way to properly thank them. Thank you to Heather Griffith for answering my questions early on—so early on that you probably don't even remember, but I do! Thank you to Mandy Abbott, Marleen Gunnerson, and Nora Gunnerson, for reading drafts and checking my work. Any errors after all that are my own.

I'm so grateful for my agent, Andrea Somberg, who believed in this story and stuck with me through submission highs and lows. I definitely won the literary agent lottery!

Thank you to my brilliant editor, Susan Chang, for believing I was capable of doing better, even when I seriously doubted it. I also won the editor lottery! Thanks too, to my copy editor, Eliani Torres, for your attention to detail. And to the team at Tor/Starscape who put hard work and time into this book: Elizabeth Vaziri, Rafal Gibek, Megan Kiddoo, Steven Bucsok, Heather Saunders, Peter Lutjen, Laura Etzkorn, Anthony Parisi, and AJ Stuhrenberg.

I'm so lucky to be surrounded by supportive friends and family, because it turns out, publishing can be pretty stressful. Thank you to everyone who kindly scheduled playdates with my little one to help me meet deadlines. My other creative outlet is guitar, and I want to give a special thanks to my guitar students for being the best distraction every time I needed it. Thank you to my local ANWA friends—I'm so grateful to have found a group of talented, fun, and hilarious writers! To my extended Esplin family, for your unwavering love and support—how lucky I am to have married into this family! To the people I grew up with—Becky, Tom, Amy, Erin, and Sara—it's no coincidence that every manuscript I've written has been about siblings. Clearly, you are my greatest inspirations. Thank you for supplying me with decades of wonderful memories. Dad, thank you for years of enthusiastic encouragement (despite what my high school English teacher had to say about it). Mom, thank you for keeping me going through years of rejection, well over a decade, and never doubting this would happen one day.

Finally, there are no words to express how grateful I am for my kids, Cord, Gus, Homer, and Elowen, and my husband, Anthony. The best thing I can come up with is that you . . . dramatic pause . . . are Battle Born.

ABOUT THE AUTHOR

J. L. ESPLIN grew up with a Secret Service agent father, who was intent on raising self-reliant kids prepared for any emergency, especially natural disasters. She lives in Las Vegas, Nevada, on the edge of town with her husband and kids. *96 Miles* is her first novel. When not writing, she enjoys teaching guitar the fun way, traveling to new places, and coming back home to the desert.